The Suspects

Katharine Johnson

"Gripping and frighteningly realistic.
The twists and turns kept me guessing to the very end."
Jo Fenton, author of The Brotherhood

"The hugely talented Katharine Johnson has, again
delivered a tense thriller! In her new novel,The
Suspects, the author weaves a gripping psychlogical
thriller which starts at a funeral. She then teases the
reader as she reveals information about her characters,
their strengths and weaknesses in the decisions they
take. This is a compelling novel - up there with
Erin Kelly and Sophie Hannah."
**Val Penny, bestselling author of
The Edinburgh Crime Mysteries series**

CROOKED
CAT

Discover us online:
www.crookedcatbooks.com

Join us on facebook:
www.facebook.com/crookedcatbooks

Tweet a photo of yourself holding
this book to **@crookedcatbooks**
and something nice will happen.

For Lucy

Acknowledgements

I have so many people to thank for their kindness and support in helping me knock this novel into shape and make it as accurate and believable as I could.

Firstly, as always to Laurence, Stephanie and the wonderful team at Crooked Cat Books.

Also to members of Book Connectors and The Book Club (TBC) who were so generous with their time and advice when the story was at a very early stage: Mark Hayden, Suzanna Salter, Stephen Hall, Lin White, Priya Prakash, Rachel McCollin, and Claire-Louise Lulabelle Armstrong Brealey; Val Penny for her legal advice and Rebeca Bradley for checking the police procedural details. To Rachel Gilbey and all the wonderful bloggers who gave up their time to support the launch. Also to Eleanor, Christine, Jodie, Jo, Bev, Cristina, Kate, Amanda, Gill, Roger, Shirley, Rosie, Helen, Stephanie, Heidi and Jenny.

Big thanks to my family and friends who put up with me while writing.

And finally but especially to you, the reader - I hope you enjoy it.

About the Author

Katharine Johnson grew up in Bristol and now lives in Berkshire. She's the author of three previous novels, all featuring good people who make bad choices. As a journalist she's written for a variety of magazines, and a history book about Windsor. When not writing, you'll find her with a book in one hand and a coffee in the other, patching up a house in Italy, playing netball or out walking her spaniel while plotting her next novel.

Connect with Katharine online:

If you'd like to be notified of new books by Katharine Johnson in the future please visit her website where you can sign up for her free newsletter.

www.katyjohnsonblog.wordpress.com

Twitter:
twitter.com/@kjohnsonwrites

Facebook:
www.facebook.com/katharinejohnsonauthor

Instagram:
www.instagram.com/katharinejohnsonauthor

Pinterest:
pinterest.com/katharinejohnsonauthor

Other Books by Katharine Johnson

The Secret
The Silence
Lies, Mistakes and Misunderstandings

The Suspects

Chapter One

The body of a young woman has been found in woods near Ashton Court in Bristol. Police are investigating a possible link with the murder of the young bride Lily Ambrose who was abducted from the same area.

November 1989

There was nothing remotely funny about Xanthe's funeral except she fulfilled so many predictions by being late for it. The ice had left potholes all over the place, so I suppose it was inevitable that the hearse would get stuck in one.

I could just see her, pale green eyes wide and alight with indignation, saying "I mean there I was…" just as she'd started most of her anecdotes.

Because with Xanthe nothing went according to plan. She'd come breezing into the office, her witchy hair blown about as though she'd been running on the moors instead of driving her 2CV, seemingly oblivious to the editor's sarcastic "Nice of you to turn up" and say "You will not *believe* what just happened…"

Ignoring the editor's pained "I don't want to know" she'd swizzle round in her chair as she recounted her latest misadventure. Covering her face with her hands like a child playing hide and seek, her laughter coming in great, gurgling gasps. The cuffs of her black jumper were stained, stiff and jagged, her black painted nails nibbled and cracked, those long, raised scars on the underside of her thin wrist just visible. A smudged phone number invariably decorated the back of one hand.

The editor usually cut her off before she reached the

climax of the tale and stuck her on Product News for the rest of the day as punishment for her lateness. The magazines in our company had the sort of titles most people had never heard of and wouldn't care about if they had. *Ice Cream Retailer, Radiator Supplies Monthly, Furniture Maker*. There's a magazine for everything somewhere – even one called *The Embalmer*. Xanthe used to love that one. It seemed funny at the time.

In the church the organ played, people whispered, a woman in front of us rootled in her handbag for tissues and blew her nose with an explosive hoot. Someone crackled a sweet wrapper. Stuart looked round in disgust. It was a large church, most of the pews still empty. There were flowers at the pew ends. Nice ones – left over from a wedding, I supposed.

Zak raked his hand through his dark mop and rubbed the stubble on either side of his face. You could hear his skin rasping. He'd been last up that morning, sitting sockless and dishevelled in the kitchen, staring into space, drinking one coffee after another. I knew he'd been awake half the night. I'd heard his floorboards creaking and the window opening and closing, and strains of Xanthe's *Everything But the Girl* album – the one he'd threatened to throw out of the window if she played it one more time.

He caught me looking at him in the pew and did a half-smile. "All right, Em?"

I managed a quick smile back – the first time we'd communicated in days. As I leaned forward to put my bag under the pew I felt him studying me.

"Is that dirt or bruises?" he asked at last.

I clapped one hand to the back of my neck, turning up the back of my jacket collar with the other. I'd hennaed my hair that morning when I was half asleep and done my usual trick of forgetting to check I'd washed all the dye off my skin. Zak looked away in an unsuccessful attempt to hide his smile.

The four of us were crammed into the pew. I don't know what people thought of us, sitting there. I'm sure they wondered how we knew each other, let alone how we'd known Xanthe. Imogen with her punky platinum cropped hair, wearing a black baggy jumper and leggings; Stuart with his sports jacket and roll-neck, Zak in his jeans and vegan leather jacket, and me in the stalwart black Lycra dress I'd worn to the office, press launches, shopping and parties but would never, I realised at that moment, wear again.

Imogen's hand on my knee alerted me to the way it had been jiggling up and down. It was years since I'd been inside a church. Just talking about religion made me cringe. Zak said to me once, "How come you'll answer any question about sex, but you go all panicky when someone asks if you believe in God?"

"It's just too big a question," I said, squirming.

"It's Yes or No," he replied. "Or I don't know."

"Just don't go there, okay? Can of worms."

The smell of dust, polish, lilies and old coats, the silky pages of well-thumbed hymn books dragged me back years. Those oppressive quiet moments I always longed to break by streaking down the aisle, shouting obscenities. It had left me with a fear of silence and a need to fill gaps in any conversation, however inappropriately.

But I didn't want to misbehave on this occasion. I'd have given anything not to. It just happened. I saw the name Charlotte Lucy Clarke on the funeral pamphlet. Jumping out of my seat, I blurted, "We're at the wrong do."

I don't even know why I used the word 'do.' It's something my Granny would say about a sherry party.

"It's Xanthe," Imogen said, tugging me back down.

Of course, the police and the press had been calling her Charlotte for several weeks, but I'd imagined Xanthe must at least be her middle name.

"See that couple?" Imogen whispered. "Her parents."

"Foster parents," I reminded her, looking over at the middle-aged couple in the front pew. "The real ones died in the plane crash, didn't they?"

The blonde brows twitched. "It seems not."

5

"And that's her sister?"

"Yep."

"The nun? The one who…?"

Imogen barely blinked and yet her cool blue eyes signalled she'd tell me later.

It made me wonder if we'd ever really known Xanthe.

Then that thing about the hearse getting stuck. I'd seen so many comedy shows about funerals – undertakers slipping in the mud, mourners sneezing out their false teeth into the grave – and I got a picture in my head of a speeded-up film, of the driver taking out the coffin and leaving it on the pavement while they jacked up the car and maybe someone else coming along and making off with the coffin and I could hear Xanthe's indignant tone "I mean, there I was…"

The vicar was apologising for Xanthe's late arrival.

"What's new?" mumbled Zak. I saw his shoulders shaking and he let out one of his Muttley laughs.

It wasn't funny. Not at all. Until Stuart leaned across the pew, his face all red and stiff and snapped out of the side of his mouth, "Sort yourselves out," like he was forty-two instead of twenty years younger.

Zak stopped just long enough to say, "Yeh, all right, Dad," and we sank to the floor, stuffing our hands in our mouths but every now and then a squeak or a snort would escape, and I could see tears of mirth running down Zak's neck.

"Please, Emily," said Imogen in that dreadful, cold, pleading tone. "Just go outside."

Looking back now, I don't know why we laughed. I realise how disrespectful and hard-hearted we must have seemed. I shouldn't even try to justify it. I could say I'd already done my crying and Zak had done his anger, kicking Xanthe's stuff around until you couldn't recognise it any more. But the simple truth is, neither of us could face up to where we were and what was happening.

Knowing she'd been so close to home for two whole weeks, lying under the frozen leaves when we thought she'd buggered off to Sweden with her boyfriend, dumping us in even more debt.

There all the time and none of us knew. All the time we were drunkenly playing Twister, falling over each other in a heap, squealing and shouting, Zak farting, Imogen's earring getting caught in my belt buckle and nearly pulling her ear off, Xanthe had been lying less than a mile away.

While we watched *The Crying Game,* danced around the house to Talking Heads, argued over whose turn it was to make the coffee. While Zak and Stuart brawled over a game of Scruples, Stuart screaming at Zak he had "no understanding of the personal space bubble."

And when the phone bill came in and Imogen went ballistic, seeing all those calls to Sweden. The way we'd slagged Xanthe off for buying shoes when she said she couldn't afford to pay her share of the electricity bill...

"Here she is," whispered Stuart. A knife twisted inside me. I'd so hoped they wouldn't be able to fix the hearse. As long as she wasn't there in the church I didn't have to accept it as real. Now it crashed in on me.

I couldn't look, couldn't think about her being in that box or what she must look like. It wasn't her, not as she had been. I curled my hands. How could they parade her like this? I couldn't help thinking back to a history lesson when one of those Norman kings had burst out of his coffin during his funeral.

One of the pallbearers stumbled and I thought, *Don't drop her, don't you dare drop her.*

To my surprise Imogen reached out and took my hand and I squeezed back so tightly she winced and withdrew hers. Seeing the red marks, I mumbled an apology. Stuart cleared his throat. The vicar burbled on about someone I didn't know, calling her Charlotte, who'd loved horses and gymnastics and had shown promise as a dancer. She was nothing like Xanthe.

He kept talking about her as though she was still alive in there, saying she was "about to make her final journey." For God's sake, she'd already done that.

I know Xanthe would have tried to contact us. She'd

have been calling for help, transmitting messages for as long as she was able. She was always trying stuff like that.

"Close your eyes and tell me what animal I'm thinking of."

Usually it ended up in a big row about coincidence – someone always saying elephant or number seven or Africa and someone else saying well of course you'd guess that. So we started coming up with answers she could never have heard of and she stomped off saying we weren't suitable subjects for the experiment.

Yet not for a moment did I doubt she'd left of her own accord to escape the bills, the soaring mortgage rates, those letters about being in arrears - and the heart-stopping guilt about what we'd done after the New Year's Eve party.

Thinking back a few weeks to when she was still there in the house, I'd do anything to be able to stop time. It was a Saturday morning, the house smelled of coffee and we were all nursing hangovers from hell and Xanthe looked up from the cards she'd spread out in front of her on the floor and said,

"Oh my God, something terrible's going to happen to me."

And we all just laughed. Later, I wished we'd paid more attention.

Even when the Swedish boyfriend rang and said she hadn't turned up we weren't that bothered. She'd have met someone on the flight over, taken a detour, perhaps changed her mind about him altogether. If she said Tuesday she meant *a* Tuesday. Or perhaps Wednesday. But as the days went on, we started to wonder. We went through every personal contact in her Filofax and they started to creep in, those icy fingers of doubt.

The thing is, she'd probably have laughed, too, hearing Stuart tell us off like that in the church. She was always trying to rile him. It was Xanthe who'd first noticed how he talked out of the side of his mouth when he got angry. She could mimic him perfectly. No one else would have dared but even Stuart seemed to find it funny.

Even now, all these years later, I can't, won't, think of her without her nose all scrunched up and her face stained by mascara tracks, making her look like a Pierrot, trying and failing to get through a story without dissolving into gulping, gasping giggles. She'd be sitting up on the window seat, knees drawn up under the tent of her skirt. Sometimes she'd laugh so much she'd fall off and lie in a heap on the floor, helpless.

She loved Stuart's pomposity, prodded away at him constantly to get a reaction. If Stuart had been in the Famous Five, he'd have been Julian, the bossy one who always took the decisions. He even looked a bit like those pictures in the early editions – tall with a firm jawline and very short fair hair. Hitler Youth was how Zak described his look during one of their rows, which as a result turned nuclear.

He always dressed in a button-up shirt and smart chinos. Xanthe and Imogen persuaded him to buy a pair of jeans once, but he wore them with polished brogues and complained he couldn't bend his knees properly, so they gave up.

But none of us laughed at his middle-aged manner that day the police called. We were all watching *Casualty,* predicting ways in which people would end up in hospital.

"The vegetable knife's going to slip."

"Nah, the cat's going to bite her. It's got rabies."

"No, she's going to trip over the cat and fall face-first onto the hob."

When Stuart walked back in, something in his face made Zak grab the controller and switch off. He didn't have to say they'd found her.

"They need someone to um – identify…"

Because at that stage of course we thought we were all the family Xanthe had. We had no idea she had one of her own, let alone a different name. We all looked down into our laps, hating ourselves for the worthless cowards we were.

"No, it's fine," he said after a moment. "I'll do it."

His face was grey when he came back but when I asked him what Xanthe had looked like, he kissed the top of my head and said. "Fine. Lovely. Asleep."

I knew he was lying but I loved him for it.

I wished I hadn't let Zak go on about the foxes digging her up and the different stages of decomposition. All those thrillers he read. Up until that moment I thought I could forgive Zak anything. But I never forgave him that.

***

When the service was over, Stuart ordered us to hang back while the family walked over to the burial plot, which was a relief because I'm pretty sure I'd have done something awful like throw up and people would think I was just doing it to get attention. It was years since I'd done that.

Xanthe's mother's eyes never left the ground but her father, stiff, dignified, stared straight ahead, over everybody as though we weren't there – or he wasn't. His coat was rucked up at the back and I wanted to tell him, but I couldn't move my legs and it didn't seem appropriate to call out.

I only noticed the two policemen as we got to the gate. Had they been there the whole time? Nice of them, I thought, to pay their respects, show their support. After all, they were dealing with deaths all the time but perhaps Xanthe, being so young, had specially touched them, reminded them of their own daughters. After all, it could just as easily have happened to them. Packing to stay with your boyfriend one moment – in a box the next. Fine line.

So I couldn't work out what was happening at first when Stuart started walking off with them. He was supposed to be giving us all a lift, after all. But I saw the back door of the police car being held open, a hand placed on his head as he climbed in. He looked back once, a strange look – helpless? Confused? Accusing? All of those things. I looked away but met Imogen's crushed-ice stare.

"This is serious, Emily. You'll have to tell them where he

was."

"Rather not," I mumbled.

After all, we'd all given false alibis. Would it really help now to tell them that on the night the police were so curious about, Stuart had been tied to my bed with silk scarves and covered in whipped cream, fruit and melted chocolate?

Chapter Two

We weren't bad people, we just made a bad choice. Or at least that's how it started.

We often asked ourselves how they'd picked us out of all the students in the country who'd applied for the journalism training scheme. Assuming there were others. We must have had something in common, something they saw in those interviews, something they liked. In one of our training sessions, the Managing Director told us it was "the hunger."

"Is that the same as desperation?" Zak asked, and we'd all laughed – a bit too loudly.

In any case, *The Hunger* became a catchphrase between us, spoken in a theatrical tone and applied to a host of situations from justifying that second Mars Bar to wanting to ask someone out.

Perhaps in reality they picked us for our differences, as part of a psychological experiment to see how long we could stand being with each other. If so, they must be at least partly responsible for what happened with Xanthe.

But my therapist told me that when something that awful happens, it's natural to look around and find someone else to blame. Mostly at the time I blamed Margaret Thatcher. If it wasn't for her government's toxic laws, the recession, the housing bubble, the soaring interest rates, the loss of society...

But the truth is, we all made the decision to move in together, although we must have all known it couldn't work. None of the stuff that came after would have happened if each of us hadn't already made some bad choices.

I still cringe now when I think back to that final interview – the Panel one held in the company's airy Bristol office on the fifth floor with a view over the docks where old warehouses were being turned into swanky apartments, galleries and art centres. I walked down a cobbled quay past people cleaning their boats watched by seagulls perched on masts, on past a line of stalls selling handicrafts, jewellery, handmade cards and espadrilles. All part of a brave new world – so much happening, so much beginning. I wanted to be part of it.

The interview started well but one of the panel had the nerve to ask me how many other jobs I'd applied for. When I told them they asked whether in that case I was serious about wanting this one.

"Serious?" I spluttered. "Of course I'm serious. Do you know how much it's cost me to come down here from Edinburgh three times? Do you know how long it takes?"

It went on a lot longer than that but it's too painful to recall. There was more I could have said. I'd been so bruised and battered by the tsunami of rejections over the last few weeks and dreaded having to go back to living at home. I knew my parents would have done their best to treat me as an adult, but we'd have driven each other mad and I couldn't take the humiliation of having failed to come out of university with anything to show for it. Going back would mean going backwards. A degree meant nothing if I was going to end up working in the bowling alley or the garden centre with the kids who'd said all along that further education was a waste of time.

When I stopped I found the Panel staring at me and I had a feeling they might be reaching for a panic button. But I suppose they saw it as The Hunger.

At any rate four weeks later, I was standing in a bedsit in the Redland district that smelled of fresh paint and had floorboards that echoed under my feet.

"It's so bright and clean," I said to the agent. "Much

bigger than the other rooms you've shown me."

He was young, skinny, wore a shiny suit too broad-shouldered for his frame. He stood looking out of the window, shifting his weight from one foot to another, jiggling some coins in his trousers.

"A short walk to shops and cafes, an excellent bus service, separate bedroom, your own bathroom…"

He needn't have tried so hard. I'd have taken it anyway. I don't know if perhaps he tried to warn me when he said, "It's one to think about anyway. Let me show you some others." At the time I thought he was trying to put me off, thought he might be trying to keep it for himself or a friend and it made me all the more determined to have it.

That first night in the flat I lay awake imagining my new life. It was a good flat for parties. Plenty of space for friends to stay over. I pictured the things I'd put in it when I got that first £500 pay cheque – a kilim, floor standing wrought iron candles, a wacky mirror… I got myself so excited I couldn't sleep.

If I hadn't been young and naive, I might have been suspicious about the fresh paint and the bars on the windows. If I'd been local, I might have recognised the address from news stories.

***

"Where are you living?"

It was the first thing we asked each other in that stilted conversation, sitting in the beige-walled Training Room that smelled of machine coffee, new carpet tiles and vinyl chairs, and had a view of boats and a cobbled quay. Imogen looked down at the table when I gave her the name of the road. Zak's arched brows shot up and he looked out of the window.

Xanthe drew in her breath and said, "You're *joking*."

"Er – no."

Stuart frowned and shifted in his seat. "It isn't necessarily the same flat."

"Same as what?"

The door opened and Mary, the Editorial Trainer breezed in, shaking the bangles down her arm and bringing with her a waft of *Opium* that made Stuart close his eyes and inhale. Zak sneezed.

"Well, hellooo my lovely trainees."

As she was setting out the goals, timetable and levels of achievement she expected us to reach, pen squeaking across the whiteboard, I caught Xanthe's eyes flicker towards me, then away again but I had to wait for the coffee break to ask her more.

"I don't know if I should say," she began.

"You've already started," said Zak. "You can't leave it like that now."

I put my money into the machine, selected a white coffee and watched the thin brown liquid froth into the cup over the powdered milk but still nobody spoke. I looked round.

"So, is someone going to put me out of my misery?"

"Look, it's just there was a murder in one of those flats a few months ago," Zak said. "Have you heard of Lily Ambrose? The Missing Bride?"

Of course I had. It had been all over the news. She never actually got to be a bride. She'd disappeared after going for the final fitting for her wedding dress. I couldn't remember the details, but I knew the story didn't end well.

"He um, he kept her at his flat," said Xanthe. "Your flat, if you mean the one on the end looking over the park."

I nodded, trying to dredge up what I'd read. Neighbours had complained about the smell and then the flies. Police found her emaciated body surrounded by unspeakable instruments of torture.

"They've caught the man now so don't go giving yourself nightmares," said Stuart as we walked back into the training room for the last session before lunch.

I appreciated his kind smile, but I knew it was already too late.

I'd never sleep properly in that place again. Each time I walked into the flat and smelled the fresh paint, it would remind me of what might lie underneath. I'd find myself staring at the blank wall and imagining streaks and blotches showing through, bloody footprints on the floor. In the middle of the night I'd hear screams, pleading.

So I arranged to be out as much as possible and invited friends – old friends who knew nothing about the flat's history – to stay at weekends so I was never on my own.

***

But it turned out I wasn't the only one who was unhappy with where they were living. Zak hated his room in a council-run B&B with a load of old men who were "almost definitely paedophiles." Imogen was stuck in a suffocating bungalow on a road that looked like Brookside Close, with an elderly woman and nine cats. "And they all hate me. I've been scratched to pieces." She pushed up her sleeves to reveal a network of angry red scars.

And Stuart's housemate left notes everywhere. *Please wipe the washing-up bottle after use…Please do NOT pull the flush after midnight…PLEASE don't use my toothpaste. I can tell!!*

If Stuart's grandfather hadn't died we'd have probably each found a place on our own, so I feel even he should take a posthumous share of the blame. Stuart put the proposal to us at lunchtime in Coffee Stop. We'd started congregating there to escape the office crowd. It wasn't a stylish place. It overlooked a car park, the tables were sticky, and you had to watch the owner, or he'd shovel sugar into your coffee without asking, he was so absent-minded, but at least we could talk freely about the course and gossip about other people in the company without fear of being overheard.

"The thing is," Stuart said, "my Gramps died."

Shrugging off murmurs of "Oh, that's awful," and "Sorry, mate," he carried on. "No, you know, he was old. But he left me a few thousand. I wasn't expecting anything. It's enough for a deposit on a flat I suppose."

"You're going to *buy?"*

I suppose it hadn't occurred to us. It seemed such a grown-up thing to do.

"Why not? Prices are going up all the time. Someone on *The Architect* bought a place six months ago and it's doubled in price. You know what they're saying – if you don't get on the property ladder now, you'll never be able to. And if I live with Helena any longer, I might just kill her."

Sympathetic nods all round.

"I'm sick of handing over all my hard-earned cash to that jumped-up little landlord who's younger than I am so he can swan around in his flash car. At least with a mortgage you end up with a house at the end of it."

He gulped his tea. "I can't afford to buy a whole house on my own. But if I could find enough people to share, we'd each pay less in mortgage than we're paying in rent."

I noticed he'd slipped from "I" to "we". The pause that followed was slightly too long to be comfortable.

"You mean, the five of us?" asked Zak pushing his hair back with both hands.

"Why not? We've all shared student digs. We know how to behave."

There was another silence as we thought about this. Yes, we'd shared flats before but not with each other. I was picturing my student friends coming down from Edinburgh, wondering what they'd make of this lot. No doubt they were thinking something similar.

"I can't stand pettiness," said Imogen at last. "People who whinge about paying their share of the bills because they're away at weekends."

"And I'm not having a chores rota," said Zak.

That led to an all-out housemates-from-hell discussion until Stuart called us to order. Xanthe was spooning her cappuccino into peaks and slicing the tops off, frowning in concentration while humming along to *Perfect* by Fairground Attraction that was playing on the radio. "What if one of us wants to sell after a few months and the others don't?" she said, looking up.

"Hmm, we'd have to agree to a certain time limit – say two years, until the training scheme ends," said Stuart. "We can get a contract drawn up, make it official."

"No need for that," said Imogen, her cool blue eyes resting on each of us in turn. "We trust each other, don't we?"

Chapter Three

In the beginning the house-hunting brought us together, gave us a common goal. The more time we spent with each other poring over property details, viewing houses and talking to agents, the more it started to make sense, us being a unit. The fact we had so little in common was a good thing – it meant we'd respect each other's space, stay out of each other's way. And we had no problem agreeing to Stuart's stipulation that none of us should date each other which would upset the balance in the house.

But the more time you spend with people the more things you find you have to talk about. Perhaps we weren't so different after all. Other people in the company had already started talking to us collectively as "you lot" and seemed amused and interested by our plan to move in together. They'd see us hanging around the photocopier or the coffee machine locked in discussion over damp courses or rewiring or how to paper a wall and seemed to enjoy giving us the benefit of their experience.

Most of the men were jealous of Stuart and Zak getting to share a house with Imogen. She was one of those women everyone falls in love with – and others just had to accept they only had a chance with anyone after Imogen had rejected them.

She was clever too. At press conferences she was the one to extract the details from the interviewee. She had a way of sitting back while we all dived in and then asking the killer question so directly and with such charm, fixing the person with her steady blue-eyed gaze and barely raising her voice, it made evasion seem impossibly rude.

She told us once the serenity thing was an act, that really

she was like a swan paddling desperately under the surface, but I think in those days Imogen just wanted to fit in with the rest of us. Perhaps in some way she already anticipated the divide that was to come.

***

It took several weeks to find the right house. The market was going crazy and most of the properties had already been snapped up by the time we saw them in the estate agents' windows. A quick glance through the property papers during our lunch hours in Coffee Stop showed we'd be hard pushed now to find enough money for the five per cent deposit we needed.

"I could ask my dad to lend me some," said Imogen.

I doubted my parents would be able to help. Both academics, they'd never been good with money and were still paying off their own mortgage on the grey flint bungalow in which I was born.

"I don't have parents to ask," said Xanthe. "Tenerife airport collision – two Boeing 747s collided on the runway? We were coming back from holiday."

Something about the note of pride in her voice when she told us it was "the deadliest air accident in history" broke my heart.

"God, how awful," said Imogen but Xanthe just shrugged and went quiet and picked at her cauliflowered sleeve. Then she looked round and managed a brave grin. "Sorry – didn't mean to put a downer on everything."

Somehow Stuart managed to steer the conversation back to the housing thing, but I thought Xanthe's story explained a lot about her. She was a lost soul looking for a family. I thought about how buying the house with us could make her feel she belonged somewhere again.

But I felt a sweep of panic when Stuart said, "Don't worry, we'll find the money between us to pay for your share."

I had no idea how I was going to pay for mine let alone

sub Xanthe but it didn't seem right to claim I was penniless. Zak once told me he'd been earning money since he was fifteen, making stuff and trading it in the playground. It made me feel ashamed. I'd taken jobs in the summer holidays to pay off my overdraft each year at uni but I was sacked from the waitress job after I dropped a pudding in someone's handbag.

I was clutched by a sudden fear that I was going to be left behind, the one who didn't make it onto the housing ladder before it was whisked away. I saw a future in which I was eternally paying rent for rooms that were more and more decrepit while the others moved on to bigger and better places.

In the end Imogen told the agent she wasn't leaving his office until he'd shown us what was in his bottom drawer. He laughed and tried to deny there was anything.

"There always is," she said. "We want to see what you're keeping back for selected clients."

Just as we thought he was about to throw us out he sighed and said, "I've shown you everything in your price range – except this one because it needs so much work."

Zak seized it. "We don't mind work."

Admittedly, it was clear as soon as we arrived that the photographs had flattered the place. Taken from a distance on a bright day, the cracks and dark stains on the plasterwork were bleached out and a tree masked the broken iron canopied balcony with its peeling paintwork. But the fact remained it was a handsome, terraced house on four floors a short walk away from bars, clubs and boutique shops in Clifton, the most desirable area in Bristol.

Georgian, the agent informed us. Regency, Zak muttered scornfully. I didn't care. I was in love.

Inside, it more than matched the description of "in need of total refurbishment." It had been run as a B&B for council tenants. The carpets had every stain imaginable and the high ceilings were yellow with what I assumed was damp.

"Nope," said Zak, clambering up on a cupboard and

peering. "Just nicotine."

The real damp was in the basement, which stank of mushrooms and had huge growths in one corner that looked like giant sea sponges.

"Easily fixed," the agent assured us. "Nothing like as bad as it looks. The tenants caused it by blocking up these air vents. All you have to do is open them up again to let the house breathe and it will rectify itself."

"We'll just keep the door shut," said Xanthe.

After all, we wouldn't be using the basement as living space anyway. It would just be somewhere to stash bikes and booze before a party. The woodchip paper throughout the house was covered in thick layers of gloss paint. More paint hid what could be a gorgeous staircase. I had to pull Imogen off before she clambered aboard the rickety banister and slid down with a whoop.

The rooms were a good size, there was a large stained-glass window at the back over the stairs and the upper floors had a terrific view over rooftops, chimneypots and towers of the city below.

Shortly after the viewing we crowded around a phone box at the docks and made our offer. When the agent got back with a 'yes' we shouted so loudly I'm pretty sure a whole flock of seagulls took off.

***

Naturally things didn't go smoothly. The survey revealed the full extent of the damp and timber work that had to be fixed before the mortgage lender would release the money and we had to fight off a developer, which meant securing an even higher sum.

It was Zak's idea to go to the company for the loan to cover the shortfall. We dressed in suits and approached the fifth floor with some trepidation as the chairman Mr Renton was a bit of a legend in the industry and seldom made himself available to humble employees. The company had a first-names policy, but he was always Mr Renton.

We let Imogen do the talking. She did a pretty good pitch about how we all believed our future in the company was worth investing in and that we were a sound investment for them. Even so, we expected to get a bollocking or at least be laughed out of the room. But we must have caught Mr Renton in a good mood because he sat back with a smile, threw up his hands and said, "Why not?"

We managed to retain a professional calm until we got into the lift and then started dancing and jumping around until we fell over in a heap. The doors opened, and the Finance Director stood there staring at us quizzically. We muttered apologies, picked ourselves up and walked out.

"Wrong floor," said Stuart.

But by then the lift was shooting back up to the top floor so we had to run down the rest of the steps.

I suppose by agreeing to the loan the management must have thought it was a good way of keeping us in the company. Too many graduates before us had left the scheme halfway through for more glamorous titles and better pay or faster life in London.

We cast our eyes over the letter stipulating that the repayments would be deducted from our salary and if we left the company before the date given we'd have to pay the outstanding sum in full. It all sounded reasonable.

My parents swooped down at the weekend to see the house before committing themselves to helping with my deposit. They accosted us with a series of observations as we went round. Had we spotted the mould in the basement? Did we realise the window frames were rotten? Were we aware the broken pane in the kitchen door was a security risk?

My mum lowered her voice, although it was still loud enough to be overheard, to ask how well did I really know these people I was buying with? What if one of them didn't pay their way? What if, heaven forbid, one of them turned out to be a criminal?

But one thing you could say about my parents was that they were never predictable. Just as they were leaving Dad asked how much I wanted to borrow again. On hearing the sum, he grimaced, clutched his chest, and folded onto the floor. The estate agent blanched and looked as though he were about to shout for an ambulance but Dad, who used to go through the same routine whenever he was presented with a bill in a restaurant, produced his cheque book.

"It's a loan," he said thrusting the cheque at me. "Don't even think of getting engaged before you pay it back because it's the money we've saved up for your wedding. And your sister's."

Hugging him, I promised him I was highly unlikely to get married within the next two years as I'd have to find someone to marry me first. I'd left my student boyfriend on a train platform in Zagreb a few months before after three stressful weeks of Interrailing. For all I knew, he was still there.

I didn't mention that it was even less likely my sister would be getting married unless same-sex marriages were to become legal, which in those days seemed a long way off.

"I know they're a bit eccentric but they're good people," I said to the others after my parents had left and we were sitting in the pub that we hoped would soon become our local. It was one thing for me to laugh at them, but I was damned if anyone else was going to.

"Don't worry," said Zak with a grin, "when it comes to embarrassing parents, I think you'll find I win that one."

"Really? How's that?"

He gave the name of a sex therapist who'd made a name for herself on morning television with her eye-wateringly frank advice and piercing questions and her less than subtle revelations about past lovers in the tabloid press. "My mum."

Xanthe spurted her beer all over the floor.

***

For the first few weeks in our jointly-owned home we were all on our best behaviour, trying to conceal our flaws and not be the one who upset everyone else. We were polite about each other's taste in books and videos, didn't impose our choice of music on everyone else, and trod carefully around political issues.

Xanthe made an effort to clear up after she'd used the kitchen, I restrained myself from experimenting with other people's bathroom products. Stuart offered us lifts to work and didn't blow his top if you forgot to leave the car seats tidy. Imogen didn't spend too long in the bath; and Zak didn't bring home a succession of waifs and strays he'd just met.

We were united against the slippery estate agent, the incompetent surveyor, the grasping building society and the curtain-twitching elderly couple next door who for all our efforts to be friendly seemed determined to find fault. Nosy Mrs Parker was regularly to be found stationed at her window watching us. She complained whenever we played music and yet her television reverberated through our living room to the extent that we often found ourselves watching one programme while listening to another.

We received a few sour remarks about the state of the garden but when we spent a weekend tidying it up she started moaning about the broken fence although our solicitor had made it clear the boundary belonged to the neighbours.

Stuart mended the fence anyway, but this seemed to raise more suspicion and Mrs Parker stood watching us from an upstairs window as though she suspected we were burying a body or something.

"Shame to disappoint her when you think about it," said Zak noting that she hadn't moved from her watch post for at least half an hour.

So, he and Stuart staggered out into the garden with a rolled-up rug while Xanthe and I dug a hole in the vegetable plot with exaggerated gestures, folding over the spade in laughter. We'd have loved it if she'd rung the police.

But bit by bit of course this honeymoon period unravelled. It didn't take long for us to start falling out, usually over the silliest things. Imogen's boyfriend Rick who she'd been seeing since uni rubbed the rest of us up the wrong way. From the occasional visit he was starting to spend more and more time at the house and behaved as though he owned the place, helping himself to beer from the fridge, taking charge of the TV remote and poking around inside Imogen's clothes or whispering lewd suggestions in her ear that were just loud enough for you to catch while you were trying to hold a conversation with her.

He also took it upon himself to go through our cupboards and chuck out anything that was nearing its sell-by date, which sometimes left us with nothing to eat over the weekend. I got the feeling he hoped we'd all move out one day, so he and Imogen could take over the house and have it the way they wanted.

It soon became clear Imogen viewed the house in a different way from the rest of us – less as a base, more of an investment. I think it's also fair to say, too, that we lacked her sense of style and thought the place would look all right with a lick of paint, so we pointedly ignored the brochures she left lying around.

Although during the first weeks we'd pussy-footed around political differences, you can only bite your tongue for so long. Zak was outraged when Stuart said, "the miners really should embrace change" and the IRA soldiers in Gibraltar had been "asking for trouble in the first place" and Stuart was infuriated when Zak called the salmonella egg scandal "a Tory trick."

But it was the personal questions that caused the most damage. Being journalists, we all suffered from an inability to know when to stop asking questions.

During one of those idle evenings in front of *Blind Date* Zak playfully asked Imogen if he was her type. When she said no he could have left it at that – but he had to ask why. There were so many reasons she could have given that would have been acceptable – he was too short, too stubbly, too much of an eco-warrior or she only had eyes for Rick.

But instead she turned her ice blue eyes on him, drew on

a cigarette and said with that lovely smile, "Sorry but you're too much of a slag for me."

Zak choked on his beer. He smiled too, just about maintaining the light-hearted air of the conversation but said, "What's that supposed to mean?"

She shrugged. "Just that you've had a lot of sexual partners if we're to believe all your stories."

He laughed. "I should be so lucky. Most of the stories are about the same few people. Anyway, this is outrageous. How would you like it if I said that about you?"

Imogen blew a coil of smoke up to the ceiling. "People say things like that about women all the time – if a man sleeps around he's a lad, if a woman does she's a slapper."

"All right but I don't."

"The point is, you can't be too careful these days."

His brows lifted. "Oh, now you're saying I'm an AIDS risk?"

The AIDS thing was always there at the back of our minds in those days. You'd have to have been in a coma for the past few years to have missed the advertisements with the falling tombstone, the leaflets that came through the door and the signs everywhere.

"You'd be more of a risk to me than the other way round," said Zak. "I got tested a couple of weeks ago after that heroin addict bit me down at the soup kitchen so I know I'm negative."

Imogen smiled apologetically. "I'm still not interested I'm afraid."

He looked appalled. "I wasn't asking. You're the last person on Earth I'd sleep with."

Stuart moved the conversation on but Zak couldn't leave it alone.

"How do you know you haven't got it?"

She rolled her eyes. "I don't need a test. I make sure I know a person's sexual history before I sleep with them. Rick was a virgin before I met him. And before him I went out with Jake for four years and I was his first girlfriend."

Zak laughed at that. "And you believed them?"

Imogen looked seriously pissed off but Xanthe jumped in with another question.

"Would you cover up a crime to protect a friend?"

At the time I was more concerned about those two needling each other to death. We had no idea how Xanthe's question would come back to haunt us.

***

After their first row the tension between Imogen and Zak built up. Zak had a thing about Imogen being a secret slob. She took such care over her skin and hair and yet her room was a bomb site. She had a drawer full of mugs sprouting mould that looked as though an alien invasion was taking place. She'd hide full ashtrays under cushions and kick old knickers under the bed. She wasn't even great at remembering to flush the toilet. And Zak of course delighted in pointing these things out.

But perhaps if we hadn't been so short of money things wouldn't have fallen apart as quickly as they did. We could have distracted ourselves more easily. The bills that came in after the first quarter were a shock and it didn't help that the mortgage rate had gone up twice by November. Doubts started to creep in about whether we'd be able to keep up with the repayments if they went any higher. The housing market had already started to slow. At first that seemed to be no bad thing but then people started saying prices would never recover. We started to wonder if we'd bought a very expensive white elephant.

Stuart got twitchy about wasting energy. If you popped upstairs for something he'd come bustling out and turn the hall lights off, plunging you into darkness, and turn off the television while you were out of the room. When he discovered Imogen had a portable electric heater in her room he reacted as if he'd found out his wife was having an affair.

But the biggest row was when four of us came back after a weekend and discovered Xanthe curled up on the sofa with a huge red dog.

"Is this a joke?" Zak asked.

She smiled sleepily. "No. He followed me home from the shops."

"Well he can't stay here."

She ruffled the dog's fur. It reminded me of the bad perm I'd had when I was sixteen.

"No collar, look. He's a stray."

"I'll ring the dogs' home," said Stuart.

"No!" Her scream made us all jump back. "If they can't rehouse them in three days they put them down. Do you want to be responsible for that?"

We looked at each other. As if he knew we were talking about him the dog pawed Stuart who crouched down and ruffled big, wiry head and the dog nuzzled his hand.

"He is rather delightful."

"No way," said Zak. "I'm allergic to dogs."

To be fair, I thought he was making it up – allergies weren't so common back then. We eventually agreed to let Xanthe keep the dog on the condition he'd be re-homed as soon as possible. Imogen and I cycled all over town putting up posters, but a month went by and still no one had claimed him. Xanthe insisted it was no problem because one of the secretaries at work had said she'd take him but every night when we got back home Rufus was still there and he'd caused a whole new level of havoc.

Cute as he looked, the dog chewed through electric cables, sofa covers, socks and a market report that Stuart was analysing for an article. Xanthe tried to get home at lunchtime to walk him but she sometimes didn't make it on time – and neither did he. It turned out when we talked to the secretary she'd only said she'd *like* to take him. If she didn't already have a staffie who hated other dogs.

After six weeks Rufus was driving us mad. Stuart got agitated when the dog's barking drowned out the TV and fretted constantly about the damage Rufus caused and the mounting cost of repairs. The Parkers next door complained about the noise and accused us of "neglecting the poor animal" for long hours while we were at work.

Zak was having regular asthma attacks which he blamed on Rufus. He banned the dog from coming upstairs but Xanthe used to sneak him up to her room anyway. But by eight weeks we'd pretty much resigned ourselves to having a sixth housemate and to tell the truth I was becoming attached to Rufus.

So, it was such a shock when Imogen, Zak and I got in from work one evening and found him wild eyed, careering round the house. At first we thought he was just having one of his exuberant romps, but it became obvious it was more than that.

"There's something wrong with him," said Imogen. "His heart's pounding."

She tried to hold him still, but he scrabbled and sank his teeth into her arm. She screamed, and he leapt out of her grip and took off around the house again.

"Thank God for that," said Zak when he finally stopped.

But when Imogen went up to her room much later she found the dog slumped halfway up the stairs, all stiff and lumpy next to a patch of vomit on the carpet.

"He's dead."

I couldn't believe it. I bent down and stroked Rufus's head fighting back tears, but he didn't respond. I thought of all the times I'd been angry with him. We hadn't given him a chance. But I couldn't understand it. He'd been fine only that morning, his usual crazy self. I noticed the froth around his mouth.

"It looks like he's been poisoned."

"He can't have been. He's been here all day," said Imogen. She shot a look at Zak, comprehension dawning. "Unless…"

Zak was clutching his hair. He murmured. "Shit. I'm sorry. I'm really sorry. I suppose he must have been attracted to the shiny wrapper."

"*Sorry?*" I said. "Is that all you can say? Look what you've done. Xanthe's going to be heartbroken. Why did you have to leave pills lying around?"

"He wasn't allowed to come upstairs."

"But you know he did anyway."

Zak dragged his hands down his face. "She'll think I did it deliberately. She knows I didn't like him. This is bad. I wouldn't, you know, I'd never do that."

Gently, he scooped the body up. I thought he was taking him outside to bury him.

"Shouldn't you wait until Xanthe gets back?"

"Damage limitation," he muttered. "I can't bring him back to life, can I? But there's no point making things worse than they are. He might just as easily have been run over."

Despite our protests he took the dead dog outside and laid him down on the road. An hour later we heard Xanthe's scream. She hammered at the door and when we opened it she dragged us outside to look. The poor dog looked a lot worse than when we last saw him, but she flung herself down on him. Stuart had to prise her off or she'd have ended up getting run over too.

"How did he get out?" she kept asking. "I can't believe none of you noticed."

We did our best to make it up to her over the next few weeks, cooking her dinner and bringing her gifts, but nothing worked. None of these events sound much, I know, but they were all tiny parts of a whole. While we were dealing with the cracks in the house, the fissures in our relationships were starting to deepen and sprawl.

But it was the party on New Year's Eve that changed everything.

Chapter Four

I don't remember much about the housewarming party we had the first weekend or the ones that followed at the end of most weeks until the one at New Year. With the state the house was in it was the ideal venue and with us all having such different circles of friends it soon became a gathering point for a large number of people.

The impression I have of the New Year's Eve party is like an old video with some moments of clarity but lots of scenes that hop and get stuck and keep replaying, of voices that fade out or are drowned by buzzing and crackling and faces that merge and morph.

I remember the air being thick with smoke and all kinds of stuff being passed around, the music so loud you could feel it slam through your body and someone falling or getting pushed against the wall when carrying a pizza up the stairs, plastering its face like a clown with a custard pie and defensively saying the place couldn't look any worse than it already did anyway.

Most people were pleased to see the back of 1988. We were all still reeling from the Lockerbie air crash so there was a lot of talk about that. I worried about Xanthe and the memories the disaster must be dredging up for her, as well as the poor people of Lockerbie which wasn't a million miles from where I'd grown up.

I remember the police coming round twice after our neighbours had complained about the noise and "suspicious smells" from the garden. They'd visited our parties so many times by then we were almost on first name terms.

I was drunk but not to the point of idiocy because

experience had taught me how far I could go without bringing on a fit and I hadn't yet told the others about my epilepsy. The last thing I wanted was the humiliation of them finding out in such a public way.

I didn't take the pills at the party either. On the one occasion I'd experimented as a student I'd been fine at the time but had a seizure the next morning during the comedown, which freaked me out a bit.

A small, skinny man with hunched shoulders and an Adam's apple that bobbed up and down, reminding me of a gecko, wearing a grey hoody and jeans that looked like they'd been sprayed onto his legs, kept appearing at odd moments asking for Fitz.

"Sorry," I said. "Don't know anyone called Fitz,"

"You must do," he yelled in my face. "He said he'd be here."

I took a step away and wiped spit off my ear. "Well we don't know him."

That seemed to satisfy him for a while but every now and then he'd pop up again with the same question and asking other people who didn't seem to be able to help him either.

Xanthe's eyes were drooping and she was throwing her arms around everyone. I even saw her kissing The Man Who Was Looking For Fitz, but she must have changed her mind because they seemed to be having a disagreement. She shoved him backwards and he stumbled into me, knocking my drink onto the floor with his backpack. I helped him pick up the bits of broken glass, cutting my hand in the process. From the blood on his lip I guessed Xanthe had bitten him.

"Can you take this stupid thing off?" asked Stuart getting hold of the straps. He tried to pull it off the man but was very nearly punched in the face for his trouble.

Zak said to Backpack Man, "Looks like you're at the wrong party. Try number thirteen – the one with all the bikes outside."

I saw Stuart accompany Backpack Man out of the room, but more bodies spilled through the door, sliding across my vision and I don't remember seeing him again. But I do remember Stuart telling a group of girls that the basement was out of bounds because the stairs weren't safe, and I remember Imogen and her boyfriend Rick dancing and thinking how cool they looked. And I remember being struck by how beautiful Zak was – the way his hair refused to be tamed, the contrast between his bright eyes and dark olive skin, the plumpness around his mouth and his expressive arched brows.

How had I not seen it before? I think I must have done during those long days in the Training Room but not allowed myself to think about it – partly because I knew there was no way a relationship with him would work. Now we lived together a fling would make life awkward for everyone afterwards. Besides, Stuart had decreed it was against the rules which was probably just as well. I knew Zak liked me, but I also knew I'd turn out to be a disappointment to him.

I hadn't, like Xanthe, lived in a squat or, like Imogen, trekked across Peru on my own and been stabbed by robbers. Hadn't thrown myself in front of a truck carrying live animal exports or been arrested for hurling missiles at a speaker from South Africa when they came to my university – or in fact done any of the principled things people he usually hung out with had done.

So, I'd convinced myself that it was better to have his friendship, which would last much longer than a relationship. He remarked once that we knew each other better than a lot of married couples did. We certainly saw more of each other, living in the same house and travelling into work together on the bus. To which I replied that I had no intention of ironing his pants. He agreed and said he didn't want to know about my morning breath.

Even now we'd been given our placements on different magazines we still phoned each other several times during the day to meet up at the coffee machine even though neither of us could stand the drinks that came out of it and we timed our lunchtimes so we could be together. We'd take a walk around the docks, share a bag of chips, look around the art gallery making irreverent observations and falling about laughing at the avant-garde exhibits or sit on a bench in front of the boats unpicking each other's life stories.

But there was something about Zak that night at the party – his eyes so full of light and laughter, his brows so expressive and that infectious laugh... I couldn't stop noticing him. He seemed, despite the people that were hanging round him, to be comfortable with me – at least he kept gravitating back to me to point out someone making a fool of themselves or to take up some half-finished thread of conversation.

Someone put on a track by the Fine Young Cannibals and he said with his heart-stopping smile as he appeared by my side, "My song to you, Em. You Drive Me Crazy."

"Er – thanks. Not sure which way to take that."

"Anyway you like."

He leaned in and said, "Stuart's little rule about not dating among housemates – rules are there to be broken, right?"

But the next thing I knew Stuart had flumped down on the floor on the other side of me.

"Have they got any idea what they look like?" he demanded, glaring at Imogen and Rick. "Have you ever seen such a plonker? Of all the people she could have chosen..." He was waving a half full whisky bottle as he spoke. "Not interrupting anything am I?"

"Yes," replied Zak but Stuart carried on. After a few moments Zak shrugged and melted away and I felt a stab of hatred for Stuart but I hoped he might keel over and go to sleep if he kept swigging from that bottle so I sat back against the wall while I waited, watching bodies twisting and sliding in and out of focus, trying to make out shapes in the dark. I gradually became aware Stuart was still talking.

"You don't mind, do you?" he was saying.

"Um, sorry?"

"Sometimes you remind me of her. I had to tell someone. It's been killing me."

"Right," I said, trying to catch up.

"I've never talked about this before. Never thought I'd be able to."

I've often replayed that scene in my head because I know now that if I'd made more of an effort to listen everything might have turned out differently but as it was all I got was, "I should never have…" – "She kept saying …" – "Dear God, I didn't mean it to end up like that" – "Of course if I could go back I'd do *anything*…"

Now when I think about it, it's obvious I should have suggested we go out into the garden or up on the roof where I could have heard what he was saying but at the time I was so worried about giving him the wrong signal and I was also fixated on Zak.

Every now and then I'd hear Zak's laughter rise up or see him stumble past and we'd share a look but as Stuart talked on, I saw a girl running her hand up and down Zak's arm. He was carrying on talking, not taking it off. He placed one hand on her hip and lifted her hair with the other while saying something into her ear, making my own hair lift up at the roots.

I didn't have the heart to keep asking Stuart to repeat himself, but the music was very loud, and my hearing had never been all it should be. Luckily, I'd mastered the art of raising my eyebrows or knitting them, smiling and nodding at these occasions, mimicking the expression on the talker's face. I hoped to God I wasn't getting it wrong because he was obviously telling me something important and I didn't want to hurt his feelings.

"You hate me now, don't you?" he said at last. "You think I'm scum."

"No, of course not."

I was running out of ways to answer. The next thing I knew he was crying. His head slumped against my shoulder and I could feel his tears tickling my neck and his body was heavy and unbearably hot. I thought there was a real chance I might suffocate or have a fit.

Zak shot me a quizzical look. I wanted to shout, "Not

what it looks like!" but tried to convey it all in a glance. He shrugged and turned away. The next thing I knew he was stumbling off towards his room with a German girl from the language school down the road.

"But what do you think I should have done?" asked Stuart.

"Well," I said helplessly, "it's hard to think what else you could have done."

"Really? You're not appalled? You don't hate me?" He waved the now empty bottle and smacked his head back against the wall but didn't seem to notice. "You're the only person who'd react so calmly."

Doubt crept up through me, but I managed to say, "We've all done things we regret, haven't we?"

I thought perhaps he'd be satisfied now he'd got whatever it was off his chest and shuffle off to his room but then it all started up again. I'd initially assumed he was confessing to illicit sex with another boy at school or possibly a master, knowing the school he'd gone to. But I began to think I'd been wide of the mark.

I had an uneasy feeling that this was more serious than just drunken rambling and started to question what I'd just sanctioned. As he shook against me, saying "You have no idea how much it means to me to hear you say that" I realised I couldn't possibly ask him to repeat the story now.

Eventually he fell asleep on me. I was getting a searing cramp in my legs but there didn't seem any way to get him off me except for waking him and I couldn't face him going through it all again.

I looked across at Xanthe who was lying in the lap of a man I'd never seen before on the window seat, having a deep and barely coherent "Is any of us really here?" conversation and decided it was pointless trying to get her attention.

At around four o'clock, just as I thought I was about to pass out from cramp, Imogen and another girl from *The Photographer* came over, took one of my arms each and pulled me out from under him, laughing.

But as I stumbled over dark shapes of bodies to the sanctuary of my own room my mother's warning question swam through my head – how much did I actually know about the people I'd moved in with?

***

The German girl stayed for brunch the next day. She sat sideways on her chair in the kitchen wearing one of Zak's campaign T-shirts, her slim, golden knees lodged between his legs, feeding him bits of croissant.

"Drink this," said Imogen. She passed me a concoction made with raw egg – the one food I'm slightly phobic about – and I had to fight against retching, which she seemed to take personally.

A man I didn't know had his head in the fridge, and the bathroom had been busy all morning. At odd intervals someone would stick their head round the door and say they were off. Xanthe bumbled in wearing her pyjamas and made herself something to eat. Stuart went around closing the doors and drawers she'd left open, switching off the light in the hall every few minutes in between crunching his bowl of cornflakes. I could feel his eyes on me but refused to look at him. I had a sense he was waiting for the others to leave. A chill crept over me as fragments of that conversation from last night swam back:

"It was as if it wasn't really me, as if I was watching someone else do it."

Zak and the German girl got up to leave. I scrambled up at the same time.

"When they came to arrest me, it was actually a relief."

"Arrest me" – he'd actually said that, hadn't he? I started to mumble something about getting in the bathroom while I had the chance.

"That thing I told you last night..." Stuart's face was pink, his eyes tauter than ever.

I froze, forcing a bright smile and zipping my lips. "Forgotten."

He wasn't having it. "Have you told anyone?"

I felt a frisson of fear. "No."

"Why not?"

"Because we're friends," I said, picking up my empty mug and slinging it in the sink.

He looked at me wonderingly, full of relief and gratitude that made me feel wretched. "You're not normal."

I managed a laugh. "Now you're not the first person to tell me that."

When I eventually got the chance to leave, I bumped into Zak in the hall. "You okay?" he asked.

"Of course, why wouldn't I be?" I must have said it a bit more sharply than I intended because he held up his palms in a sorry-I-asked way.

I pushed past him to the bathroom and sat on the floor with my head in my knees, thoughts whirling through my head. Stuart's unheard confession played on me over the next few days. We behaved like normal people, going to work and coming home but I kept stealing glances at him and wondering what it was he could have done that had got him sent to prison and that could make him so certain I'd be appalled. He'd made it clear that he was deeply ashamed and whatever it was he wouldn't be doing it again but so many criminals say that and yet can't help themselves.

I was tempted to tell Imogen, to gauge her reaction. With her cool head she'd know what to do but if Stuart suspected I'd told anyone, I had no idea how he might respond. He might, I thought, studying him, be a psychopath. A paedophile. A serial killer. And whatever he'd done, I'd told him it was okay.

The elderly couple next door accosted us outside the house about the noise at the party and asked innocently if that was the police they'd seen. Imogen went round with a box of chocolates to apologise but came back fuming. Mrs Nosey Parker had grabbed the chocolates off her, given her another lecture and shut the door in her face.

It wasn't until a week later that we made the gruesome discovery.

***

The boiler packed in on the Monday. We woke up shivering and found all the radiators were off and there was no hot water. In the kitchen Imogen gave the boiler a beating but it refused to come to life. The breakdown was compounded by arctic outside temperatures, a scarcity of heating engineers, prohibitive call-out charges and our total lack of funds.

The house with its high ceilings and rattly windows was so cold ice formed inside the windows. We were forced to make do with boiling kettles of water for washing and wearing coats and gloves inside the house. We stayed out as much as possible, impressing our editors with the extra hours we put in and went to the local swimming pool to linger under their hot showers.

The only room that offered any warmth was the living room which had an open fire, so we went on a wood gathering mission in the woods after work although we couldn't fit much wood in Xanthe's 2CV and Stuart refused to let us muck up his Capri. Stuart and Zak nearly came to blows over fire-building tactics but Imogen calmly built a pyramid and got it going.

Zak brought his duvet down and we huddled under it on the sofa telling ghost stories and playing Scruples until late in the night. There was a trace of perfume on the duvet and a stain I tried not to notice. I couldn't help thinking about the German girl in his bed and what she must have done to him and what he'd done to her. But then I reminded myself it wasn't my business, and in any case why should I care?

Our first hint of Stuart's explosive temper was when Zak laughed at an old school photo which he'd dropped while carrying a box upstairs and asked if he'd felt a prat dressed in the cloak and stockings that had been his uniform. "Or do you still dress like that when we're not looking?"

Stuart sprang at him. "You know nothing about me. Nothing!"

Zak looked shocked but tried to laugh it off. "All right, sorry."

But Stuart wasn't letting go. "You think it's all right to make assumptions about me purely because of where I went to school?"

"Again, sorry." Zak turned his head and murmured as an aside, "I seem to have touched a nerve."

Stuart grabbed him by the throat. "My stepfather sent me to school so he could beat up my family in peace. Are you happy now?"

He stormed out, slamming the door with such force the glass panel exploded into shards. Moments later he was back, glass crunching under his feet.

"And just so you know, people don't have a monopoly on poverty just because they come from oop north," he shouted as though they'd been having a completely different conversation. "Are you so bloody ignorant you don't know that there's been as much poverty here in Bristol? In High Wycombe? In London? And plenty of fat cat lords of the manor in Yorkshire and Manchester and…"

"Right. Got it," said Zak. When Stuart released his grip, Zak pulled a face. A moment later we heard a crack. Zak's nose steamed blood from a Glaswegian kiss.

"What's his fucking problem?" he breathed when Stuart had gone. He was obviously having to try quite hard not to cry.

"I guess school days are a sensitive subject," said Imogen handing him a tissue. "It might help if you didn't deliberately wind people up."

***

On the Wednesday we got the letters from the building society.

"How can we be in arrears?" Stuart was shouting, waving a letter around the kitchen like a dispatch paper.

"Two missed payments," said Zak, taking the letter off him and reading it.

We looked at each other, all hotly denying any knowledge of it.

"Ah," said Xanthe looking into her mug of tea.

"Send them a cheque," said Imogen. "Today."

"I can't. We don't get paid until Friday. It will bounce right back where it came from."

"Then borrow. Beg. Steal. Or we'll get repossessed."

"They don't really do that, do they?"

"Of course they do. They're not a charity."

Xanthe didn't eat for three days, which we tried to ignore until Stuart caved and lent her the money. He must have known he wouldn't get it back.

Zak insisted he cook a meal for all of us, which was the only way he could get her to accept food and produced an amazing Lebanese feast he'd picked up from his travels. Imogen and I made a very unsuccessful banoffee pie for dessert. I think we got a vital ingredient wrong so it didn't set and looked like sick but it tasted fine.

"This is fun," said Stuart uncorking the wine like a benevolent host and looking more relaxed than he'd done in days. "We should make it a regular thing. I'll cook next time. How about Friday?"

He seemed to have forgotten the way he'd attacked Zak and none of us wanted to remind him, so we found ourselves agreeing. What he didn't tell us was that he'd never cooked before. He borrowed a book from the library and swotted over it for most of the day before embarking on a complicated shopping mission after work.

He spent ages peering at the instructions, following them to the letter despite my assurances that measurements didn't have to be exact for a risotto. Like an old-fashioned housewife, he barricaded us out of the kitchen, refusing offers of help.

Hours passed. Stomachs groaned. We tried to take our minds off our hunger by playing Trivial Pursuit, but it only half worked.

"I can't think of the answer," Xanthe whined. "All I see is food. Even these wedges are making me think about cheese."

There were some half-empty bottles left over from the

party which distracted us for a short time but when they were finished the hunger gnawed away even stronger.

"Do you think he'd notice if we sneaked out to the chippy?" Zak whispered.

"Sadly yes," I said. "But perhaps if we create a distraction we might be able to sneak in and make a sandwich."

"Hmm, not sure I want to risk the Wrath of Stuart twice in a week," he said, nursing his swollen lip.

"I've got some chocolate in my room," Xanthe said, but she barely made it out of the door before Stuart came out of the kitchen.

"Won't be long. Where are you going?"

"Er - can I help?" she asked brightly.

"Certainly not. Get back in the living room."

She came back wincing an apology.

"Actually, I tell you what you could do," he called out from the kitchen. "Open a bottle of red to let it breathe. There's a nice bottle in the cellar I got given at the Bologna press launch. I hid it before the party. Far too good for riff raff."

She spun round on her heel. "Right you are."

Liquid food. It was something. Zak and I turned back to the game but I was so hungry I'd nearly lost interest - I had a stomach cramp and my head ached. Xanthe's footsteps disappeared down the hall.

A scream shattered the silence. Something clattered in the kitchen.

Zak let out a low groan. "Noooo. He'll have to start all over again."

"It's coming from the basement," I said. "Xanthe?"

I expected to see a rat or spider or be treated to one of her ghost stories, but nothing could have prepared me for what lay at the bottom of the stone steps. It took my brain a little while to catch up with what my eyes had already taken in but yes, it was a human being.

Chapter Five

The small figure on the floor caught in the wavering beam of the torch Stuart grabbed from the hook by the door wore a familiar grey hoodie, through which his shoulder blades stood out like wings. His ratty face was turned away at an odd angle, but the angry red complexion he'd had was now grey, and his mouth curled up into a snarl revealing long, gappy teeth. Dried vomit crusted around his mouth. He was very still.

"Shit."

"Jesus, the poor bastard."

Xanthe was standing with her hands clamped to her face, hyperventilating. "I nearly stood on him," she whispered, covering her face.

I couldn't work out if the smell in there was the stench of death I'd heard people talk about or simply vomit and other excretions mixed with the basement's awful mouldy reek. There was a dark stain under the body that I didn't even want to think about.

"It's that bloke from the party," said Stuart after a few moments. "The one who was looking for someone."

"Fitz," I said, remembering.

"Is he definitely dead?" asked Xanthe from behind her fingers.

Zak snorted. "Looks pretty dead from where I'm standing."

He moved forward but Stuart shot out an arm. "Don't. Not yet. Not until we've decided what to do. We have to stick together and agree how to handle this."

I swallowed. "Yes. We need to call a doctor."

"Bit late for that."

"No, I mean – doesn't someone have to sign a death certificate? Take him away? The police then."

Stuart's voice was quiet but firm. "No."

"*No?*"

"Think about it. How's it going to look? He died at our party. Probably fell down these steps in the dark because we hadn't fixed the light." Stuart's voice shook, and he leant on the wall for support. "I kept *saying* we needed to do something about it. Or someone hit him. Or…" He lifted his head as another scenario presented itself. "Or he reacted badly to something he was given."

Zak backed away, shaking his head. "Don't look at me."

"I *am* looking at you."

"Fuck off, I didn't give him anything."

"No? Prove it then. Because believe me, if they do tests on his blood and find he's taken something, and the police start asking around you'll be the first person they want to talk to. Everyone knows what happened to Xanthe's dog…"

"What?" Xanthe's face drained of colour. I held my breath.

"What are you—?" she began. She looked from one to the other of us, her eyes huge and glistening.

"Not now," said Stuart. But apparently, he couldn't stop himself adding, "Did you really believe it was a road accident?"

Zak was looking at Stuart as though he'd like to kill him. "Thanks for that." Turning to Xanthe he said, "I'm so sorry. I swear to God he was already dead. I didn't…"

"I hate you," she whispered. She turned to me in horror. I sensed what was coming. "Emily did you *know?*"

Stuart cut across her. "Can we just focus on what's happening here?"

I felt furious with both men at that moment. I couldn't take my eyes off the body, still couldn't believe it was happening. During the period when I'd had most of my fits I could sometimes sense them coming on and I'd try and get away somewhere quiet even though I knew it made me more vulnerable to injury. This could have been me – a group of strangers recoiling from my dead body, wondering how to dispose of it, my parents and sister never finding out, wondering for the rest of their lives if I'd really gone or if I was going to walk back through the door. I clamped my hand over my mouth as bile crept up.

Xanthe's breathing was forced and shallow. "Whatever happened, it's not our fault. We didn't do anything. We'll explain to the police —"

A tic moved at the side of Stuart's face. He closed his eyes and whispered, "God, you're stupid."

Zak moved and I thought he was going to hit Stuart. But instead we watched in silence as he walked down step by step. You could hear the creak of his shoes and the grit on the stairs crunching under them. He circled the body, knelt down beside it, shielding his nose and mouth, choking into his crooked arm. Gently, he went through the pockets under the wavering beam of Stuart's torch while we watched from the stairs, peeling the shirt fabric out of the vomit crust with such care tears stabbed the back of my eyes.

As he lifted the body an arm flopped out towards me. I jumped back with a scream. I was having trouble keeping my breathing steady. He pulled out a train ticket from Leeds and a door key. The train had the same date as the party and was an open return.

"No wallet," he said, frowning.

"He had a backpack," I remembered. "One with a smiley face on."

Shining the torch onto every inch of space we concluded that the backpack had vanished.

"So, I'm thinking either someone killed him to get the backpack or found him dead and took it," said Zak.

We digested what this meant. Someone else from the party knew he was here. One of the people who we'd invited, who'd been drinking our booze and eating our crisps, had not only killed this man – or stolen from him – but they'd left the body here knowing we were the ones who'd end up as prime suspects. What sort of person would do that?

"We've got to get him out of here," Zak said.

"No, we've got to call the police," I argued. "We don't know what we're dealing with. If we don't tell them and they come looking for him…"

"Why should they?" asked Stuart. His voice sounded far away. "There's nothing to link him to us. We didn't know him. He didn't know us. He was at the wrong address, looking for this Fitz who none of us knows."

"Perhaps he found him – or her," said Zak. "And this is the result."

My stomach was roiling. To think of someone committing murder while we were upstairs dancing and fooling about, Stuart slumped on my shoulder wasting his breath shouting his stupid story into my ear, Zak being chatted up by the German girl and Xanthe high as a kite in the arms of someone's friend's brother while Imogen and her boyfriend were doing their frenzied dancing. None of it seemed real.

"But for God's sake hundreds of people saw him here in this house." I could feel the hysteria rising in my voice. "Someone will remember him, and the police will come here, and I don't know what you get for disposing of a body but I'm pretty sure…"

I looked round for support. If Imogen had been there she'd have backed me up, but she'd gone up to London to a concert with Rick, and Xanthe was in her own world, still reeling over what had happened to her dog.

"This is mad. What about his family? Surely they deserve to know what happened to him?"

"Will you shut up?" Stuart demanded in a stage whisper, grabbing my shoulders. "The neighbours don't need any encouragement to dob us in to the police. There's nothing they'd like more than to see us carted away."

Suddenly the spoof burial we'd carried out in front of their eyes didn't seem so funny after all. I was shivering so violently now I thought I might have a seizure.

"We can't risk him being found here," he said more

gently. I flinched as he laid his hand on my arm. "You might be prepared to take the chance but I'm not. In case you've forgotten, I know what the police are really like."

The others looked at him and then at me, but he didn't elaborate, and I couldn't.

My head swam. "I'm sorry, can we talk about this upstairs? I keep thinking that door's going to swing closed and…"

I had visions of being trapped down there with the corpse, unable to open the top or bottom door, trying and failing to devise ways of getting out of there and Imogen coming back from London but not having any need to look in the basement for ages when she'd find five bodies down there instead of one.

We bolted up the steps. Xanthe locked the door, which took forever because her fingers were trembling so much. A hissing sound sent Stuart running into the kitchen to rescue the charred onions.

"I'm guessing nobody's hungry anymore?" he called over his shoulder.

"I'll make some tea," said Xanthe.

Ignoring Zak's "Yeh, tea – that'll solve everything," she went into the kitchen and we followed.

The light in the room seemed harsher than usual. The windows were steamed up from Stuart's culinary efforts and there was an acrid smell of blackened onions and dry-boiled rice. I switched off the rings. I suppose we were lucky not to have burned the house down but I didn't feel lucky. The clock on the oven said nine-forty-five.

Xanthe opened the window to release the smell. Stuart shoved her out of the way and hauled it closed. "Do you want the whole world to hear what we're saying?"

Zak fell into a chair, rubbed his hands over his face, then pulled them backwards and forwards through his hair. "Fucking fuck-faced *fuck*, why did this have to happen to us? Whatever we do we need to decide fast."

He drummed his fingers on the table. "The longer he's here the more chance there is of the police being tipped off and coming round. Even if they don't, he'll decompose and pretty soon the neighbours will get suspicious. I mean the Parkers were suspicious of us *before* this. So, do we tell the authorities or pretend he was never here?"

We waited for the kettle to roar. Xanthe poured hot water into the mugs and slopped a teabag from one to another, an economy measure that Stuart insisted on. She made the usual mess on the counter and down the front of the units but for once he didn't say anything. My arm was shaking so much I spilled half my tea down my top, but it seemed such a pointless thing to fuss about just then.

"Okay," said Zak, stretching out his fingers and studying them. "Dream scenario is that the police come, agree it was an accident, take away the body and apart from a small piece in the local paper about someone dying at a party in Bristol there's no publicity."

Xanthe started to interrupt but he held up his hand. "*Nightmare scenario* is that the police come, get suspicious, take us all in for questioning, take statements from everyone who was at the party, question our employers, our friends, our neighbours, inform the press – and we get done for keeping the body hidden in the cellar for a week anyway."

"But we weren't hiding the body," I objected. "We didn't know it was there."

"Yes, but are they going to believe that? They might not be able to get a conviction for murder or even manslaughter, but our careers would be wrecked, we'd lose the house, then there's the effect on our families…This is fucking *shit*."

"We can't afford to take time out if it goes to trial," said Xanthe. "We can barely pay the mortgage as it is."

My head pounded as I thought of the reaction in the company. They'd thrown a reporter out a few weeks before for forgetting to pay for his petrol. Reputation was everything to them. They were hardly likely to give us a second chance after this.

Zak pressed his knuckles into his temples. The fridge hummed. The puerile messages spelled out in magnets on the front seemed to have been put there by a different set of people in a different lifetime.

"Stuart's right, it doesn't look good," he said at last, wiping his face on his sleeve.

"And wake up, Emily – do you think PC Plod and his chums are going to take our word for it? They're probably on bonuses – nothing they'd like more than to take down some journos. Have you ever been to a football match? Seen how they treat people at demos? At Orgreave they were bludgeoning people who were on the ground. Or even walking away. When they raided the sect one of them dragged a disabled woman out by her hair."

"Sect?" I asked, distracted.

He shook his head like it was perfectly normal. "Where I grew up."

Questions flew around my head, but I shelved them for later.

"He's right," said Xanthe. "You can't expect the police to be on your side. You should have heard the things they said to me when I reported something bad that happened in the foster-home. They laughed. Called me a liar, called me names – made me feel worse than I did before."

"But not all police are like that," I said. And yet at the same time I was reliving the lecture I got from the officer back home after the firework throwing incident. It had made me feel so small and stupid and frightened. And they'd been wrong then, too.

He'd made it clear he would like to have taken it further and it was only the boy's parents' – in his opinion misguided - generosity of spirit that stood between me and criminal proceedings.

How much worse would it be now that I was an adult, trying to explain away a dead body in my possession? I was impressionable, always had been. If someone accused me of borrowing or breaking something, I'd always get a clear mental image of doing just that while I was denying it, which made me act guilty even if I wasn't. I couldn't see myself coming off well in an interrogation.

"Not only that," said Stuart, "but we've all been in

contact with the backpack chap. We'll all have left a trace. They'll find the evidence they want and make it fit."

I caught Stuart staring at me, daring me to object. I thought about his secret and the way he'd flown at Zak the other day, the damage he'd done to Zak's face in those few short seconds and wondered how he'd react to not getting his way now.

"You have no idea what it's like Inside," said Stuart. The others probably thought he was talking about things he'd heard or read about but I noticed him shudder at some recollection. "The whole dehumanising horror."

I thought about the body in the cellar below us ticking away like a timebomb. The longer we left it the grislier the task would be. There was murmured assent around the table.

"We have to agree on this," Zak was saying. "Whatever we do we have to stick together and see it through. Otherwise we'll all end up with a police record or worse still behind bars."

"Emily?" said Stuart.

Three pairs of eyes looked at me expectantly. I pressed my hands to my head. Tension roared in my ears. I wished it would all just go away. Backpack Man meant nothing to us. He should never have been at the party. What did we owe him? Nothing. And yet he had the power to destroy our lives. Indignant anger swept through me. How dare he muck up everything I'd worked so hard for?

"I suppose so," I said at last.

"But what are we going to do with him?" asked Xanthe in a small voice. "The Parkers will definitely get suspicious if we start digging up the garden. Again. She's onto us if we just nip to the shops for some booze." She closed her eyes.

"Who said anything about digging up the garden?" said Zak.

"What then?"

"We take…" He froze as we heard footsteps and laughter in the street outside. A group of young people enjoying themselves. It could have been us on any other night. We waited for the noise to die away.

"We take him away from here and make it look like a suicide."

Not the most detailed plan, but this thing had been sprung on us and we weren't in the habit of plotting ways to get rid of bodies. Now I think perhaps everyone should have a contingency plan because you never know when it might happen to you. We were all quiet, thinking about it.

"We'll need a car," Zak said. "He's too heavy and awkward to carry far."

But we'd have to get him into the car somehow. I couldn't bear the thought of touching the body. I kept thinking about things I'd read – bodies on the battlefield falling apart as they were picked up.

Stuart and Xanthe were the only ones with cars and Dollie, Xanthe's 2CV, was barely capable of getting across town. If a trip involved a hill she'd have to circle round it – and that was without a body in the back. The driver's door had been held together with gaffa tape since she opened it without paying attention while trying to get a jammed cassette out during the middle of an anecdote and the door had been ripped off by passing traffic.

Her car also had a tiny boot and the thought of having to hack off limbs in order to origami the body in was too horrendous to contemplate – not to mention hardly fitting the appearance of suicide.

Stuart scraped his chair back. "No way, not mine. I'm not risking getting the blame for everything this time. If I'm going down, you lot are coming with me."

Zak fumbled for his cigarettes. "For God's sake, you've never been down anywhere. And have you got a better plan?"

Stuart sank his head into his hands. The Capri might have been an ugly orange rust bucket but I knew how much it meant to him. It was the only possession he really cared about and there was no way he'd be able to afford another car now we were stuck with an ever-increasing mortgage, the cost of a new boiler and an ever-mounting pile of bills.

That legacy from his grandpa had been swallowed up, largely because of his generosity in helping Xanthe out as well as paying his own bills. The car was all he had left.

The hand on the clock clicked forward several times.

"All right," he said at last. "Two of you take the car. Don't bring it back and don't tell me what you've done with it. I'll report it stolen tomorrow morning. The other person needs to stay and help me clean up. We're in this together, all equally culpable."

"I can't drive," I said. I didn't add that I'd never learnt because of my fits. It didn't seem like the right time to get into all that.

Silence hung between us. Zak took a long draw on the cigarette, ground it out in his empty mug and said, "Fine, okay, I'll do it."

He turned to me and he suddenly looked so young and vulnerable. "Come with me?"

I felt like someone had driven a stake through me. It wasn't fair to leave him to do this alone and yet I was terrified. If we were caught…

"It would give us a better chance of success," Stuart said. "A couple will attract much less attention than a young man driving on his own in the dark. Especially, no offence but," he squeezed Zak's shoulder, "one with your colouring."

Xanthe's eyes on me were huge, round and unblinking. I was never sure what to expect with her. As useless as I knew myself to be, I felt Xanthe would be even more likely to freak out and do something daft – especially with the level of hatred she was feeling for Zak at that moment, now she'd found out about her dog. I put my head in my hands. I don't know how long for, but I suddenly became aware of the stillness as they waited for an answer. I shrugged and nodded. What else could I do?

We waited another hour, then another. It was one thing having the idea – quite another doing it for real. Eventually, having discussed all manner of scenarios and solutions, the other three located the key to the external door and hoisted the body up the cellar stairs while I scraped the car windows except for the boot. It took them ages and it was such a cold night the ice was packed hard and refroze as fast as I scraped.

I was shivering so violently I dropped the scraper more than once and had to scrabble for it in the dark. A rosy glow emanated from the bedroom window next door and I kept thinking someone was watching us but whenever I looked up there was no sign of movement.

The boys walked to the car with the backpack man draped around Zak's shoulders like a drunk, whispering instructions to each other and doing the occasional forced laugh to make the whole thing look like typical weekend behaviour. The breath of two men froze in the air.

I lifted the boot as quietly as I could. The car was parked side-on so with the boot up our actions were shielded from the Nosy Parkers' house on our right and the one on our left was empty but there was still the very real likelihood of passers-by hearing us through the hedge.

We stood in a huddle around the car while Stuart wrestled the corpse into the boot. It wasn't easy – a tight fit – and involved a lot of grunting, panting and swearing. I heard the crack of a bone breaking and had to run back into the house to be sick.

Xanthe was standing in the hallway when I came out of the bathroom. Her eyes looked like huge hollows in her white face.

"Is this really happening?" she asked.

"I suppose it must be."

She pulled me into a fierce hug and whispered, "Be careful, won't you? Don't do anything unless you're absolutely sure no one can see. And make sure Zak doesn't do anything stupid."

I clung to her skinny body for what seemed like a long time. The truth sank in – that this could be the last time we'd see each other. If only I could persuade her we shouldn't be doing this and that the two of us should just walk away but in the end I knew it was useless. She'd had trouble from the police when she was living in the squat and found them no help at all when she'd reported abuse while she was in care. She wouldn't trust them any more than she trusted Zak but oddly she seemed to trust me which I found strangely touching and terrifying.

When I came back out into the darkness I could just make out the orange glow of a cigarette in Zak's hand. "Let's go," he muttered, tossing it to the ground and grinding it underfoot.

My legs felt like concrete. I was surprised I was even able to walk. The whole thing felt like a ghastly dream. Mechanically, I opened the passenger door and climbed in. This could only happen to me, I kept telling myself. My life couldn't have taken a more bizarre turn. I was in a car with the man I was in love with – and a corpse.

"So where shall we go?" Zak's voice sounded unnaturally loud as though he was suggesting a day out.

"The gorge?" I suggested.

He nodded as though it was where he'd had in mind too. Clifton Suspension Bridge was the obvious place for suicides but far too public for staging one. There were however lots of dark crevices and steep drops around Avon Gorge, clumps of bushes for concealment and at least one point where the netting put up to prevent falling rocks had broken.

We tried the area around Sea Walls but just as we found an ideal location we spotted a car already parked by the trees.

"Shit," Zak whispered.

The car was rocking, and its windows were steamed up so there was a chance the occupants would be too busy to notice us, but it was too big a chance to take. We tried another place near the Observatory. The same thing happened only this time there were several other cars.

"Fuck." Zak's head thumped against the windscreen. "Don't any Bristolians do it in their own beds?"

"We could try later?" I whispered.

He shook his head. "We can't keep cruising round. Someone will see us and think we get our kicks from watching."

"So where do we go?"

He looked straight ahead. "Away. As far as we dare before it gets light."

It was the last thing I wanted to hear. I was desperate to get rid of the body as soon as we had the chance, so we could put the whole thing behind us and pretend it had never happened, but I had to accept the chances of abandoning it around the gorge or parks of Bristol without being seen were now pretty slim.

The roads glittered with frost. The city lights were dazzling and disorientating against the dark night as we left the Downs behind and descended the steep hill back into town. We passed all the places that had become part of our lives – the bus stop, the curry house, the Spud U like, the laundry. I thought about the people in the houses we passed living their lives, washing the dishes, curled up together on the sofa in front of *The Late Show*, putting the bins out, sleeping, checking on their children, making love.

Everything appeared in sharper clarity than usual. I noticed pointless details like carved figures over doorways; the pattern on a stained-glass panel, a couple hanging out of a window smoking, a pair of shoes left out on a step.

We filled up with petrol on the outskirts of town and each took out as much money as the hole-in-the-wall would allow. We didn't talk about it, just did it. Zak bought a bottle of whisky. I hoped he wasn't planning to drink himself into oblivion while he was at the wheel, but he placed it in the glove compartment. Neither of us spoke for a long time. I could hear Zak's breathing, watched the windscreen cloud. He wiped a circle with his gloved hand.

I reached out to turn the heating on but he caught my arm.

"Don't."

"Just to clear the windows."

"No. The last thing we want is him heating up." He jerked his head back as though I might have forgotten who he was referring to. My legs felt like they were made of ice.

I stretched my skirt over my knees clad in opaque tights, but it kept springing back. I wished I'd changed into jeans and a chunky jumper, but sartorial matters hadn't been uppermost in my mind when I'd left the house.

After a while the silence between us was unbearable. Zak shoved in a CD but after a few Enya songs muttered, "Christ, what is this shite?" and fiddled with the radio until he found something he liked. I wish he hadn't because I can never hear songs like Tracy Chapman's *Fast Car* without being back on that road knowing what we were about to do.

The speedometer lurched to the right as we joined the motorway. Dark shapes of trees and buildings flickered past. The lights on the opposite carriage swarmed towards us like searchlights.

"What year?" he asked when a song by Squeeze came on.

I looked at him.

He looked down at the wheel. "Sorry. I'm just trying…"

He was right – we'd go crazy just sitting and thinking about what we were doing.

"I know, yes. Sorry. Um, no – can't think straight. Nineteen seventy-six? Seventy-seven?" I said at last, trying to stop my teeth from chattering.

He frowned. "I was thinking a bit later."

We raced to guess the songs by their intro and sang on when we went through tunnels, so we could try and hit the right word when the sound came back. But the singing and the guessing were subdued. I panicked every time a car drew up close to us or we saw a police car. It seemed like everywhere people were leering in through the windows. Lights were too bright, other cars were accidents waiting to happen. Zak must be over the limit. We'd drunk a couple of bottles of wine between us while trying to stave off our hunger while Stuart was cooking. Funny how that desperation to eat had seemed so real. Now so trivial. My stomach was knotted so hard I didn't feel as though I'd ever want to eat again.

"Are you all right?" he asked after a while.

I almost laughed. "Been better."

He nodded and said quietly, "It's shit, isn't it?"

"Do you think this is going to work?"

After a long pause he said, "Honestly? No idea."

I looked out into the night. "If we get caught do you think the others will stick with us?"

He gave a short, bitter laugh. "Would you?"

I imagined Stuart and Xanthe staring blank-faced at the police, denying any knowledge of anything and appearing shocked to discover there'd been a body in the car their housemates had taken. But we who were driving the car with the body in it were surely never going to get away with protesting our ignorance. Fear sat like a stone in my stomach. I just kept praying to something to get me out of there, make it all stop.

He squeezed my hand. "We'll get it right."

Fields of darkness spread out around us. I wished we could go back but we were on this road now and Macbeth's argument came into my head about returning being as risky as carrying on. Riskier even. It had been bad enough getting the body into the car in front of the neighbours. How much harder would it be to try and get it back into the house? And what would we do with it then?

Nobody had walked down the road as we were getting him into the car. We couldn't hope to be that lucky twice. And we could hardly leave it in Stuart's car, taking it to and from work as if it was a perfectly normal thing to drive around with a body in the boot. I had to fight off an unhelpful cartoon image of the car being pursued by dogs everywhere we went.

I was so cold I'd lost all feeling in my legs and my lips were so stiff I couldn't talk properly. Road signs came and went and each time I wondered if the name would be significant. We hit traffic around Taunton but after that the road was clear.

An hour passed and then another.

In the middle of nowhere Zak pulled over. "Sorry, got to pee."

"What? Where? You can't leave me here. With *that*."

He raised his brows. "Want to come?"

"I've had better offers. Didn't you go before we left?"

He gave an incredulous laugh. "Strangely I had other things on my mind."

"Can't we stop at the next services?"

"Who says there'll be any? I won't be a minute."

I've never felt more alone than sitting there watching his figure being swallowed up by the darkness. At first the silence roared. Then the rain started, drops spattering onto the windscreen like machine gun fire. Was he ever coming back?

A knocking. My blood froze. I was getting horrible flashbacks of an urban myth that had gone around our school about a woman turning round and seeing a crazy man banging her husband's decapitated head on the car.

Surely I must have misheard. But no, there it was again. For God's sake he wasn't dead at all! He was awake and banging on the boot to be let out. A part of me wanted to punch the air - and a part was too terrified to contemplate what he'd do to us when he got free. And who he'd tell…

At the corner of my eye something moved. My heart exploded as I snapped my head round. A luminous jacket flashed past the rain-streaked window, then a face appeared. I screamed. No sound came out.

"Can you open the window please, madam?"

Heart lurching, barely able to breathe, I leaned across and fumbled with the catch. All the time I was looking desperately for Zak.

"Are you all right?" asked the police officer as he shone his torch in.

Trying to control my trembling I forced a smile and assured him I was fine.

He poked his head inside the car. I drew back.

"We thought you'd broken down."

"Oh. No. My friend had to – you know, he needed the bathroom." I could hear myself jabbering.

He frowned. "The hard shoulder's not for parking."

"Sorry. I'll tell him."

The officer took a few steps away and spoke into his phone. This was bad. If one thing led to another and he asked to look inside the boot I couldn't think of a single plausible explanation. Yes, I'd try and feign surprise but given the way I was behaving I didn't stand a chance of convincing him.

I stared at the place where Zak had disappeared. Where had he got to? Was it possible he'd seen the police car and legged it?

"Going far?" asked the policeman popping his face in at the window again.

I gave the name of a place I'd seen on a road sign.

"That's nice. Visiting for the weekend? Made an early start, haven't you? Where are coming from?"

What was this? Despite the cold, I felt a bead of sweat run down my face. Why were we having this casual conversation? Didn't he have more important things to do? Or was he working up to the real question?

I mumbled something about a friend's birthday.

He moved round to the back of the car, his feet crunching on the asphalt. I counted the steps towards the boot. My breath was coming in juddery gasps. All I could do was wait for him to spring the catch.

Then out of the darkness walked Zak. He stood haloed in the headlamps and I read his expression. The police hadn't seen him yet. He had a chance. He could melt back into the darkness, run into the trees and afterwards deny he'd ever been in the car with me. Join the others back home and they'd all say they knew nothing about a body in the house. It must have been Emily.

Zak seemed to be thinking about it for a long time but slowly, trance like, he walked up towards the car. "Everything okay?" he asked the officer casually, but I could hear the catch in his voice.

"Are you the owner of this vehicle, sir?"

"Yes."

"What's your name?"

"Stuart Mountford."

"Can I see your licence please?"

I heard Zak mumble something about it being at home.

"Do you have your insurance details?"

"Not on me either, I'm afraid."

"You'd be able to produce them though at your nearest police station?"

"Yes of course."

I couldn't hear the rest of the questions and answers because they were turned away from me and the wind was buffeting the car.

"One of your rear lights isn't working, Mr Mountford," the officer said, turning back again. He pointed out the offender. They were standing inches away from the body.

Zak bent down and examined it. "See what you mean, officer. I'll get it fixed."

"You certainly will and at the first opportunity. Do you realise how dangerous it is to drive without a light? It means cars behind can't tell if you're slowing down. If you had to brake suddenly someone could easily smash into the back of you. You could end up causing a serious accident or even death. Think how you'd feel about that."

The dreadful irony of causing someone's death while trying to conceal another death we hadn't caused…I'd been wrong when I thought things couldn't get any worse.

"Yes, I understand. I'm sorry, I didn't realise. I'm sure it was fine earlier. It must have just gone on the way here this evening."

But unfortunately, the officer wasn't going to leave it like that.

"Given the time of night, I'm considering whether I should let you drive the car on to your destination in that state or have it taken away."

I closed my eyes. This couldn't get any worse. I had to press my hand against my mouth to prevent myself from being sick or crying. Zak was silent, waiting for the police officer to come to the decision that could make all the difference to whether we slept in our own beds that night or never saw them again.

"On this occasion I'm going to let you drive on."

I wanted to kiss him. I could hear the relief in Zak's voice as he thanked him.

But it wasn't over.

"You'll need to get it fixed first thing in the morning. You are not allowed to drive the vehicle until you've done so. I'm going to issue you with two tickets. The first is for the light. You need to get it stamped by your garage during the next seven days and brought into the station to show the work's been done.

"The second is for you to produce your licence, insurance details and MOT certificate also within seven days, so you can do that at the same time. If you don't the prosecution process will begin. Do you understand?"

"All right, that's fair. Thank you."

I sat rigid, waiting. As Zak was about to open the driver's door to get back in the officer called, "And don't stop on the hard shoulder again unless it's a real emergency. I should be giving you a ticket for that as well."

"Right. I'm sorry, thanks."

As Zak sank into the seat he blew through his cheeks and slumped over the wheel. He fumbled for his inhaler and took a long drag.

"Thought we'd had it," he said between puffs.

"What kept you? I thought you weren't coming back," I told him.

He started the car up and manouvered it out towards the road.

"I wouldn't do that to you."

"But you thought about it, didn't you?"

He coloured and dropped his gaze. "Yeh. Sorry."

We kept checking the mirror to see if the police were following us. Surely it had been obvious I was a nervous wreck? The way they'd appeared so suddenly made me certain they'd do so again at any moment.

Zak was fuming about living in "a fucking police state" and saying we'd have to change direction now.

"You gave him Stuart's name," I said after a moment, trying to keep my voice level.

He shrugged. "I could hardly give him mine, could I? I doubt Stuart's car's insured for other drivers. Anyway, he's going to report the car as stolen, remember? Hopefully not while we're still in it."

After a few moments I said, "So you're not insured to drive this car. But you do have a driving licence, right?"

He shook his head and laughed "Emily, we have a body in the boot and you're worrying about whether I have a licence? Look, I can drive for God's sake. We've got this far haven't we? I have had a licence before, it's just, well, I'm sort of banned."

"*Sort of* banned?"

"Only for a year. Bit of an accident coming over a hill - I hit a queue of cars at the top and they all went into each other like dominoes. But look if you'd rather take over please be my guest…"

I shook my head. "I can't."

"Right so you're stuck with me, aren't you?"

We drove on until we reached some services where Zak filled up the petrol again. The lighted windows looked so inviting. It made me think of being very young travelling with my family to stay with my relations, snuggled in our sleeping bags with the back seats down. What would they say if they could see me now?

"Can we go in?" I said. "I'm desperate for the loo and I'm so cold."

He sighed. "Better not be seen together. You go. But keep your face down in case they have video cameras."

I was afraid of him falling asleep at the wheel, so I bought two coffees on my way out and nursed mine between my knees for the next few miles. We left the motorway and drove for some way on an A road. We came to a crossroads and after a few moments of indecision he chose a smaller road.

We drove across miles of moorland and in and out of small towns and villages. We followed a series of narrow lanes with high hedges surrounded by darkness. I could make out sheep and gorse and trees.

After miles and miles we could see the sea like a cold, grey metal sheet. We drove through more villages and small lanes and eventually followed a sign to a headland. Zak drove through the car park and ignoring the boundary rammed the car up over some grass. We bumped along a track and across more grass. The car protested but he floored the accelerator and we ploughed on.

"This'll do," he said at last, cutting the engine.

Silence filled the car. I tried to work out how far we'd have to walk back to find any sort of civilisation if we were to leave the car here. We sat for a while on the cliff top to make sure we hadn't been followed. My heart slammed against my ribs as though I'd been running. The only sound was our breathing and the waves booming. The wind rocked the car so hard I thought it might blow it over. I was trying not to remember my dread of heights.

I described my idea of moving the body into the driving seat and pushing the car off the cliff as though The Man Who Was Looking For Fitz had driven it over. Zak sat very still, thinking about it.

"Hmm," he said at last. "I think the important thing is to get the car as far away from the body as possible. A car's going to draw attention and will be linked back to Stuart immediately whereas a body might take a while to get washed up and then identified. Anyway, we'll need some means of getting away from here."

When I opened the door, the wind tried to rip it off. It tore at our hair and clothes and filled our lungs with salty air. Below us the sea was thundering against the rocks, sending up towers of spray, ghostly white in the moonlight. We staggered round to the boot, pressing our bodies against the wind. I really didn't want to see inside but at the same time I couldn't wait to get rid of the burden.

The face was turned away, the body in a foetal position, much as it had been in the basement. Thank God for the darkness and the fresh wind. I could almost kid myself the cargo was and always had been inanimate.

Zak leaned in and shovelled the body up into his arms. "Help me with the feet." They kept getting caught.

I didn't look at the face this time. Somehow, we got the body out of the car. Zak heaved it towards him in an embrace and walked – or dragged – it over to the cliff edge which now seemed much further away. I was terrified he'd lose his footing or be blown off the overhang.

"Check there's no one around," he panted.

I strained my eyes. Only dark nothingness for as far as I could see. The sky was sprinkled with stars and I wondered how I could appreciate beauty at a time like that.

I looked back at Zak and the backpack man. The pair stood there locked in each other's arms like a couple of lovers. They shuffled closer to the edge of the cliff, toppled dangerously, then one pitched forward. I watched it fall. The body tumbled through the air, almost beautiful, the arms spread out like wings. The jagged rocks and the sea rose up to take him.

I waited for the smash as it hit the water. It didn't come.

Zak sank to his knees. He raised his hands to the sides of his head.

"Shit."

He rocked forward. I thought for a moment he was praying but he kept looking back over the edge as if he thought he might have been mistaken. I looked too, going as close to the drop as I dared. My head lurched as I saw the problem. The body was still there, not even halfway down the cliff.

"Have to leave it," I shouted above the wind. "Come away from the edge."

"No, no we can't. I'll have to —"

"Don't be stupid. You'll die."

He wiped his hand over his mouth. His breathing was all over the place and his face was twisted with fear.

"Zak, you're not going to. Please don't." I grabbed hold of him but he shook me off.

Slowly, he started his descent. He shouted something

65

back up to me but it was lost in the wind. I watched, frozen in horror as his feet slipped from under him a couple of times and he perched on perilous ledges, grasping crumbling bits of rock. The wind was whipping his hair and clothes, trying to tear him away from the cliff.

Every time I looked down my stomach roiled and my head spun. My brain felt as if it was sliding around. It took ages for him to get to the body and the wind kept pulling but somehow he reached the crumpled figure lying on the outcrop.

Pressing himself back against the rock Zak kicked hard. Then again and again, putting all his weight into it. The violence shook me even though I knew the body was past feeling anything. Eventually, after several attempts the corpse dislodged and rolled over the edge. This time it hit the water. But how was Zak going to get back up?

For the second time that evening I was terrified and alone. I prayed over and over to a God I'd long since abandoned to get me through this nightmare. I kept looking round, expecting to hear sirens and see a barrage of blue lights. Was I going to have to answer for this on my own? I hadn't realised up until then that it was possible to feel this scared and not die.

"Shit." I jumped at the panic in Zak's voice. I heard a skittering and a splash as rocks fell.

My head swam as I crawled on my front to the edge. I was almost dragged over just looking. I could just make out Zak's shape in the darkness, swinging, scrabbling, sliding.

"There's nowhere to hold," he shouted.

I could see a ledge just above him to the right, but he couldn't get a grip. He was fighting against the wind. His face was frozen in panic, his feet flailing at the rock. I stared down past him. The moonlit sea was thrashing against the dark rocks. No sign of the body. I looked back at Zak – if I didn't do something he'd go the same way.

"Wait," I shouted.

"No – it won't work," he yelled back, a note of resignation in his voice. "There's no point you…"

Ignoring him, I inched down one level, sending more stones bowling down to the sea. I'd never been so scared. This was crazy. Surely, we were both going to fall? And be found close to the body which police would obviously work out had been transported in the car we'd left at the top. After all our efforts such an ignominious end. I almost gave up.

But something took over, a voice that told me to shut up and concentrate, and somehow, eventually, I managed to reach the ledge above Zak.

I anchored myself around a piece of rock that jutted out from the cliff, and held out my waivering spare hand for him. My teeth were rattling too hard for me to speak but even if I had he probably wouldn't have heard with the waves so loud. He grabbed my hand and I screamed at the ripping sensation as he hauled himself up, but the wind swallowed my voice. From the ledge we managed to scramble back to the top, hugging the rock and guiding each other's feet, trying not to let ourselves think about how the wind could pluck us off at any moment. At last we flung ourselves down on the short grass at the top.

We clung to each other for a long time. I could feel his heart banging against my chest. He was laughing and crying, and his chest was heaving. Around us, the light had changed. The sky had a pale blue band and the caves on the other side of the cove were visible like blank staring eyes. The water rippled like fish scales. In the growing light there was no sign of the body.

"Come on," he whispered. "We'd better get going."

Back at the car he spent a while fumbling around inside the boot.

"What are you looking for?"

He checked under the car but eventually said, "Nothing. Just making sure. Come on, let's go."

I looked back once, hugging my arms around myself and then walking around to the passenger side. I had no idea what the future held. I'd crossed a line and it was impossible to imagine ever being able to get back.

Chapter Six

Driving away, I was sure the police would be lying in wait for us in the car park at the start of the headland. I held my breath as Zak swung the car back down the bends in the road. So many of them. I wanted to tell him to hurry but I also knew we couldn't afford to draw attention to ourselves or risk an accident by speeding.

"How's your shoulder?" he asked after a few silent miles.

It was the first time the pain had really registered. "Hurts like hell."

"You saved my life back there."

I couldn't help smiling. "Don't be so dramatic. Keep your eyes on the road."

But I'd surprised myself. Amazed myself, actually. The sad thing was I'd never, ever be able to tell anyone about the one heroic thing I'd done in my life without risk of imprisonment.

"Thanks," he said. "I won't forget."

Eventually we rejoined the motorway but instead of coming off at Bristol continued north and eventually headed off to the east. I was increasingly nervous about Zak's driving. He'd strayed over the cat's eyes more than once and his face had a fixed expression. Still, with the sky brightening I knew we couldn't afford to hang about.

"That thing about the sect," I said, hoping talking would keep him awake.

He shrugged, apparently happy to talk about something other than the obvious. "Anything seems normal to a child doesn't it? We lived in a big old manor, about thirty people including us children."

"And what did you do?"

He pulled a face. "Normal stuff really – or it seemed normal anyway. At weekends we hung around town centres giving out leaflets and asking for money. Some people went to work and we had meetings where people gave testimonies about their experiences and we meditated. The little children were given jobs like polishing the fruit and cleaning the shoes. Then as we got older we helped with the DIY and the gardening. They didn't like asking for outside help."

So that explained his practical skills. "But what did you believe?" I asked.

"The usual – peace, love and understanding. Giving up your worldly wealth to the cause – you couldn't join unless you did that. Of course, the guy at the top was driving round in a Bentley and shagging anyone who took his fancy. Nobody else was allowed to sleep together."

"So, this man – was he your father?" I asked trying to keep up.

He grinned. "Doubt it – he was paler than Stuart. But I didn't even know who my mother was until the day we left."

I digested this. "How could you not know?"

"They didn't have a concept of family the way most people do. Thought it was an unnatural construct imposed on people by the state. All the women looked after the children and you weren't allowed to know who gave birth to you. Funnily enough I always thought it was this other woman called Blue. I liked her. She spent the most time with me and I felt safe with her. She had dark skin, and hair a bit like mine. It just seemed to make sense.

"But on the last day Rosa came and told me she was my mum and I could either leave with her or get put into care. It was quite surreal – she was the person I'd had the least connection with. But suddenly we were this cosy little unit in the outside world we didn't understand. I'd never even watched television."

It explained why he never joined in when the rest of us

69

reminisced about *Rainbow, Rentaghost, Carrie's War* or *Grange Hill*.

"That must have been weird."

He nodded. "She'd been living in the sect since she ran away from home as a teenager. No qualifications, no work experience. Didn't have a clue about finance. We took the boat over to Dublin and moved in with her parents at first where she'd grown up but that didn't work out – too much resentment built up on both sides. Eventually we were given a council flat but getting used to each other was the hardest thing. Those first few years were very difficult – I found it hard to settle and she found it hard to fit in. She had no idea about discipline, so we rowed all the time. We're closer now."

I shielded my eyes from the sun, which was starting to rise above the fields.

"Sod it," he said, "we'll have to get a move on."

I was thrown back against the seat as he stamped on the accelerator. But somehow tiredness got to me in the end and I must have drifted off. I woke up with a sick feeling and a horrible ache in my neck.

"Where are we?" I said, choking on the thick fug of his cigarette smoke.

"Sandy."

"Where's that?"

He lifted his shoulders. "Fuck knows."

We circled the town a few times until we found some wasteland at the edge of an industrial park. Again, we waited to see if anyone was following us.

"Got everything?" he asked as we got out of the car.

He searched the ground for a suitable stone. I jumped at the sound as he smashed the rear window on one side, then the other. He stripped off his upper clothing, revealing his skinny frame covered in goosebumps.

"Get back," he said, replacing his sweatshirt. "Right back as far as you can."

"Do you know what you're doing?"

"Yes."

I didn't ask. He'd obviously thought this all out at some point. From a distance I watched him reach into the glove compartment and take out the bottle that he'd bought at the garage earlier. He soaked his T-shirt with the whisky, spread it out on the back seat and took out his lighter.

"Run."

At first nothing happened. I was thinking about fireworks and how you should never go back to them and I had a sudden vision of that boy's face after I'd thrown the rocket back at him.

Who was I kidding, thinking tonight's events were so different from the rest of my life? I'd been bad before. Something in me, however much I tried to blank it out, felt a magnetic pull towards trouble.

Zak started to move towards the car. I went to grab hold of him and pull him back but just as I did so the car went up with an enormous whump. The air filled with acrid smoke, the smell of burnt paint and the crackle of flames. I could feel the heat even from where I was standing. What was he thinking? For God's sake, it was hardly a subtle way to dispose of a car.

"Let's go," he shouted, propelling me round.

Our feet pounded through the wood at the edge of the wasteland. We had no idea where we were running but kept going as long as we could. We passed a blocked-up stream and an abandoned children's playground and the backs of a row of houses.

Frenzied barking broke out from one of them. Zak froze. I grabbed his arm and pulled him along. Each of his breaths was followed by a high-pitched whine. He stopped, folded over, gasping, took a long puff of his inhaler and stumbled on.

We reached a wide road with lights heading back into the town centre. From there we followed signs to the station but a look at the timetable told us it was still a couple of hours before the first train. We slumped on the floor against the closed waiting room and watched the clock inch forward.

Zak's face was grey, his whole body shuddering with the effort to breathe.

When at last the station office opened we bought two tickets to London. From there we could travel back to Bristol as though we'd spent the weekend in the Capital, miles and miles away from where the body had been left. The adrenalin was now starting to recede and tiredness taking over. I felt stiff, grubby and exposed, as though I was wearing a t-shirt proclaiming my guilt.

"We should spend the day in London," said Zak when we were sitting on the train but moments later he was asleep.

I thought I was dropping off too but the heat rising from under the seats scorched the backs of my legs after being so cold and I began to feel nauseous. A numbness crept up my stomach, the sort of feeling you get when you're on a fairground ride. I had a strong sense I'd been there before, sitting on that same seat on that same train thinking that same thought. I was getting an oddly familiar metallic taste in my mouth although it was ages since I'd eaten anything. Realisation struck before I could do anything about it.

"Emily, are you all right? Fuck. Em!"

Zak's anxious face hovered just above mine. He had tears in his eyes. I tried to make sense of what was happening. What was he doing up there and why did my head hurt like it had been split with an axe? I imagined a series of tiny people climbing out of it like an old legend I'd read about a god giving birth.

I was gradually aware of shapes and colour. Sound. Legs. And, higher up, faces, concerned and then relieved. Swaying. I was lying on the floor of the train. I covered my face with my hand. Could I have picked a worse time to have a seizure?

"It's okay, don't worry, you're fine," Zak was saying. He seemed to be choking back tears. He'd tried to get me into the recovery position but there wasn't much room for manoeuvre in the aisle and I was now twisted at an uncomfortable angle.

Turning my head, I found myself looking into a dark

space. I could just see a sticky trail of liquid. In a panic I shifted position, feeling the floor beneath me, but it was reassuringly dry. An empty coffee cup rolled towards me and relief swept through me.

I felt as if I'd just landed back from outer space. My face prickled round the edges and my brain felt full of lead. From a long way off I heard someone ask if they should call an ambulance.

"No. Think she's all right now, thanks." He sounded scared. He was clutching his hair, wiping his mouth on his sleeve.

"Sorry," I kept saying, trying to sit up. "The thing is — the thing is you see —"

"Please shut up," he whispered.

"But I'd just like to say —"

He planted a hard kiss on my mouth so I couldn't talk any more. His unshaved face was rough against mine and I felt my skin burn. My lips were numb. Oh God what else had I said? As I opened my eyes people shifted their gaze. Zak hauled me up onto the seat and spread his coat over me. Someone offered to get me some water but I thanked them and told him I'd be okay.

I felt incredibly tired as I always did after a fit. He put his arm round me. I could feel his body trembling against mine. All the time the question was going through my mind, were the seizures going to become a regular occurrence again? Even yesterday I'd have jumped at the chance of being on a train with Zak's arm around me and yet I could never have imagined this. Nothing in my life would ever be the same.

"Sure you're all right?" he asked in a low voice.

I nodded. "Thanks."

"I think you had some sort of fit."

"Hmm."

He pulled back. "Has it happened before?"

"No." I sat up. "Well, yes. But not for a long time. I thought they'd stopped." I screwed up my face. "Sorry, I should have warned you."

He looked relieved. "No. Yes. I just wish I'd known what

73

to do - I felt so useless."

My head still felt heavy and I slept until he woke me at St Pancras.

"Do you need anything?" he asked as we got off the train.

"Food."

He nodded. "Sandwich?"

"More."

We stumbled through the mass of bodies and sat in a burger bar and I made short work of a meal deal with a milkshake while he sat watching. I still felt woozy and in another place. Zak tried to get me to describe what it had felt like, but I could never remember the fit itself.

"I sometimes get lightheaded just before so I know it's going to happen. Afterwards it just feels like my brain's been switched off and then back on again. As if a tiny bit of my life's been erased. The kiss was a bit of a surprise."

He coloured, dipped his head and looked up with an apologetic smile. "I wasn't taking advantage. I had to stop you rabbiting. You sounded like you were about to launch into a speech."

I winced. "Yes, I do that."

He sunk his face into his hands and looked up at me. "Really? Always? Fuck, this is serious. I'm going to have to keep an eye on you."

"Sorry."

He exhaled, cupped my face in his hands and said, "I thought I was going to lose you."

I managed a smile. "You don't get rid of me that easily."

I could tell he'd obviously gone through the whole scenario of being left alone in all this, just as I had earlier. In view of the fit we decided against spending the day in London, but we bought two tickets for an exhibition and a film and picked up a *Time Out* to look at the reviews. I slept for most of the journey back. Engineering works meant we had to get a bus for part of the way, which took ages. From the station we got a cab back to the house. I couldn't wait to collapse into my bed, draw the covers over my head and pretend the worst night of my life hadn't happened.

But as I stuck my key in the lock I got a warning feeling. I opened the door and found myself staring at a police officer.

Chapter Seven

My first instinct was to turn and run but I knew I wouldn't get far. My legs felt hollow. Xanthe and Stuart's white faces stared at us from the hall. It was horribly like the scene I'd imagined. Was this a setup? Had they called the police while we were away and dumped us in it? Or had the policeman who stopped to see why we'd parked on the hard shoulder passed on his suspicions to the Bristol police? Had the body been found? Could they have made a connection that quickly?

"My car's been stolen," said Stuart.

Zak was the first to recover. "Stolen? When?"

"Some time over the weekend. I haven't used it since Friday."

The policeman seemed to be studying us, following the conversation and watching our responses. Zak did a pretty good job of acting shocked. I thought it best to stay quiet except to make sympathetic noises.

He asked us when we last remembered seeing the car and went over our activities during the weekend, times we'd been in and out of the house. "Did you see it yesterday when you left for London?"

"Sorry," I said, "I can't remember. I wasn't really looking."

He wanted to know who else lived in the house. Was there any chance Imogen might have borrowed the car? What time would she be back? I'd felt jagged tiredness as we arrived. Now I had to swing into the cheery housemate role as Stuart asked casually about our weekend in front of the officer.

"Yeh it was good," said Zak. "So much to do in London."

"Do you normally lock your vehicle?" the officer asked Stuart.

"Always."

He closed his notebook. "We've had a few car thefts recently. Most often it's just kids joy riding and the car turns up eventually although it's usually a write-off, I'm afraid."

The officer paused inches away from the door to the basement. I was trying to regulate my breathing. Did the police usually make the effort to come round when a car theft was reported? Or did they already suspect something? I felt my eyes travel over to the basement door and forced them away to look at the ceiling, the floor, the jumble of shoes and bags, Stuart's golf clubs, a couple of umbrellas with company logos and a potato. But whatever I tried to focus on, it didn't feel natural.

When the police officer finally left we slumped to the ground.

"What the fuck was all that about?" breathed Zak looking up at the ceiling.

"Sorry. There was no way I could have warned you," said Stuart. He looked done-in too, bags under his eyes and a scarlet patch over his throat. "I wasn't expecting them to come over. Looks like they don't have enough to do at the moment."

"If they only knew," said Xanthe with a wry smile.

"What if they do?" I asked. "It's not normal, is it, to come round in person over a stolen car?"

She shrugged. "What's normal anyway? I don't know any more."

She threw her arms around us both and clung so tightly I nearly choked. I became horribly conscious of my sorry state.

Stuart's face was tight and anxious. "What happened? Where the hell have you been? Tell me everything."

I wanted nothing more than to retreat into my bed, but we gave them an account of our night. We left out the encounter with the police and didn't mention my fit on the train. No point in alarming them with stuff we could do nothing about.

"What about you two?" Zak asked.

"Take a look." Stuart led us to the basement. I shrank back but I realised I couldn't live the rest of my life in that house afraid to go in or even walk past the basement. I gripped the handle and pushed the door open. The first thing that hit me was the choking smell of chlorine. Now I thought about it perhaps I'd been aware of it all along when we were standing outside with the policeman. Perhaps he'd noticed it too.

Stuart's arm snaked around me and snapped on the light. Tadah — a new fitting. The walls had been scraped and painted, the giant mushrooms removed, but the biggest change was the floor. He and Xanthe had made a couple of trips to Texas Homecare in the 2CV and bought a job lot of laminate flooring. It gleamed innocently under the bright light.

"Wow," I said, reining in my thoughts. Was it just me or did the revamped space look glaringly suspicious? I doubted the planks would have fitted across the little car without having to stick out of the window, where they'd have been seen by countless people.

Zak stood in the middle of the space, looked around him and nodded. He inspected the joins. "You must have been working non-stop."

"We were. Still got that corner to finish. We need some more planks. I wasted a few getting the cuts right."

"I'll give you a hand with the rest," Zak said. "Have you been listening to the news?"

Stuart nodded. "Nothing so far. We've had the radio on constantly while we've been working."

But when the phone rang he was jumpy as hell. I began to see that being left behind in the house hadn't been an entirely easy option. He seemed grateful when I answered the phone but looked ready to seize it from me if I slipped up.

"Em." It was a shock to hear Imogen's voice. So normal, oblivious. "How was your weekend? And don't say crap because I can guarantee mine was worse."

I smiled weakly at the unlikeliness of this.

"I'm waiting for a bus. Sodding engineering works. Won't get in to Temple Meads station until nine-thirty. I was wondering if there was any chance Stuart might pick me up?"

Because of course in her world everything was different. Stuart's car was sitting on the driveway. It hadn't been used to transport a corpse and wasn't now a smouldering heap in a wasteland in a place we'd never heard of.

"Um – not sure," I said. "We don't know where Stuart's car is at the moment. Xanthe's here though."

There was a pause. "Has she been drinking?"

"No."

"On the whacky backy?"

"Don't think so."

"Hmm, beggars can't be choosers I suppose."

Xanthe looked relieved at the chance to get out of the house. I had a fleeting vision of her just keeping on driving, windows down, long hair flying, jumping aboard a ferry and never being heard of again. But just as she was about to open the door Stuart grabbed hold of her.

"Wait. We need to think first. Do we tell Imogen about this?"

We looked at each other.

"We have to, don't we?" I said at last. "I don't see how we can keep it from her when we're all living here. She's bound to notice something's up."

"But think. What if she tells Rick?"

"She will," said Xanthe after a pause. "She tells him everything. And I don't trust him. He's a lawyer for God's sake."

"And if we tell Imogen we may as well tell her dad while we're at it because she tells him everything too," said Zak. "And I definitely don't trust him."

"We can't have her tell anyone," said Stuart. "It's not worth the risk. The fewer people that know about this the better. That means not telling anyone ever."

I leant back against the wall and closed my eyes. Already it was getting worse. Keeping secrets from each other in the house. It would get more and more complicated as time went on and different people moved in and out of our lives.

How long can you keep a secret? Would you keep it from your husband or wife and your children? What if you tell just one special person and you split up in twenty years and they tell just one other person? Who tells just one other? The only solution was to keep it from every single living person outside the four of us but that meant spending as much time with each other as possible and hoping that didn't drive us insane. We needed each other in order to survive but I couldn't help the creeping thought that one of us wasn't being honest.

As I passed the bathroom ten minutes later on my way up to my room I heard a noise. The shower was full on, but the water couldn't completely drown out Zak's crying. Even with my bedroom door closed I could still hear those shuddering, heaving sobs and I imagined him cowering on the floor under the deluge, face turned up, water as hot as he could stand. It went on a long time.

I thought about calling to him but decided he probably wouldn't hear me and if he did he'd pretend not to. So I went into my room and lay on my bed, stuck in a Eurythmics CD and turned it up loud in the hope it might transport me back a few years to my much simpler previous life.

But it was impossible to ignore the snapshots that flickered through my head of the body on the floor, the body in the car, the body falling and Zak kicking it to hell. Or the smell of the burning car, or the fear that my seizures had returned.

A quiet knock at the door shook me back into the moment.

Zak stood there, head down, black hair flat and dripping. He glanced up at me and I knew his look mirrored my own. It was so many things – shared knowledge, revulsion, regret. No sense wishing things had been different.

"Can I sleep here tonight?" he whispered.

The difference a day made. "Not sure it's a good idea."

"I don't mean with you, I mean next to you. Please? I don't want to be alone."

He looked so desperate and I didn't have the energy to argue about it, so I stepped back to let him in.

We lay together in the bed, curled into each other, clinging like children and cried some more; more than I ever thought was possible. I was worried the violence of that crying might shatter a rib or do some permanent damage to my body. Perhaps I wanted it to. Zak fell asleep before I did. I lay listening to him breathing, envying him that oblivion but resisting sleep myself for as long as I could because I was terrified of what I'd see in my dreams.

But at some point during the night we must have reached out for each other because somehow we ended up making love. Looking back, it's a hard thing to justify in the circumstances but I can only say love and lust were the furthest things from my mind at that moment. I think we did it to prove to ourselves we were still alive, that we could still breathe and feel. To annihilate images of that grey, emaciated, vomit-encrusted body, to shut out everything and exist purely in that moment.

Afterwards, I lay with my head on his chest, his arm draped around me, my hair damp and stuck to my face which was caked in dried tears, the familiar but unfamiliar smell of his skin and sweat in my nostrils.

Every rise and fall of his chest assured me we were still living, and every breath felt like a small triumph over death and for a few moments before I fell asleep I felt like everything was going to be okay after all.

Sometime before dawn I heard Zak shuffling about, picking his clothes up off the floor.

"Where are you going?"

The only reply was a softly closing door. I lay waiting for him to come back but heard the front door click shut and his feet on the gravel outside. Looking out of the window, I saw him go over to his bike. I wondered if he'd look up and see me, but he started up the bike and rode away.

When I went downstairs I found Imogen and Xanthe drinking coffee in the kitchen. Xanthe looked remarkably serene as though she'd forgotten the incident already.

"It's a bugger about Stuart's car being nicked," Imogen was saying as she spread butter on her toast. She picked up a piece and crunched. "Still, they'll probably find it. They can trace number plates in seconds these days, can't they?"

My stomach burned as I met Xanthe's eyes. "Guess so," I said. I felt too sick to eat.

"Zak's gone out on his bike," Imogen continued. "He's acting really weird today."

"Is he?" I busied myself choosing a mug.

"Haven't you seen him? I thought I saw him coming out of your room earlier."

I shrugged but I was too battered by recent events to put up a fight. Her sandy brows shot up.

"Seriously? You and *Zak?*"

"Yes. No. Maybe - I don't know."

Stuart was busy in the basement finishing off the floor. Xanthe and I spent the day curled up on the sofa watching children's television programmes, trying to cocoon ourselves in a happy, make-believe world and not allow ourselves to think about the car being discovered or police examining the tyre tracks on a Cornish cliff or a body being washed up alongside the surfers. A few times, I thought I heard Zak coming back but it turned out to be the wind rattling the door.

***

By midnight Zak still wasn't back. The next morning, I thought he might have gone straight in to work from wherever he'd been. The rest of us travelled in Xanthe's tiny car and when we got there I heard someone saying Zak had rung in sick. Walking back into the office, I felt as though I'd aged twenty years. It was like waking up from a dream and having to readjust your eyes to assure yourself that everything was still the same.

One or two people mentioned the New Year's party, saying they'd had a good time or conjecturing about who had got off with whom, but there had been other parties that weekend and the conversation moved on to future events and plans for the week ahead. And yet one of these people hunched over their typewriters or sitting back and speaking into their phones or gathered in small groups discussing circulation figures or page proofs – any of them who'd been at our party – might be the killer. It made me suspicious of everyone I spoke to. I found myself watching for signs of them watching me. How could they live with themselves, knowing what they'd done, knowing what we'd discover, wondering what we planned to do?

Halfway through the morning Stuart accosted me by the fax machine.

"Where did Zak go?" he whispered. "What the hell's going on?"

"No idea."

"He didn't say anything to you? What if he's gone to the police?"

He wiped sweat off his face. He was having trouble breathing.

I touched his arm. "He wouldn't. Let's talk about it later. We can't here."

But of course it made it almost impossible to concentrate.

"Did you actually read this proof?" my editor demanded. "Because this here," he jabbed at it with a Tipp-Ex-encrusted finger, "isn't a word that I've ever heard of. There's a whole paragraph repeated here," another jab, "and the piece ends mid-sentence. How can you not have noticed?"

The veins at the side of his head bulged as he spoke. I took it back off him. I could hardly blame him for still thinking a few errors on a piece of paper were worth risking a heart attack over. It was a piece about a man being banned from a public swimming pool because he was HIV positive and a study into a drug that could potentially slow the disease. Interesting and important, and yet nothing on the page was familiar although I'd been staring at it for the best part of an hour and had put my initials at the top to show I'd read it.

I knew Zak wouldn't have gone to the police, but I could imagine him making a getaway, putting as much distance as he could between him and the body. Which left me as the only traceable person who'd been in the car with the corpse. I felt horribly alone.

"Tell me it's not true," whispered Stuart when we met in the corridor on the coffee run later.

"What isn't?" Was he referring to the body in the basement, the way we'd got rid of it, the lies we'd told the police? It was hard to keep up these days.

"Are you sleeping with him? Zak?"

It seemed such a pointless and trivial thing to ask in the grand scheme of things.

"That's a rather personal question."

His eyes flashed with triumph. "I knew it. I knew something was going on between you."

I pressed the button for black coffee and watched it pour into a cup. He didn't walk away, just stood there breathing too loudly.

"Look Stuart, nothing's *going on*. Nothing that concerns you anyway."

Surely, he wasn't going to bring up the no-dating among housemates agreement? Our lives had moved on so fast now the idea seemed quaint.

He put a hand on the machine and leant on it. "But that's just it, isn't it? It concerns me very much. There I was thinking we were four individuals. Now I see you two have been secretly a couple. It alters the balance of things."

He stopped as the guy from *Carpets* who looked like Jason Donovan came up behind us. "Jason" seemed in a hurry and was obviously relieved when we suggested he go ahead of us as we were each getting in a round.

"You must know where he is," said Stuart as the man from *Carpets* walked away, clutching his coffee. "Are you going to join him? Is that part of your plan?"

I pressed the machine again, this time for white without sugar. "There is no plan. I don't know where he is and we're not a couple. Has it even occurred to you something might have happened to him?"

To be honest it hadn't really occurred to me until that moment. I'd been so confused and annoyed with Zak for doing a runner without telling me but now I was thinking, what if he'd been so preoccupied by everything that had happened that he'd overshot a bend or pulled out in front of a lorry or taken an overdose?

Stuart pressed the hot chocolate button before I'd had a chance to remove the last coffee cup and dark, smelly mocha fountained up and dribbled down the machine.

"Stop. Stop!" he shouted, realising his mistake. He started kicking and thumping the machine. I was afraid he'd damage it. The last thing we needed was to attract attention to ourselves. One of the ladies from Reception came clucking over and told us off for making a mess. She fetched a wodge of paper towels from the loos and oversaw us cleaning it up and I took the opportunity to leave with her so he couldn't ask any more questions.

***

Four days passed. I was living on a knife edge. On the Wednesday night voices on the stairs ripped me out of my sleep. For a moment I panicked thinking it was a police raid but as I came to, I recognised Stuart's headmasterly tone followed by Zak's Dublin drawl.

"Where the hell have you been?"

"Look, I had to get away. Clear my head."

"Where did you go?"

There was a pause before Zak answered, "What's it got to do with you?"

"Everything. We didn't know if you were planning to come back. We're paying a mortgage together in case you'd forgotten. For God's sake we didn't..." He whispered the next bit so all I could hear were staccato sibilants. I could imagine his hands cutting through the air and a bit of spit flying.

Zak whispered something in return. Then he said, "Can I get past?"

"No."

Another pause and Zak's voice took on a harder note. "Sorry, who do you think you are? You can't tell me when to come and go. You've got issues, do you know that?"

Stuart's voice trembled as he said, "Don't you think you at least owe Emily an explanation?"

A wave of heat rushed over me. This was excruciating. It sounded like I'd been crying on Stuart's shoulder and declaring my feelings for Zak which by now were very confused anyway. The last thing I wanted was for Zak to think I was bothered by his disappearance.

"What's Emily got to do with anything?"

"Oh, let's see now, let's suppose you spent the night in her bed just before you ran off."

There was a long silence before I heard, "Is she okay?"

"What do you think?"

Zak's voice tightened. "I think I don't need your advice."

"Oh, I think you do." And then it all came out. "I cannot believe that you would use an occasion like *that* to get your leg over. Did you get some sort of sick thrill out of…?" The next bit was whispered but must have referred to dumping a body. "Did it turn you on? Did you feel you had to *celebrate?*"

Zak's voice rose. "Get out of my fucking way."

There was a scuffle, a couple of thumps and an alarming creak. I pictured Stuart forcing Zak back against the rickety banister until he was leaning over the edge.

I jumped out of bed. I got halfway across the room when Imogen's door opened on the second floor above me. The landing shook as she stomped to the top of the stairs.

"What the hell is wrong with you two? Pack it in. Some of us are trying to get some sleep. I've got to be up at a crazy hour for a product launch in Stoke."

"Ask him," said Zak, getting his breath back.

But I heard Stuart going down to his room and Zak going towards his. I thought I heard his feet pause outside my room, but he didn't knock. Moments later his door clunked shut.

**

"Stuart had a point," Imogen said the next morning before running to catch her train. "What if Zak doesn't come back next time? If he buggers off and doesn't pay his way we're all going to have to cover his share or get repossessed."

"It was only a few days," I pointed out.

"Yes, well you're not thinking very sensibly at the moment, Emily," she said, and I couldn't really think of an answer to that.

Eventually Zak agreed to let us know if he was going to take off again for longer than a weekend although he muttered something again about how he hadn't expected to feel as if he was living in a police state when he was *in his own home.* Over the next few weeks we tried to function as we'd always done. It was a relief when Imogen was around because there was no possibility of someone raising their latest concern:

You didn't take off his clothes? Tell me you didn't pay for the petrol by card? Did you look out for cameras? What did you do about the tyre tracks?

Sometimes we told the truth, sometimes we lied because it was easier. Sometimes we genuinely couldn't remember. On more than one occasion Zak lost it with Stuart.

"But you didn't take off his clothes?" Stuart asked yet another time.

"Of course we fucking didn't. What weirdo takes their clothes off before they throw themselves off a cliff? In case you've forgotten it was your idea in the first place and I don't recall you volunteering to strip him down at the time."

Stuart made us rehearse our stories over and over. "Tell me again, from the beginning. What time did you leave here to go to London? How did you get there? Why did you only get singles back? Where did you stay and with whom? No, that's not good enough. You're sounding glib now, Emily."

If we stumbled or gave conflicting answers or even answered too easily he brought his fist down on the sofa. "You've got to think this through. You have to give exactly the same story. Be a hundred per cent sure of what the other person is saying. They'll try to imply other things. Trip you up. Confuse you so they can divide and rule. Don't fall into the trap. You need to be absolutely sure of what the other person will have said and don't let anyone fool you otherwise."

Of course, we had to carry on with normal things like going to work, doing the food shopping and putting up shelves. We went to someone's birthday bash and the leaving drinks for someone from Accounts. Went to press launches, saw a local band down at the harbour pub and *The Unbearable Lightness of Being* at the waterfront cinema.

Without Stuart's car we had to rely on Xanthe's 2CV which wasn't a comfortable ride for four people and would be even worse with five on a wet day when Zak's bike refused to start. Imogen kept insisting Stuart should put in an insurance claim for his car despite the fact he kept telling her it would be a waste of time. I wished she'd stop bringing it up. I could see his facial muscles tense a bit more each time.

That wet Thursday morning after Zak came back from his travels Stuart was concertinaed into the front seat and the rest of us were squeezed onto Dollie's back seat. We were halfway to the office when the engine gave out. Xanthe hunched over the wheel and wailed, "*Now* what?"

Stuart looked across at the petrol gauge. "When did you last fill this car up?"

We ended up pushing Dollie to the garage, arriving at work late, aching and dishevelled – just what we didn't need when we'd hope to stay under the radar.

But the strange thing about the office was that even after something so horrendous had happened it took you over. We had pages to fill, press releases to sub, people to interview. The phone trilled, typewriters clattered, page proofs landed on your desk. Life carried on.

I felt as though I'd been split in two. There was a life in which we were still young, hopeful trainees embarking on our journalism careers and another life in which we'd conspired to conceal a death and rob a family of its chance to grieve. I grasped any opportunity to be busy and I welcomed the tedium of writing product news and churning out stories about the Channel Tunnel, trading-up, and how companies were preparing for the Single European Market in 1992 – anything to take my mind off my other self.

"Oh my God! When did this happen?"

My heart lurched as I came downstairs one morning and found Imogen standing in the doorway of the basement. A shiver swept through my body. For a ghastly moment I thought she'd found a bloodstain or a shoe or something.

I battled to keep my voice under control. "What is it?"

But she gave a great whoop and I realised she was looking at the newly-decorated walls and floor. She hadn't noticed before because she had no reason to go down to the basement.

"Why didn't you tell me? I'd have helped. Although wouldn't it have been better to start with the kitchen?"

She gave Stuart a crushing hug when she found he'd laid the floor. "You're good at this – you can do my room next."

"Not a chance," he said with a laugh.

Perhaps it sounds silly but there were brief moments when I almost forgot it had happened. IRA bombs, rail disasters and a fatwa placed on Salman Rushdie for writing *Satanic Verses* made the world seem a dark and dangerous place but also made you see your problems weren't the biggest thing going on in the world.

But just as you thought you were coping okay it came back and hit you. You'd see a poster for a missing person or a bunch of criminal faces on *Crimewatch* that reminded you that you were now part of that sector of society. I began to go over and over how we could keep up our mortgage repayments if we were sent to prison. And if we lost the house because of it where would I go when I was released and how would I get a job?

And even if we got a non-custodial sentence how would having a criminal record affect our lives? Would we have to disclose it every time we applied for a job, opened a bank account, applied for a mortgage? Or would we be forced into a lifetime of lying?

We were strong at different times. One of us would be on edge and the others would have to cover for them but we were always aware that one of us could break down and bring things crashing down around us in a moment. In an odd way it drew the four of us closer together, making us look out for one another, although Zak and I avoided being alone together as much as possible. That night he'd spent in my bed hung there between us but was never mentioned.

It turned out that on the morning he went missing he'd got on his bike, crossed the channel and kept going until he reached Metz where he remembered a friend was living. I hoped the friend wasn't Ellie, a girl who'd featured in a number of his anecdotes and wasn't a girlfriend but with whom he always seemed to end up having sex when they met up.

Not that I wanted a relationship with Zak any more – I didn't want to repeat anything from that disastrous weekend – it would always be impossible to think of that night I'd spent with him without also thinking about the events that had led up to it. I guessed it was the same for him.

And yet we were bound together by what we'd done. It would always be there between us, this shared knowledge. No one would ever understand me as well as he did because they couldn't be allowed to know everything about me and yet ironically it was also that knowledge that kept him and me apart.

***

"We ought to give the body a name," Xanthe said as we drove back from work on the Friday in the 2CV. Imogen was in London with Rick so we could talk freely.

"Just between us so we don't have to keep calling him Backpack Man. How about Chris or Steve?"

"What if he really is called Chris or Steve?" I asked. "Loads of people are. It would have to be something none of our friends is called but that isn't so uncommon people pick up on it."

Outside, sleet was falling, and the roads were dark and wet.

"All right then. I wondered about Bib?" she said.

"Bib's not a name," Zak objected.

"It's short for Body In the Basement."

"Still not a name."

After a while she said, "All right – Bob then?"

"I think Bob could work," said Stuart. "We don't know any Bobs and it's not a name that jumps out at you."

After much discussion we settled on Bob. In a way I didn't like giving the body a name because it made him seem more human but on the other hand it made it easier to talk about without resorting to winks and hand signals. We'd talk about "the week Bob came over" or "after Bob left town."

Once or twice Imogen asked, "Who's this Bob anyway?" but it was easy to dismiss as she so often spent her weekends with Rick

Every day brought a sliver of hope. When we were sure no one could hear us, we whispered about our chances. The more time elapsed before Bob was found, the less easy it would be to identify him and establish any connection to us. With every week that passed another few thousand missing persons joined the files that the police would have to trawl through while searching for Bob, however briefly, before looking in our direction, putting a bit more space between us. I seemed to be permanently holding my breath.

If they'd done a post mortem the day we dumped Bob they'd have known from his lungs he was dead before he

91

reached the water. But after a few weeks surely it wouldn't be so easy to identify him? How long would it take for the lungs to decompose? For fingerprints to be undetectable? Wouldn't all the forensic proof have washed off?

I found myself slipping off to the big library by the cathedral in my lunch hour and scanning the reference books for any information that could provide answers but there wasn't much available on forensics and it wasn't the sort of thing you could ask about without raising suspicion. I bumped into Zak there once and we shared a look as we revealed the covers of the books we were reading.

It struck me it was quite sad that the only time he and I really talked to each other now was when we were discussing Bob in whispered conversations that a few weeks before we could never have imagined having.

"It says here bodies always rise to the surface eventually," I said.

"Not always." Zak looked around and nodded his head at a child sitting on his mother's lap as they turned over pages together of *The Very Hungry Caterpillar*. We moved down the lines of bookcases until we found a quiet one. If anyone noticed they probably thought we were going in for a snog.

"Not if they get trapped in a cave," he said. "Or eaten by fish. Or broken up. A body without a head or hands is hard to identify."

It wasn't a nice thing to hope and I felt awful doing so but it was all we had. Once or twice I caught myself wondering if our last night with Bob had really been as unplanned as it had seemed. It struck me that Zak might have already done his research and chosen that way to dispose of the body because it gave us the best chance of getting away with it. But that led me into thinking all sorts of worse things about him. I suppose it was all part of the paranoia that was developing in all of us. There was always that nagging doubt that you'd wake up one day and find the others gone and you'd end up taking the blame for everything.

Or that you'd end up as the next Bob.

What appalled me most was that we were starting to think like killers now, as though by doing what we did we'd stepped into their shoes.

We were used to reading all the newspapers between us for work and ordered the main ones so we could follow up on relevant stories for our magazines but now we were scanning them feverishly and leaving radios on in all the rooms.

"For God's *sake* who turned this on again?" Imogen would say. "The electricity bill's going to be mental."

It worried away at me, the fact we were keeping something so enormous from her and I wondered how she'd react if she found out. But I envied her too – for being able to sleep without nightmares, for being able to see a future that didn't involve court cases and prison cells. And perhaps most of all for her clear conscience.

***

"Are we okay?" Zak asked in the curry house one evening after work when Stuart had gone to the gents, leaving us alone together.

The question took me by surprise. I played with my food, not sure how to answer. "I wasn't aware there was a We."

"Ouch." He dragged his hands through his hair. "I thought we were heading that way – you know, before…"

I nodded and shrugged. But that was Before. Everything had been different Before. And then he'd disappeared without a word.

"I'm sorry," he mumbled. He tried to articulate his feelings a couple of times and eventually came out with, "Look, it's not like Stuart says. It wasn't about that at all."

"I know that."

"I mean, that's not how I normally do things."

"Zak, nothing about that weekend was normal."

He nodded. "It's just that I can't think about that night – any of it – without remembering the other things that went before." He snapped a poppadum and ground the piece into crumbs under his thumb. "It's messed everything up."

It was a relief to know he felt the same way as I did although it wasn't great to know that being with me reminded him of death.

"But it doesn't have to stop us being friends does it?"

I forced a smile. "No, I suppose not."

***

A few evenings later when Imogen was at her Callanetics session Stuart called a house meeting in the kitchen. He was holding an envelope. His face was white.

"You were stopped for a broken light? Why for God's sake didn't you tell me?"

Zak and I looked at each other.

"Ah, that," said Zak.

"Yes, that. Don't tell me you forgot about it. How many times did I ask you to go over everything that happened that night? I told you it was essential that there wouldn't be any surprises. This is what trips people up. And then it turns out you kept quiet about something as major as this."

"We didn't want to worry you," I told him.

"Worry me? I have every reason to be worried. You nearly gave the game away."

"It was never a game, Stuart."

He was pacing the room now, red-faced and ragged-breathed. "You realise they could have taken the car off you? They could have opened the boot and bingo, they'd have got you."

"Yes, but they didn't," said Zak.

Stuart dropped his voice and put his face close to Zak's.

"No but they now have a record of someone driving my car on that road at that time - someone who apparently *gave them my name.* Is there anything else you'd like to tell me?"

Zak shoved him away. "What choice did I have? If I'd made up a name and they'd checked the car ownership details and found it was registered to a different name they'd have arrested us there and then for stealing the car. Is it my fault that your stupid light needed fixing?"

"You won't have to pay the fine anyway," Xanthe said. "The car's reported stolen."

Stuart slammed his hand against the wall. "That is not the point. How would a random thief know my name?"

Zak threw his arms up. "I don't know. I didn't know what else to say. We were caught by surprise. Why didn't you spot the broken light yourself? Then we wouldn't have got stopped. They'll most likely think there was something of yours in the car with your name on."

Stuart's head was nodding fast as though he'd forgotten how to stop. "*Or* that it was someone I knew."

"Okay but that could be lots of people. Just try and stay calm about this."

"Calm? Are you out of your mind? I never thought you'd be so bloody stupid. Now are you sure there aren't any other little secrets you've been keeping from me?"

We assured him there weren't. But I was beginning to wonder if he was losing his sanity. I swung between thinking it was only a matter of time before we were discovered and, by making a series of feverish calculations, concluding that even if the body was found our chances of avoiding detection were fairly good simply because it had all been so random.

But in a way I found these moments of optimism more frightening than the doomful feeling because it seemed so dangerously deluded, like a soldier who stands in the middle of the battlefield convinced he won't get hit.

And then in February the worst happened.

Chapter Eight

February

After we finished our first magazine placements we were sent up to Birmingham to a trade show at the NEC. Together we had to produce a daily exhibition newspaper from stories wrung out of every stand. It was a hectic schedule as there were hundreds of stands to get round. Exhibitors often weren't free to talk to us or only wanted to talk to sales reps so we had to keep traipsing backwards and forwards between different halls until we found a good moment.

We were given a stringent set of rules including not being allowed to eat garlic, onions or curry, get drunk, swear, use the phone in our hotel rooms or take anything from the mini fridge without paying for it ourselves – in short anything that might have made the experience bearable. The company would pay for two drinks only in the hotel bar, after which we'd have to buy our own at extortionate prices.

In the middle of one of these afternoons in the press room at the exhibition hall Xanthe had one of her hysterical outbursts, questioning what she was doing busting a gut over a story about roof felt and had to be peeled off her typewriter in tears.

The Awards dinner held on the final evening was a major opportunity for hobnobbing with the big cheeses from the industry and our publishing director issued a decree that nothing short of death should stop us attending – words that came to have a dreadful irony.

We had around twenty minutes in our hotel rooms after

being dropped off from the exhibition hall by the courtesy bus before meeting back down at the bar in our gladrags for our transfer to the dinner.

I'd just come out of the shower, wrapped in a hotel bathrobe, hair in a turban. My feet after traipsing the exhibition halls for hours felt like someone had hammered nails into them and my mouth ached from maintaining a smile but there was just about time to change into a different set of clothes.

I flicked on the TV while scrabbling through my travel bag for a pair of tights and was halfway through untangling them when I saw it. The camera panned across a wide section of coast and then zoomed down the rocks to the churning sea and a little cove. It could have been anywhere but there was something about the outline of the cliffs, the gorse and the little coastguard hut. Even before they showed the map I knew I'd been there.

My stomach dropped. My legs gave way. I sank down onto the bed. The world seemed to shrink around me until I found myself in a tiny, hostile space struggling for breath. I turned up the sound.

Police don't know yet how long the body has been in the water or the cause of death, but tests are being carried out to establish the man's identity...

A harsh sound jarred me to my senses. It took a few seconds to register it was the phone. I stared at it stupidly as if it was a bomb, thinking about the most likely callers. The police? The managing director? A work colleague who'd been at our party and had pieced events together? Imogen?

The body had been found by a couple walking their dog on the beach. My head filled with irrational hatred. Why did they have to walk their stupid dog on that beach of all places and at that moment?

I realised the telephone was still ringing. I pounced on it – but then had second thoughts. Very quietly I replaced the receiver. I jumped back as it started up again. How long would they keep trying before they gave up? But then what would they do – come round in person? I moved towards the phone but wheeled round as someone knocked at the door.

Had it definitely been this door? Hotels are disorientating places and it's easy to mistake a knock a few doors down from my own. I stood frozen halfway across the floor trying to come to a decision. The phone stopped ringing. Started again. I kept thinking if I answered the phone I'd immediately know that I should have answered the door and vice versa.

"Emily?" said a voice outside the door. Low and urgent.

I opened it. Stuart looked more agitated than I'd ever seen him. I stood back to let him in and he swept through, looking lovely in his dinner suit, his blond hair gleaming and smelling of citrus shampoo but his eyes fixed on the TV screen. He grabbed the remote and turned up the volume.

"The north Cornish coast near Bude. Does that sound right?"

I shrugged and nodded, my eyes also glued to the scene.

He sank onto the bed and brought his curled fist up to his mouth, pressing his knuckles against his lips. "That's it then. This is where it ends."

"Not necessarily." Although I was aware I was grasping at straws. "They might come to the conclusion he lost his footing, or he jumped. Or that he'd been out partying, he was high and walked off thinking he could fly like that student did off the Suspension Bridge a few weeks ago. Even if they suspect, they can't do anything without proof."

Stuart didn't seem to hear me. "Tell me again how you did it," he said. *Not this again.* He was breathing through his mouth as he listened – short, tremulous breaths. His right thigh was jiggling as though he'd lost control of it and he had to lean down hard with his forearm to stop it.

"You're sure no one saw you?" he said when I'd finished.

"I don't think so."

His face filled with panic. "You *don't think*?"

I closed my eyes. "I'm sure."

"And nobody followed you at the other place, the spot where you left the car?"

98

"Not as far as I know."

He shot me another look.

"No, they didn't."

"And you definitely removed his clothes before he went into the sea?"

"What? No, we never said that. We've been through this."

Stuart looked aghast. "*No?* He was fully clothed?" He gave a groan and fell back on the bed, setting his mouth into a tight line. In a strangely calm tone he added, "That's it then. They'll identify him by his clothes in no time at all. They've got us. We might as well hand ourselves in."

"They'd identify him anyway from his dental records," I said. My stomach was churning, and I felt as if I was going to be sick.

Stuart's face was contorted as he chewed the inside of his cheek. "Too soon. This has happened too soon. Seven weeks – it's nothing. This is where our luck runs out."

The phone started up again. "Shall I answer it?"

His face was ashen as he nodded. I could feel his eyes boring into me when I picked up. I couldn't speak.

"Em?" said Imogen. "What the fuck are you doing? I've been ringing for ages."

My voice caught. "Sorry, I was in the bath. I'll be a few minutes. You go on down."

She finally agreed but said, "Don't be late. Donald's just given Xanthe a bollocking for that piece on Gibsons. Turns out the man she quoted has been dead ten years."

"What?" I said, not really listening.

"It was his son she spoke to. He said he was Mr Gibson and she didn't check his first name and used his dad's name. Donald's *apoplectic*. If we're late to the dinner he'll probably fire us all."

I laughed weakly. What difference would it make now?

"Don't you dare leave me alone with that prick from the sauna company. He keeps trying to feel my bum."

"Right. Okay, no I won't."

As I put the phone down I felt another surge of nausea. "I

don't think I can do this."

Stuart grabbed hold of my shoulders. "No, we must. It's not over yet. We absolutely must go and act completely normal." I tried to wriggle free, but his fingers were digging into my shoulders through the bathrobe. "Listen to me, Emily, you're going to put some clothes on and we're going to go down and smile and get through this evening."

"But that's just it. I can't act normal. Not now. Not knowing —"

I felt winded, as though I'd been punched in the stomach. I sank to my knees. "It will be worse if I go and break down or have a fit or something."

He twisted me round to face him. "Stop it. Look at me. Pull yourself together. That isn't going to happen. Because you're not going to let it."

But then he didn't know, did he? I'd never told him about my epilepsy and the fit on the train. It could happen again and I might blurt out the truth amid the gibberish I usually spouted as I came to.

"Please," he was saying, "you have to do this. You can't let everyone down."

Seeing he wasn't going to leave the room without me, I grabbed my clothes and went into the bathroom to get dressed. When I came out he was sitting on the bed, eyes still glued to the TV screen although there was a completely different programme on now.

"I think you're sitting on my hairbrush," I said.

He shifted position without turning his head and passed it to me in silence and I noticed how much his hands were shaking. I hoped until the last minute that he might see sense and let me stay in the room, but he stood up and steered me out with his hand on the small of my back. I felt like a hostage, but I also knew he was right. We couldn't risk drawing attention to ourselves by not going.

Chapter Nine

Zak was already in the bar downing a vodka when we got there. He'd just showered, his hair was still damp, and he smelled of after-shave. I'd never seen him in a dinner suit before. Stuart tutted at the state of the tie and retied it for him, but his hands were still trembling, and he kept getting it wrong.

Imogen was perched beside them sipping a mineral water, dressed in a black fishtail dress and heels. Her cropped hair gleamed gold under the lights.

"Xanthe's not coming. She's not feeling too good," Zak said, signalling with a discreet twitch of his eyebrows that he'd seen the news.

"Since when? She was right as rain this afternoon," scoffed Imogen.

Stuart looked like he was about to explode but said, "Come on, let's go," and marched off across the foyer to where the taxis were waiting. Stuart was twitching, springing on his heels as we shuffled towards the front of the queue.

"He's going to be a liability," muttered Zak.

Sitting pressed up next to Zak in the taxi, it was the first time we'd touched since that night we came back from our mission. I think he could feel me trembling when I thought about the television coverage of that night because he pushed his leg firmly against mine to stop it and gave me a small smile that didn't disguise his fear. I wished Stuart had sat in between us but there wasn't much he could do. Imogen was singing along to the Whitney Houston song on the radio but none of us could bring ourselves to join in.

At the reception in the Majestic hotel we entered into the

ridiculous charade of keeping up with the jollity, laughing at the innuendos, conjecture and attempts to out-pun each other in order to break the ice.

When we found ourselves alone for a few moments Stuart put an arm around Zak's and my shoulders as though giving a drunken embrace and said quietly,

"Did you take the plates off the car before you set light to it?"

We looked at each other. Zak closed his eyes. "No," he admitted at last.

"But you checked the car for any of our belongings before dumping it?"

"Yes," I said, waving back at the woman from a rival magazine who'd been with me on a press trip to Belgium. She signalled that she liked my dress and I indicated that her hair looked great.

We had checked the car although perhaps not as thoroughly as he'd have liked. It was only half light and we'd been in such a panic to get away.

Stuart threw his head back and looked at the ceiling or heaven. "All right. And you stayed until the car was burned? Until the number plate was unrecognisable?"

"No. We never said that," I told him.

"No?"

"Did you suggest that at the time? Hindsight's a wonderful thing," Zak snapped. He smiled clench-teethed at the managing director of Ace Kitchens. "And anyway, if we'd hung around we'd have been spotted."

But Stuart wasn't satisfied with that. He was silent for a few moments, pinning us into the hug until it was difficult to breathe. "I can't believe, can't *believe* you didn't think of it."

"Look, Stuart, shut up, please. This is not the time or the place. We did the best we could," I said. "We agreed to trust each other and that's what you'll have to do."

"Hey, what's this?" asked Donald, the publisher, appearing from nowhere like some unwelcome genie. "I'm not paying you to stand around gossiping amongst yourselves. Get out there and mingle – bring back some useful insider info."

He looked from one to the other of us. "There's one missing. Where's Xanthe?"

"Not feeling well," said Zak. "She sends her apologies."

Donald looked disappointed. I suspected he was planning a reprisal for when we got back to the office.

We drifted away, and I found my place name on a table of tanked-up people from some of the leading rival industry brands. On one side of me a red-faced man from a well-known appliance manufacturer. On the other the bearded CEO of a shower company.

"So, I'm next to the lady in red," he said, breaking into the Chris de Burgh song as though I wouldn't have understood the connection.

I laughed jovially. It was going to be a long evening. But this was normality I reminded myself. This was where I wanted to be. I had to hang onto this.

He asked if I was married or living with someone. His eyes lit up when he heard I was sharing with several people. "So, tell me how it works," he asked, wiggling his eyebrows. "Who's sleeping with who? Or do you all change round?"

The more I denied it the more he was convinced he was onto something so in the end I let him have his little fantasy.

A good-natured argument broke out over the chronology of some events. A woman whose friend worked for one of the tabloids was telling anyone who'd listen how her friend had been offered a ludicrous sum to trick a footballer into bed and give them a story.

A man next to her was dating a woman who knew for an absolute fact that a well-known member of the royal family had been having it away with a pilot and now had Aids. "I swear to you, everyone in the press knows. They're just not allowed to print it," he kept saying.

All the time I was trying not to think about the post mortem being carried out on Bob's remains.

There was the usual gossip about members of the

103

industry. The MD of Ace Kitchens had been married to the owner of Carberry Kitchens but was now shacked up with the owner of Ascot Appliances. The owner of Bloomsbury Cabinetmakers had started Carberry Kitchens with Richard Carberry but Richard Carberry had stolen Bloomsbury's wife and his business from under his nose so Bloomsbury was out to destroy Carberry Kitchens. I tried to keep up.

The surprise entertainment was a well-known comedian who did a good job given the material he was stuck with. As the evening wore on the drinks were topped up and there were bawdy comments and more remarks about my house share. I drank more than I should to blot out the thought that at any moment the doors could bang open and a police squad would storm the place and strong-arm us out of there.

My thoughts were interrupted by Stuart's braying laugh. My stomach knotted even tighter. I knew that laugh. It was the one he did when he was really drunk and was about to get emotional.

I shot my chair back and grabbed Zak. "We've got to stop him drinking."

Around us people guffawed and someone kept shouting, "Straight up, I swear to God that's what happened!" and another voice squealed, "Impossible — unless she was a contortionist."

Zak looked over. "He's probably more of a danger sober. With any luck he'll fall into his cheesecake and snore through the rest of the evening."

"Yes but…"

"What?"

"He gets confessional when he's drunk. He told me something once – that time at the party – that he'd never have told me if he was sober."

Zak frowned. "What did he tell you?"

"Well that's the thing, I don't actually know."

He shook his head. "You're not making much sense."

He turned his chair round, rested his hands on my knees and I recounted the whole thing, speaking into his ear.

"Aye, aye!" said the man next to me, giving his

neighbour a nudge. Zak stuck up his middle finger, but laughed along.

He blanched as I told him as much as I'd heard of Stuart's tearful confession, his fear that I'd tell someone and his weird behaviour the next day.

Someone announced the awards and there was a scraping of chairs as people sat back in their seats and a round of applause.

"Bathroom break," said Zak as he moved his chair back round. "Meet me out there."

He slipped out and after sitting like a frozen rabbit for a few minutes I headed out too. I found him skulking in the corridor by the Ladies. He pulled me inside a cubicle and got me to repeat the whole thing. His face was etched with fear.

"Are you serious? Shit. You see what that probably means?"

"That Stuart killed him? Yes, it has occurred to me. But wait a minute, you're the one who took offence when I suggested one of us might have done it."

"But I wasn't in possession of all the facts then, was I? Obviously, this changes things. He's killed before – or come close enough to have got put Inside. They don't do that for nothing. And we all know about his violent temper."

I wasn't so sure. "It explains why Stuart's afraid of the police and being sent back Inside but not why he'd kill some random bloke who gatecrashed our party."

Zak rubbed his hands over his face. "But what if it wasn't that random? What if Stuart knew Bob?"

I digested this. "I don't see how he could have killed him. He was slumped on top of me all night."

Zak grabbed my arm. "Not all night. Only from around eleven-thirty. He could have done it before his big confession. It could be what triggered his memory and guilt feelings."

I felt the hairs on my arms rise. "But why would Stuart want to kill Bob? He didn't know him."

"How do we know that? And even if he didn't, so what?

105

You know how quickly he flares up. Suppose he lost it with Bob the way he did with me when he nearly broke my nose. What if he followed him down the stairs to the cellar and laid into him there? He'd have had the advantage because there was no light and he knew the layout of the place, how many steps there were, the ones that were broken…"

It still seemed a leap from head butting Zak to actually killing someone. I had to agree Stuart was obviously stressed to the point of near-lunacy tonight by the discovery of the body but I didn't feel so different myself. But could he have pushed Bob in a fit of anger? That was easier to imagine.

"The fact remains," I said, "that if he starts opening his heart to someone tonight and telling them what we did then we're all going down. We have to get him out of there."

We shot back into the dining room hoping to slip into our seats unnoticed, but a raucous cheer went up as we sat down. Donald sprang over to us. "Where the hell have you been? You missed our award."

Apparently, *Exhibition News* had won a surprise award but only Imogen had been there to collect it with Donald. She was none too pleased either.

"You left me looking like an arse. I had to come up with a speech just like that and Donald kissed me." She wiped imaginary saliva off her cheek. "Stuart's completely off his face. And I really hope Xanthe's throwing up everywhere because if this was just an excuse to lie in bed with room service while watching *Blind Date* I'll kill her."

"I mean everyone has something to hide, don't they?" Stuart's voice rose above the general conversation. It had that high, hysterical note. "Zak you might think is a bit odd but Emily there – looks like butter wouldn't melt, doesn't she? But she's as bad as the rest of us."

"I bet she is," said the woman next to him giving me a broad wink.

Zak was out of his chair in seconds. He put his arm around Stuart and dragged him out of his seat, winding one of Stuart's arms around his neck. "I'm sorry, he gets like

106

this."

People round the table were laughing. "Leave him alone – it's just getting interesting."

"I'll tell you what's really interesting," said Stuart. His eyes were filled with a strange light.

Zak planted a kiss on the side of his face and said into his ear just loud enough for me to hear, "Shut the *fuck* up" which seemed to do the trick at least for a few moments. Until Stuart shook him off and took a swing at him.

"Whoa!" A red-faced man from a tile company shot back as Zak cannoned back into the table toppling glasses and a half-full wine bottle. A woman from a rival publishing company shrieked as she was drenched in Merlot.

Donald appeared out of nowhere, red-faced and fulminating. "That's it. Get him out of here. In fact, you'd better leave too." At least he was on-side now. He helped manhandle Stuart out through reception and called for a taxi.

"I mean things happen, they just happen, and you can't get back," Stuart was saying as we propelled him into the back of the cab. He was slurring his words and I was hoping by some miracle they weren't as clear to other people as they were to me. "All that time and we had no idea he was there. What if Xanthe hadn't gone down there that night... He'd *still be there now*."

"I swear to God," hissed Zak. He must have dug his fingers into Stuart's gut because Stuart let out the kind of squeal that chills your blood.

Donald sprang back, wiped his face with a tissue and said, "I want to see him in my office first thing on Monday morning." He half-closed the cab door and then pulled it open again. "No, make that all of you."

"But Monday's our day off in lieu for working over the weekend," Zak reminded him.

"Not any more it's not."

The door slammed shut. Back at our own hotel I helped drag Stuart out, apologising for his teary tirade as we crossed the floor to the lifts. A group of Japanese business people inside the lift stared at us curiously.

Outside Stuart's room Zak slammed him back against the wall, searching through his clothes for his room key. Stuart who was notoriously ticklish started laughing. We jumped back as he turned aside and spewed all over his clothes. He sniffed disapprovingly. "Did I do that?"

When he was safely shut in his room, I went to my own, locked the door and lay on the bed watching the ceiling spin and waiting for the telephone to ring or the door to be kicked open. I was reminded of the night we'd left Bob and I wondered if Zak might knock on the door, but he didn't. When I finally fell asleep I dreamt of a torch shining in my face, the bedcovers being ripped off, being wrenched out of bed and marched in handcuffs past all the people I'd been at dinner with the night before, their faces shocked and hostile.

In the half-light, unable to sleep, I got up and sat hugging my knees, watching some idiotic cartoon and only vaguely aware of the light in the room changing as a weak sun struggled up. A look at the clock told me I'd made it through the night and I wondered if I'd go through this same feeling every night until it was over.

I looked out over the car park at all those business people who'd been at the dinner and were going back this morning to their showrooms and factories and offices and getting on with their lives just as they had before. Would we be the subject of their next awards dinner chit chat? That group of journalists who'd sat among them hiding a terrible secret – it would become an industry legend.

Of course, they wouldn't believe we'd just moved the body – they'd go for the full gory details of how we'd killed Bob, probably as part of a sex game that went wrong. And how they'd love it. They could spout on about it for years, competing to be the one who divulged the most sordid details they "knew for an absolute fact."

My head felt tight as though someone had stretched an elastic band around it. I was still in my clothes from the previous night. I hadn't dared get undressed. The only thing worse than being dragged out of bed by police in the middle of the night would have been being dragged out in my knickers and Snoopy T-shirt.

Perhaps they were outside the door waiting. I slid clothes off hangers and stuffed them into my travel bag. The least I could do was to be ready for them.

But no one came.

When it was time to get ready I tried to disguise my puffy eyes and pallid complexion with a heavy application of eyeliner and concealer. My skin was so sensitive it seemed to sizzle at every touch and my hand was too shaky to get a nice, even line. I looked like a ghost.

Something else was nagging at me. Something that should have happened by now, but I didn't want to give myself anything else to think about. I'd have to deal with that later.

***

An hour later I met the others downstairs in the dining room for breakfast. I had no appetite but couldn't face being alone with my thoughts any longer. Stuart sat huddled over a cup of tea with that battered, baby bird look, very contrite. Zak hovered round him, apparently solicitous but I knew he was keeping watch. Imogen sat white-faced and fuming about how we'd all gone off and left her again.

"I will never, ever drink again," said Stuart. His meaning was clear to three of us, but Imogen just laughed.

"I'll remind you of that at lunch time."

Xanthe walked in and helped herself to a full English, ignoring Imogen's incredulous stare and sarcastic comment about a miraculous recovery. She'd applied an extra thick layer of eyeliner that morning but otherwise looked remarkably serene and sat eating her breakfast as though in a trance.

The one good thing was that Donald had left early because of some crisis in the office so at least we didn't have to face him.

We got the train back to Bristol in silence. It was packed

with industry people, so we couldn't risk talking about what had been on the news even when Imogen went off to the loo or share our observations about the exhibition and after a sleepless night we were too tired for bright chitchat. But I picked up a newspaper at the station and we passed it around, trying not to spend too long looking at the story about a washed-up body.

We shared a taxi from the station to the house. As we pulled up in front of it we noticed the light in the kitchen. Something cold crept over my scalp. There was someone inside. The four of us slid looks at each other but we couldn't say anything in front of Imogen.

"Anyone fancy going for a drink?" asked Zak.

It was tempting to take off and hole up in a pub but being arrested in front of a crowd of people would be even worse than being arrested at home.

"Let's just get it over with," said Stuart.

"Get what over with?" Imogen demanded but getting no response rolled her eyes.

We followed Stuart up the path. He paused momentarily, then stuck his key in the lock. We looked at each other one last time before going inside. I had no idea what we'd find on the other side – the same officer who'd come over when Stuart reported his car missing? Or a bank of armed police? I drew in my breath as a figure appeared out of the shadows.

Rick.

Imogen squealed, dropped her bag and jumped into his arms. She caught him off balance and the two of them fell over, sprawling on the floor, ending up in a snog. My breath was still caught. I looked round at the others and their frozen expressions told me they'd had the same fear as I had.

Rick greeted us coolly. He'd cooked dinner for him and Imogen. It was as if he'd forgotten we lived there.

We cooed at the table set for two in the living room with a candle and vase of roses. Then the four of us cosied up in Xanthe's room with a bag of crisps, feeling like interlopers in our own home.

The candlelit dinner was followed by a romantic video.

"Why don't they just go to bed?" moaned Stuart. After a while he said, "I refuse to skulk any longer," and marched into the living room to play gooseberry.

Zak, Xanthe and I slept in Xanthe's bed, sprawled across each other like children.

Xanthe gave a sleepy laugh. "Your friend from the awards dinner would love it if he could see us lying here together."

Chapter Ten

We slept most of Sunday and returned to work on Monday, our cancelled day off in lieu. Donald seemed to have forgotten that he'd asked to see us when we got back and was surprised when we turned up in the office. He slapped Stuart on the back as if they were old friends, asking how he was as if they'd been on a lads' night out together.

Another thought that plagued me during those first weeks was what if Bob hadn't actually died that night of the party? What if he'd only fallen or been injured and hadn't been able to get up? What if he'd been calling out for days, getting weaker and weaker, and none of us had heard him as we went about oblivious, playing our music and arguing about the mortgage?

And what if by removing his body and staging his suicide we'd also removed the evidence that would have shown his death was an accident?

The irony wasn't lost on me that this was the second house I'd lived in where someone had died. It made me question my own judgement. Was I in some subconscious way drawn to disaster and doomed houses or were doomed people drawn to me?

Then the anger hit me. I felt furious that the future I'd once taken for granted – meeting someone, having a family, writing for one of the top magazines – had been taken away from me. No, I'd thrown it away. Instead – but only if I was lucky – I'd be stuck here in this mausoleum with these people, one of whom might very well be a killer or be shielding one, because we couldn't risk letting each other go.

But one thing I discovered is that it's not possible to

maintain fear at its highest level. So even though it nags away at you it's quite possible to function almost as normal. It was frightening in some ways how mundane our lives were and how unremarkable we must have appeared to other people. A bit distracted maybe but I doubt many would have guessed we were hiding anything at all.

I found ways to drive the whole business to the back of my mind, filling up my spare time by working, joining an aerobics class and accepting any invitation to go out with other people who knew nothing about Bob.

But every now and then a question would crop up that would plunge you back into the hellish reality. Friendly invitations from one of the other three to go for a coffee at lunch time or stay in at the weekend usually masked a frantic worry, an obstacle we hadn't foreseen. We went over the events of the party so many times and yet new worries always came to the surface.

"When did each of us last see Bob?" Xanthe asked.

No one could say for sure. I thought I might have seen him again in the kitchen, but it was very hard to remember the order of things and there had been so many people there. Every time I thought about that it chilled my stomach. So many witnesses – what would it take for them to recognise Bob?

We went over all the people we remembered at the party. Most of them we could vouch for but how well do you really know anyone? Whoever the killer was, and whether they'd killed Bob by accident or design, I hoped they were going through hell not knowing whether the body was still down in our basement or whether we'd been to the police and the noose was closing on them.

Two weeks passed.

Zak found himself a girlfriend. Chiara. She had tumbling red hair and legs that went on forever. But more importantly she had something I didn't – she was unsullied by the dead body thing. He didn't have to feel guilty when he was with her. Perhaps she even helped him forget.

At times I felt like I was on the run. Every moment of

freedom that remained before the police tracked us down was precious. I took every opportunity to experience new things. At the end of the month I went on a press trip to Brussels as part of my new placement on a brewery magazine.

During the beer and chocolates walking tour and the visit to the Museum of Modern Art I fell into conversation with a reporter called Ansel with hair the colour of sunshine who shared my love of Magritte and waffles and told me that the saxophone was invented in Belgium by a man called Sax and that the country had the longest tram railway in the world. I felt a million miles away from the claustrophobic Bristol house with its sordid secret.

I sat next to Ansel at dinner that evening in a restaurant in the old market area and afterwards strolled with him around the Grand Place, which was all lit up and looked magical. Afterwards I had my first and only one-night stand – unless you counted the night with Zak which I was doing my best to forget.

In the morning Ansel asked for my address in England. Although I was tempted to see him again I said no because it didn't seem fair to get close to someone when I was so uncertain about what my future held.

***

After we got back from the exhibition Stuart had a lock fitted to his door. He was very careful about locking it each time he left the room, even if he was just popping across the landing to the toilet and taking the key with him. He locked it from the inside too. Perhaps the discovery of the body had brought home the reality to him – that the killer might be one of us living in the house. But it also made us wonder if he had something to hide.

"What the hell does he get up to in there?" asked Imogen putting her ear to the door.

On the one occasion the room was left open I couldn't resist taking a look inside to see if I could get any clue to what he'd done in the past that made him feel so ashamed.

The room was almost bare, as if he was planning to clear out. All his clothes and belongings had been put away apart from the books which were arranged in order from Asimov to Zola. On his bed lay a book with a couple of photos on top of the open pages. Intrigued, I took a few steps towards them and picked up the picture on top of the pile.

It was of a girl – she looked around twelve with a cloud of blonde hair.

"What are you doing in my room?" Hot shame flushed through my limbs as Stuart's voice sounded close behind me. He'd come up the stairs so quietly I hadn't heard him.

"I'm sorry," I said, taking a step back. "I was about to make a coffee. Thought I'd see if you wanted one."

He held up the mug he was carrying. "I've just made tea."

"Great minds," I said, mustering a bright smile. I turned to leave but he stood between me and the door.

His eyes fell on the photograph in my hand.

"Oh. I was just looking at it," I said, putting it back as carefully as I could. "It's a lovely picture. Who is she?"

"My sister."

I hoped he couldn't detect the shake in my voice "I didn't realise you had a sister. You never talk about her."

He shrugged. "It's how I like to remember her."

"I'm sorry. Were you close?"

A funny look crossed his face. My heart pounded. I felt I was getting near to the truth at last about Stuart's past. Was this what he'd been trying to tell me at the party?

"We were. Until my stepdad arrived. He turned her against me, like he turned my mother against me."

"Sorry. I didn't mean to pry."

"No, it's all right."

His voice was terse even for him. I moved again towards the door, but he leant back against until it clicked shut.

"Actually, Stuart, I need to get on."

Wordlessly, he produced his key and turned it in the lock. I was wondering if any of the others would know where I was.

He sat on the bed and patted the space next to him.

"Sit down. I'll tell you."

He picked up another picture of the same girl but quite a few years younger with a young Stuart and a ruggedly handsome man digging a sandcastle.

"My father," said Stuart. "My real father. I don't remember much about him – a few things but I'm not sure how much I've imagined or been told. He died when I was eight. My mother remarried when I was twelve and my sister Skye was ten.

"My childhood ended the moment Paul walked in. We had a bigger house and a bigger car, but it wasn't a better life. He pulled apart everything my father had done for us.

"He hated me. He liked Skye - couldn't do enough for her – but he didn't want me around. There were always tensions. The only thing he wanted me for was as a babysitter, so he and my mother could go out for romantic evenings and weekends away.

"You should have seen him with his clients – charming, ingratiating, full of bonhomie. He was always inviting them to dinner without giving my mother enough notice and belittling her attempts to turn out something suitably impressive.

"But behind closed doors it was a different story. It began with criticisms but got nastier. I watched my mother change from a vibrant, funny person to a someone who was too nervous to contradict her husband or voice an opinion on anything without looking to him for approval. It was sickening. I asked how she could let him do it to her, but she'd fallen so far under his control she wouldn't see it.

"Skye had always been clingy – never had friends of her own - but she got worse after Paul moved in, always following me about. It annoyed me because she was too young to do the things I wanted to, and I couldn't stand to see the way he manipulated her.

"That weekend in Cornwall - Paul persuaded my mother I was a danger to Skye and I'd tried to kill her."

I swallowed more loudly than I meant to. "That's terrible. How can she have believed that?"

He gulped some tea. "They told me to keep an eye on her as usual, but I wanted some time on my own, scrambling over the rocks at the edge of the beach - I was thirteen for God's sake, it's only natural. I wanted to see if I could get to the other bay before the tide cut it off. I looked round and she was following me. I shouted at her to go back. She was only going to slow me down – she had a really bad sense of balance - and I'd miss the tide.

"She kept pleading with me to stop but I pretended I couldn't hear her. At last she went quiet. I looked round and couldn't see her anymore. I assumed she'd given up and gone back.

"It wasn't until later that I got back full of excitement about how I'd made it across that I saw the crowd of people and everyone shouting. And Skye was laid out on the beach, her hair was all clogged with sand and someone was pumping their hands on her chest.

"My stepdad persuaded my mother I must have pushed Skye in. He said I was jealous and a danger to her."

I absorbed all this. "And Skye – was it too late?"

He shook his head. "No, she was all right. She could have told the truth but she was angry with me for not waiting and I think she liked the fuss she received so she let him convince her to go along with his story.

"Which is how I got sent to boarding school."

"That's terrible," I said. "But it wasn't your fault. And Skye wasn't a baby, was she? I doubt she'd have wanted you watching over her the whole time."

He drained his mug and put it down on the cabinet.

"She has learning difficulties. Very trusting and she doesn't understand danger. But my mother believed him too. I still can't believe she let him talk her into sending me away. She shouldn't have done that. She was too weak to stand up to him. What it boils down to is that sex with Paul was more important to her than keeping her own son."

"Perhaps it wasn't the only thing," I said, "what else

117

could she do with two young children?" He didn't seem to hear me.

"I hated school. The bullying I suffered there. There were a couple of boys who made my life a misery. They identified me as a victim the moment I walked through the door. And because the other children were cowards it spread. I despise that about people."

"Did you tell your mum about it?"

He shrugged. "I didn't spell out to her exactly what was happening, but she should have been able to read between the lines shouldn't she? I told her enough to make most intelligent people start asking questions, but she didn't. And do you know why? Because she didn't want to hear the answers. She was my mother for God's sake. Mothers are supposed to protect their children. But she hadn't protected me from him and she didn't protect me from them."

"Stuart, this is so sad," I said. "But what happened to Skye wasn't your fault. So, you took your eye off her – but you didn't push her. Didn't the police believe you?"

He looked at me oddly.

"I told you, what happened to Skye was an accident. She slipped. But that's not what I went to the detention centre for. I told you about that at the party."

With a sick realisation I saw that I hadn't understood this thing at all and was no closer to finding out what he'd done in his past that he was so ashamed of.

Chapter Eleven

My stomach clutched as I saw two well-built men stop outside our house, looking it up and down. It was always at the back of my mind that Fitz, whoever he was, might come looking for us one day. But after consulting a clip board the men went across the street. A little later they loaded up a van with a television and some furniture while the home owner looked on, distraught.

"Bailiffs," said Imogen.

"Bastards," said Zak.

Repossession had seemed a distant threat when we bought the house but by the end of 1988 hundreds of homes had been taken back by mortgage lenders and the during the year that followed more and more people were losing their homes. The government's promise that mortgage rates would never rise over 9.5 per cent turned out to be worthless which didn't surprise any of us but left us with a real probability of finding ourselves homeless. Which would in itself have been a disaster but we now had the added complication of Bob.

"Perhaps we should just sell," said Xanthe, "and go our separate ways."

"We can't sell," said Stuart. "Are you mad? The more people that come traipsing round here the more chance someone will sniff something out."

"There's nothing left to find," Zak argued. "At least we'd have a chance of making a new start, each of us."

But Stuart shook his head. "We can't afford to sell the house yet. Haven't you heard of negative equity? And with interest rates going up none of us is going to be able to afford to live anywhere else."

The solution he proposed was to fix the repayments before they went up even more. But the new rate was more than any of us could afford and the thought of being tied to paying thirteen and a half per cent for the next two years was unbearable, so we took our chances. "It's got to come down some time," Zak said.

It did. But not before it had gone up.

***

Around a week later I had a rare evening to myself. I'd had a bath and was shuffling around in my dressing gown making some dinner. I opened the kitchen door to take the bowl of pasta and a magazine into the living room. I caught my breath as something moved in the shadows. Someone was standing in the hallway.

"I didn't know you had a key," I said, recovering, as Rick turned around. I knew he'd borrowed Imogen's key while we were at the exhibition but hadn't realised it was a permanent arrangement. "Imogen's in Hertfordshire – an overnight press do."

"I know," was all he said. "So, how is everybody?"

"Fine." I rambled through a list of barely-relevant achievements, without mentioning the real developments. Whatever the others said I had my doubts about Rick's innocence in all this.

I could feel his eyes travel up and down over me and I wished I hadn't decided to get ready for bed at such an early hour. I felt vulnerable and dishevelled standing there in my nightwear. He looked like he was about to say something about my appearance but in the end he didn't. Most disturbingly, he was standing by the door to the basement, and it was open. I was suddenly aware of how tall he was.

"You've done this space up," he said, watching me for my reaction.

My stomach flipped but I tried to keep my voice even. "Yes, it was a bit dank. We just wanted to brighten it up a little."

"New flooring," he said peering. "And you've painted the walls."

I nodded, trying to look as though it was of no importance, but my heart was crashing against my ribs.

"When did you do this?"

I shrugged. "Can't remember exactly. Quite a while ago now."

His conker-bright eyes flitted round the space again. "It wasn't like this at New Year."

"Um – no, probably not, I can't remember."

"You've put in a lot of effort. But you've filled it with junk - what's the point of that?"

I kept my tone light. "It might look like junk to you but it's valuable to us."

He eyed the conglomeration of junk and pulled up the corners of his mouth. "Really?"

He didn't move. "The bikes I get. It makes sense to have them down here – but what's in all the boxes?"

"I don't know about all of them. I only know what's in mine. Old school books, stuff from uni, things my mum and dad stored for me while I was a student but refuse to hang onto any longer. Nothing exciting."

He wrinkled his nose. "Do you really need to hang onto that stuff? What's wrong with the attic?"

Was he trying to get me to admit something? I was desperate to move away but forced myself to stand there.

He took a step inside. "You know, this space could be much better used. You could make it into a studio flat and let it out. That would help solve your financial situation. You're struggling, aren't you?"

He must have noticed my face flood with colour because he asked if I was all right. I insisted I was.

"The basement gets damp," I said. "And there's no central heating. What we've done's only cosmetic. We haven't sorted out the problem."

But all he said was, "These things can always be put right. Let me show you what I'd do to sort out your situation."

I made excuses about being pushed for time. No way was I going to set foot in the basement, especially with Rick. Either he knew nothing about Bob and would become suspicious or he knew everything about Bob in which case I didn't want to be on my own with him ever. Besides, my pasta was getting cold.

"It will only take a second," he said. His eyes glinted with excitement.

Once I'd recovered my voice I said, "No. Sorry, I can't. Not now."

He looked disgusted. "That's the trouble with you lot – no vision. I've never understood what Imogen's doing here with you. The way you treat this house like a dump. No respect, no aspiration. I can see you all dragging her down. She deserves better."

I didn't feel like getting drawn into an argument in which I'd probably say something I regretted so I just said, "I'm sorry you feel that way."

I flinched as he reached out towards me. He laughed.

"You see? You're so neurotic. And Xanthe's so ditsy, Stuart's a pompous prick – and don't get me started on Zak. Why are you all still here? You don't even like each other."

"That's not true."

"Imogen's the only one who actually cares about this house. But from what I've heard everything she suggests gets ignored. If any of you had troubled to ask her she'd explain why it's so important for her to create a happy home, like the one she remembered as a child before she found it was all a sham."

It was news to me, but it made me realise that we didn't know that much about Imogen. She'd always seemed the uncomplicated one – sorted, stable. It hadn't seriously occurred to me that she might have problems other than her paranoia about catching Aids which wasn't that unusual at the time. But still, whatever it was, it was Imogen's story and I didn't see why Rick should be the one telling me it.

He grabbed my wrist. He was holding it more tightly than anyone would think necessary. "Come on. What are you afraid of, Emily?"

"I'm not."

I yanked my hand free from his and retreated towards the phone in the hall.

He laughed. "You are. Why do I get the firm impression you've been working on Imogen, trying to put her off me? What have you got against me being here?"

"Nothing. We haven't said anything."

"Good because it won't work."

I turned to go again.

"Is it my imagination or have you put on weight?"

I ignored him.

"You're all so close," he said suspiciously. "There's something unnatural about it."

"Sorry?"

I looked at his fingers drumming on the basement door, looked down the steps and back at me. I felt skewered by his stare.

"There's something you've done, all of you, some collective guilt. Don't try and deny it. You forget what I do for a living. I'm a lawyer – I can sense these things. You're all covering for each other in some way. I will find out. And I'll make you pay."

"Don't threaten me," I said as coolly as I could, but my heart was thumping as I walked away. With the help of my chest of drawers I barricaded myself into my room that night but even so I didn't sleep much.

∗∗∗

"Rick knows," I said when the others were back. "He knows about Bob."

"Calm down," said Stuart. "Why do you think that? What have you told him?"

"Nothing."

I told him what Rick had said and the feeling I'd had about him in the basement.

"He was trying to get me to say something, I'm sure he

was. He thinks we killed Bob. Or he killed Bob and is testing to find out whether we know. Either way, I didn't feel safe."

Stuart seemed most concerned about Rick having a key. "We never agreed to that. I'll speak to Imogen about it."

"We have to tell her about Bob," I said. "That's if she doesn't already know. We can't let her carry on oblivious, sharing a bed with Rick. Not if he's dangerous."

Stuart caught my arm. "No. We can hardly ask him how much he knows without telling him more. And we've no evidence it was him who killed Bob or even that he knows anything. You can't base a theory on the fact someone's obnoxious. And Imogen trusts him. For now, we should too."

"I'd trust him as far as I could throw him," muttered Zak.

But Stuart had a point. We didn't say anything to Imogen. She already knew we didn't like Rick and she'd told us he liked her less when she was with us.

***

At work a few days later we saw Xanthe heading in the direction of Donald's office half way through the morning. She rolled her eyes as she passed my desk and I assumed it was some minor problem. The blinds in his glass-walled room were down and the door shut but you could hear Donald's ranting tones even if the words were indistinguishable from across the open plan office.

Stuart sat up like a meerkat. Zak, in the corner, looked up from under his brows and caught my gaze. Imogen busied herself gathering some pages and took them over to the photocopier outside the publisher's office. I saw her take a step back as Xanthe came out, pink-faced and holding back tears.

Xanthe was escorted to her desk. Donald stood over her as she collected her belongings without making eye contact with any of us and disappeared out of the door leaving a long, powerful silence trailing in her wake. We all joined

Imogen at the photocopier where she confirmed by drawing a finger across her throat that Xanthe would not be coming back.

"No warning?" said Stuart. "That's against procedure. She can sue them for that."

Imogen shook her head. "There are some things you don't even get warnings for. She was up to her silly tricks with the false names. This time someone spotted it."

I closed my eyes. Xanthe had often inserted silly names for people who were prepared to comment as long as they weren't identified. Imogen was fuming. "I can't believe she even tried to get away with R Soul, Dick Head and Hugh Janus all in the same issue. She must have a death wish or something."

Zak broke into a grin. "It actually went into print? Oh shit."

"It's already been spotted by a couple of major advertisers," said Imogen. "They've pulled out and are placing all their ads for the year with the competitor journal but that won't be the end of it – they'll sue the company. It's made them a laughing stock. Donald had no choice but to fire her on the spot."

"But what's she going to do?" I said. "There aren't any other jobs around – they all say you need two years' experience."

"More to the point, how's she going to pay her share of the mortgage?" asked Zak.

The full impact dawned on us.

Stuart gripped the stair rail by the photocopier. "We'll have to get them to change their mind. Granted it was silly, infantile behaviour but she's only a trainee. Ultimately, she shouldn't have to shoulder the responsibility. Someone should have spotted the names before the pages went off. They must have been first- and second-read. We can't let them get away with this."

"They already have, Stuart," said Imogen.

He didn't listen. "Come on, let's go and see Mr Renton."

But if anything, we made it worse. The Chairman let us

know in no uncertain terms that not only did Xanthe not stand a cat in hell's chance of coming back, he would also be calling in the money she owed the company for her share of the top-up loan.

"Well that's going to be impossible if she's unemployed," pointed out Zak.

"In which case, if you care to read the agreement you'll see that you're all jointly responsible for the money owing," said Mr Renton. "I'll have a word with Accounts and make sure your salaries are adjusted accordingly."

"Wait, hang on, this isn't fair," began Stuart but Mr Renton waved his arm and looked down at his paperwork signalling he had things to do – more important things than considering the future of a bunch of immature trainees.

We thought about staging a walk-out, refusing to come back unless Xanthe was reinstated but after taking advice from the union we had to concede the idea stood very little chance of success and was most likely to result in the four of us being thrown out too.

"Why didn't she *think?*" Imogen asked as we drove home later.

She stopped the car on the way and bought Xanthe some flowers and a box of chocolates although it was doubtful they'd do much to lift her mood. As we opened the door the house shook with the sound of her James CD playing at full blast. We called her name several times on the way up the stairs, but she didn't respond. Worried she might have done something silly we opened the door anyway and found her curled into a ball on her bed, the floor strewn with balled-up tissues that had missed the bin. We finally coaxed her downstairs, but she wouldn't talk. She spent all evening on the sofa with her head buried in Zak's shoulder leaving snail trails all over his shirt.

It felt strange getting up for work the next day without Xanthe. She was always hanging about the kitchen in the mornings and we normally chatted about the day ahead, but she was nowhere to be seen and her car stood in the drive. We took the bus into work and back again. The 2CV stood outside the house.

We knocked on her door and persuaded her to come out to see *Field of Dreams* with us and although it was the worst film I'd ever seen we had a good evening laughing about it but afterwards she retreated again.

***

The next few weeks were a nightmare. We were all cutting back as much as we could as it was, living off pot noodles and value sliced bread but it was still a struggle. When my editor airily told me to pay for my train ticket to Durham and "just pop it on expenses" he probably had no idea that meant not eating for days except for the odd chocolate bar. Sometimes I look back now and wonder how we functioned.

Stuart started to get twitchy about Xanthe using the electricity and the heating during the day when we were out. Imogen had flown into mother hen mood immediately after the firing, circling ads in the newspaper and spotting cards in shop windows. "Dog walker? Nanny? Catering assistant? Barmaid?"

But each suggestion brought tears of frustration from Xanthe and comments like, "I thought I was finally getting somewhere, doing something I was good at."

We felt bad asking Xanthe if she'd mind tidying up downstairs or cleaning the kitchen during the day, putting on some washing or cleaning the bathroom and she never thought to do these things herself. After another trip to the job centre she said it was all a waste of time and she'd prefer to work freelance. She'd met some Swedish PR man at a trade fair who said he might be able to get her some work doing their brochures and there was an environmental magazine that had just started up and was looking for freelancers. Which was all very well but as Zak pointed out, even if she got a commission the following day she wouldn't get paid for at least three months.

At the end of the month she still hadn't received her first

unemployment benefit and got weepy when asked for a contribution for the water rates.

"She can't keep sponging off us," Imogen said, fuming.

So, it came as a surprise when Xanthe bought herself a new jacket just after Stuart had subbed her for a pizza. It was a thing of beauty – we'd admired it several times in a shop window as we'd passed. It cost nearly a month's salary and was hardly a necessity.

When questioned Xanthe said it was a gift from her sister – it was news to us she even had one – but Imogen said if her sister wanted to help her out she should pay us back some of the money Xanthe owed.

The upshot was that Xanthe retreated more into herself which made us all feel bad. We thought at least her mortgage payments would be taken care of now she was unemployed, but it turned out things weren't as simple as we'd thought.

"It takes weeks before they step in," she said after coming back from the DHSS, "and then they only pay a quarter, then half and then eventually all of it."

Imogen was incandescent. "We can't wait that long. If we do, we'll default on the mortgage and the house will be repossessed."

When the phone bill came in it was obvious that Xanthe had spent many hours on long-distance calls to Erik. She said it was nothing serious but I couldn't help wondering if she'd disappear to Sweden one day. We couldn't risk losing the house but we couldn't afford to pay Xanthe's share of the mortgage and bills either. When would we be able to move on from this? It was like being stuck in an unhappy marriage without the advantages.

***

After long conversations with her boyfriend Imogen came up with a solution.

"Rick says he'll buy your share of the house."

Perhaps I should have seen it coming but the idea of Rick moving in filled me with horror. From the looks on their faces the other three felt the same. Xanthe was aggravating sometimes but compared to Rick she was a joy to live with.

If he had a share in the house he'd have a say in how we did things which would have been unwelcome at the best of times – but with the Bob situation the very last thing we needed was Rick nosing around while a disgruntled Xanthe waited outside to spring her revenge.

"That's if I want to sell," said Xanthe.

"You can't expect us to carry you forever."

I could see Xanthe shrink. "How much?" she asked at last.

Imogen's tone was cool and reasonable. "We can't give you any money for it – your share's not worth anything now that house prices have come down. But you'll get your deposit back. And it will free you up to move on somewhere else, make a new start."

"Er – that would be *my* deposit," Stuart murmured.

Xanthe looked from one to the other, her eyes huge and desperate. "You can't just take it off me."

Imogen sighed. "The house is worth less than we paid for it. Rick would be taking on the debt. We're actually being quite generous."

"In that case I'm not selling."

But Imogen's voice took on a steely tone. "I'm afraid you don't have a choice. Sorry but we can't put the house at risk by defaulting on the payments."

We looked at each other.

"Hold on a minute," said Zak. "You can't make a decision like that without our agreement. The house belongs to all of us. And I don't agree."

Imogen rolled her eyes. "You wouldn't. Are you saying you have a problem with Xanthe giving up her share or Rick having it? Because at least you know him. It's not like a stranger coming in. And he's away in London most of the week. We've got to do something about it and it's going to be pretty difficult to find someone else who's willing to buy a fifth of a house, isn't it?"

"Especially this one," said Rick. I thought I saw a look of

129

triumph flash through his eyes.

But Stuart refused too. "It's nothing personal but if Xanthe sells – or even gives – her share to Rick that in effect gives you two votes instead of one for every decision we make, which isn't democratic."

Imogen clutched her head. "Not this again."

"I'm not selling," repeated Xanthe.

What is it you're afraid of?"asked Rick. The look he gave me sent a shiver right through me. "If you have a problem with me taking on Xanthe's share, why don't you all buy out Imogen's share instead so she and I can buy somewhere of our own?"

His expression dared us to come out and say the reason we couldn't sell the house.

"Or let Rick and I have your shares - then you'll be free to go wherever you like," said Imogen.

The idea was attractive in a way. I could ditch the job and start a new life somewhere else, miles from Bristol and Bob. Zak could travel and do charity work and join environmental campaigns, and Stuart would be in with a chance of getting a job on a national paper if he moved to London.

But when I thought about it, it just wasn't fair. We couldn't leave Imogen there in the house that had been a tomb – especially if Rick was dangerous. What if the police unearthed another clue in the future and came to investigate and she ended up getting blamed for everything?

"You can't do this, Imogen," I said.

She gave an indignant snort. "What do you mean, can't? We're offering you an opportunity you won't get again."

"But think about it – you'd be taking on a massive debt between you and who knows if house prices will ever recover?"

She smiled. "Please don't worry on our account — Rick's not badly paid and prices will recover one day – they always do. These things are cyclical as I'm sure Stuart will tell us. It's an investment for us. My dad says he'll help us out."

We exchanged looks. Trust her bloody father to interfere.

"What about the agreement?" I asked feebly. "We said we'd all stay for two years."

Rick laughed. "Did you sign anything? I thought not."

"You know what I think this is, Emily?" said Imogen. "Sour grapes. You don't want to hang onto the house, but you don't want me and Rick to have it either. You're like a spoilt child sometimes."

Her hand shook with tension as she lit a cigarette.

"Rick and I want to get engaged. You lot are holding us back."

Engaged? It was the first I'd heard of it – although perhaps that wasn't so surprising given that we'd had other things on our minds.

"Aren't you rushing things a bit?" asked Zak.

Imogen gave him a withering look. "I wouldn't expect you to understand."

He shrugged. "So, get engaged if you want to – we're not stopping you. But we're not moving out."

She drew on the cigarette and curled her feet up under her. "Why not? You don't care about the house. None of you understand what it means to me to be able to create a lovely home. I know this place is just bricks and mortar to you – but it could be so much more than that. It's a beautiful house and it could be a lovely family home one day. I grew up in a house like this in Cheltenham, but we lost it. I don't mean to lose this one."

Her words reminded me of something Rick had said to me on the basement steps that time.

"You always say I'm materialistic, but it has nothing to do with money – and as it happens I do know what it's like to have nothing."

Her outburst took us all by surprise.

"Christmas 1983. Everything was normal – perfect, actually. I remember looking around and asking myself if it was too perfect. And then telling myself it wasn't. My dad had taken a few days off. We did all the things we used to do as children like picking out our tree from the forest and

131

bringing it home. Hanging stockings up by the fire.

"My dad gave Mum a pair of earrings. We'd all known about them for weeks – we helped him choose. God, I was so excited waiting for her to open the box. The look in her eyes when she saw them...

"I got a Human League album, some makeup and a Swatch watch with different coloured straps. My sister had a Care Bear."

Zak looked as if he was about to make a comment, but she stopped him with a look.

"The radio was playing *Only You* by the Flying Bloody Pickets when the doorbell went. I opened it. She was standing there staring at me. A girl I'd never seen before. I kept thinking she looked a little bit familiar, but I couldn't think how I knew her. Anyway, I thought she must be a friend of my sister.

She just said, "Is my dad there?"

"I said no, it was only us. But then my dad came out, pushed past me and marched her away. I could hear them arguing down the road. She called him Dad too."

"He had a secret love child?" asked Xanthe.

Imogen gave a short laugh. "He had a whole secret family. They believed just like we did that his work took him away for a week here and a week there.

"My mum came out and stood in the street watching them disappear down the road. I suppose she must have had her suspicions, and this was the final confirmation. She went to pieces. I followed them to the girl's home. It was only a few roads away and a carbon copy of ours – except they had a beagle instead of two Labradors. They even had the same car. I thought honestly, why bother?

"But in that moment everything we had became worthless."

"You never told us," said Xanthe.

Imogen waved her arm. "I'm over it. I learned from it not to judge my worth by other people. I'd never put myself in that position of depending on someone else for my survival. Dad thought Mum wouldn't throw him out because she had us and no income. She was his secretary, you see, so she'd have to lose her job as well as him.

"But she did anyway. And in the end, although the first year was hell, I think it's made us stronger. My sisters and my mum and I are always there for each other. We thought we needed him to complete everything, but it turned out we didn't. It was a struggle for my mum to find a job, but she did it. And I know from watching her that I can too.

"I didn't see my dad for three years, but he suddenly popped up again when I was a student, wanting to be friends. He tries to make it up to me by buying me stuff – so you see I'm not quite as privileged as you seem to think. And you lot are holding up my life."

She left the room in disgust. Rick followed her, giving us a parting glare.

"Wasn't expecting that," said Zak at last.

But it was obvious the matter of Rick joining us in the house wasn't over. Neither were our money worries going to go away.

"Perhaps I should join my sister in the convent," said Xanthe, throwing her head back against the sofa.

I laughed at that. "Sorry but I can't see you as a nun."

She grinned. "It would take a bit of getting used to but at least I wouldn't starve."

"And me?" I couldn't help asking.

She touched my arm. "You'll find something. You don't need to worry, Em."

If only that were true. But there was nothing, absolutely nothing else, I could do if I moved away. Besides, I was increasingly beginning to suspect another problem was about to present itself.

But oddly enough the next monthly payment went through without any nasty letters and so did the next. Xanthe had reduced her diet to one tin of soup and a couple of apples a day but insisted on paying her share of the bills. I suspected Stuart was still helping her out even though he said he wasn't. After all, it was in all of our interests to keep the house with its secret inside it.

Chapter Twelve

It was a Thursday night and we had half an eye on the television during a game of Scruples. Imogen had drawn a question along the lines of if you saw your best friend's partner cheating on them would you tell them, and the debate was getting quite heated. And suddenly there was Bob's face on the screen, staring right out at us.

You could almost feel the air being sucked out of the room. My heart crashed against my ribs. Xanthe's arm jerked involuntarily and her drink spilled over the board.

"Watch out, look what you're doing!" said Imogen.

"Ssshhh!"

"Don't shush me."

It was a holiday snap – some boys backpacking in the Greek Islands. The face could only have only been on the screen for seconds, but it seemed like forever. It must have been taken a few years before our New Year's Eve party. He was a bit fuller in the face and his hair was longer. He was wearing a black t-shirt with tour dates, holding a can of something and standing in front of a taverna. You couldn't see his crooked teeth because he was smiling with his mouth shut. His expression was heart breaking – so happy, so unaware. He must have thought he had a whole life ahead of him. But how in the world had the police identified him?

Imogen crunched her crisps throughout the report. I wanted to grab them off her, but I took the remote instead and turned up the sound, ignoring a glare from Stuart.

"For God's sake, what's wrong with your ears?" said Imogen between crunches. "It's like an old people's home in

134

here."

They showed a reconstruction. Someone who looked a bit like Bob was shown working behind a bar in Leeds. An interview with his mother cut in, saying what a lovely son he'd been, and the ex-girlfriend talked about how he'd been through a rough time when his parents divorced but he seemed to have got over it. She got tearful, recounting how they'd split up a few months before he disappeared. He'd lost his way, got into drugs and hooked up with some bad people. His name was Oskar Bramley. He was twenty-four.

Xanthe gave a whimper. Stuart stiffened. Imogen looked at her strangely, then went back to crunching her crisps.

There was no mention of getting a train to Bristol or any connection with Stuart's car. The police were concentrating their investigation on Cornwall and Leeds. Perhaps we'd be all right after all.

But the problem now was that we had details. Bob now had a real name, an age. Parents, a brother. An ex-girlfriend. He was a human being.

"I think I might know him." Imogen was pointing her crisp packet at the screen.

I felt something die inside me. I caught Xanthe's eye. She made a play of looking out of the window before asking, "How?"

Imogen was frowning. "Don't know. He just looks a bit familiar. I feel like I know him from somewhere. I wonder if Rick's watching this. He might know who he is."

Eyes flicked round the room. We were all thinking the same thing – hoping to God Rick had found something better to do that evening than sit around watching *Crimewatch*. The last thing we needed was a lawyer poking his nose in, especially one whose father was a High Court judge and who'd made it pretty clear he didn't like us and would prefer to have us out of the house altogether.

My stomach squeezed so hard I thought I might be sick. How long would it take her to recall the party and the man who'd been looking for Fitz? As wrapped up in each other as Rick and Imogen had been, there was every chance he'd come up to them and asked them the same question.

"Does he look familiar to you?" she asked, looking round.

We all shrugged.

"He looks like lots of people," said Zak after a while.

"Hmm." She was still staring at the screen, running through the different ways she might have come across him. "I wonder if he went to my university."

We tried to deflect her by talking about all the people we barely knew at university. It had surprised me on the day of our graduation photograph to see a number of students I hadn't known existed who must have been holed up in their rooms for the three years.

"I never spoke to the chap who lived next door to me," said Stuart. "I only knew he was there because he'd play that dreadful Jennifer Rush song over and over again. I'd thump on the wall and he'd turn it down but twenty minutes later he'd start again."

"There's something about that guy though," Imogen said, tossing the crisp packet into the bin.

"She knows," said Xanthe after Imogen had gone.

I wasn't so sure. "If she does why doesn't she come out and say so?"

"She's testing us, waiting for us to say something."

"Unless," said Zak, "she's the one with something to hide and she's testing to see what we know. Perhaps the reason she and Rick are so keen for us to take over the house is that they want the chance to get away without having to put the house up for sale. What if one of them killed Bob?"

I laughed. Zak didn't.

"What, you're serious?"

"Think about it. Imogen wasn't there when we found the body but that doesn't mean she didn't do it. She's like Macavity the cat, isn't she? Never at the scene of the crime."

"Look, I know you don't like Imogen but…"

"I'm not that petty, it's more than that – there's something about her. She's so cold, it's unnatural. I still think she's capable of something very bad. I can't stand living here with her, and if Rick's going to be here on a semi-permanent basis I plan to spend as little time here as I can."

It sank in that of course he'd be able to move in with Chiara. His living costs would be halved, and he'd be away from this mess. But where did that leave the rest of us?

"It's all right for you," I couldn't help saying. "Some of us don't have a choice. I can hardly afford the mortgage for my share, let alone the rent on somewhere else."

He looked apologetic. "Something will turn up."

But that was just it – I wasn't sure that it would. I began to think about swallowing my pride and going back home to Scotland and camping out in my old bedroom again until this nightmare was over. My parents would be appalled at the mess I'd made of my life, but I didn't think they'd turn me away. There had to be an end to this, had to be some way to feel safe again.

March

In March we went to a fair on the Downs. It was the best evening I'd had in ages. We walked up there after work as it was starting to get dark. The barrel organ music, the bright, gilded paintwork and the smell of hot dogs and candyfloss filled me with nostalgic excitement. We'd proved ourselves rotten shots with a rifle, laughed ourselves silly in the ghost train and had a go on several rides. But seeing the sign in front of the gravity ride, I hesitated.

Zak turned back to me with an incredulous smile. "What's up? Are you chicken?"

"No, I'm…"

"What?"

He looked so lovely I almost didn't want to say because I knew it would bring everything crashing down for him. But in the end, he guessed anyway.

"Oh shit." He brought his hand up to his face.

The music, the colours, the laughter, everything seemed

to freeze.

"And I'm afraid it's..."

He was nodding. "Yes, I got that." He was quiet for a really long time. Then he just said, "Wow."

At least he didn't say the usual insulting things men are supposed to say on these occasions like "Are you sure?" or worse "Are you sure it's mine?" He just said, "Chiara's going to kill me" which was probably close to the truth although under the circumstances not a good choice of words.

"Sorry."

Xanthe called to us from the queue but he waved at the others to go on ahead.

"No, don't be daft – it's as much my fault as yours. But shit."

"To be fair, it happened before you met Chiara."

He leant back against a tree. "No, I know – it's just, she's bloody intuitive and well she's quite insecure."

"Is she? She doesn't seem it." I couldn't imagine her having anything to feel insecure about.

"About you."

"Me?"

"Well, us – sharing the house. She thinks we spend too much time with each other as it is."

I smiled at the irony and he shook his head and said, "Yeh, I know."

After a while he said "Wow" again and then regaining control he said, "How long have you known about this?"

"I wasn't sure for a while. I've never been very regular, and I had my mind on other things. Then I thought it might just be stress that was sending things haywire. But I know now. I've taken a test."

He frowned. "A home test? They're not that accurate though, are they?"

I couldn't blame him for clutching at straws but I had to break it to him that the latest ones were highly accurate. Besides there was the sickness and the hardness I felt at the pit of my stomach that for a while I'd told myself was nerves. There was no doubt.

"It doesn't show."

I hadn't been eating much and the weight gain had been easy to conceal under a loose cardigan. But with the weather getting warmer it would soon become more obvious.

He was obviously working up to ask something but didn't know how. At last he came out with,

"And what do you want to do about it?"

I watched a family with two small children fighting over a shared candyfloss and it all seemed so surreal. "I don't know."

"Only the thing is I think you're going to need to make up your mind pretty quickly, aren't you? It's been a few weeks now and, I mean, if you decided to have an abortion I think there are different types and an earlier one is a bit less traumatic."

I closed my eyes. "I suppose so. I know people have them every day, but I -"

I'd been reading up about it and it seemed there were two types of termination, one that could be performed in the first few months and a surgical option done later. The thought of either filled me with revulsion and guilt.

He put his arm round my shoulders and I wished he wouldn't because at that moment the warmth and familiarity were unbearable. It wasn't the answer he'd been hoping for. I could hear his heart thumping against me.

But he lifted my face up gently. "Look, if you don't want to do it, don't. Whatever you want to do, you get my support, okay? You don't have to do this on your own."

"No, it's fine. You don't have to be involved either way. I just thought you had a right to know."

He frowned. "I am involved though, aren't I? Either way."

He managed a brave smile, but I could tell he was terrified. A baby certainly wouldn't fit with his free-spirit lifestyle. Perhaps he felt a little bit proud too that he'd proved he'd be capable of making it happen when the right time came along but he was wise enough not to say that. I felt tears pricking the back of my eyes and blinked them away.

He rubbed his free hand over his face and I knew he was thinking about Chiara, how he'd have to tell her and how she'd react to knowing he'd fathered my baby. He'd tell her of course it was a moment of madness, a drunken grope that went too far after one of our silly evenings and that it hadn't meant a thing. After all he could hardly explain the real circumstances – but even so it hurt.

Not that it was any of Chiara's business – it had happened well before she was on the scene. But it would make things awkward in the house with her questioning if there really had been more to it and whether any of that feeling still lingered, especially now Zak and I had a shared interest.

She'd be even more suspicious of him sharing the house with me and he wouldn't be able to set her mind at rest by telling her the truth – that I was safely out of temptation's way since I was as much a reminder of death as a horned owl.

But I didn't think she'd take kindly to him giving me emotional support when I needed it or to an ongoing involvement in our baby's life.

Our baby. It sounded so strange. Me and Zak who barely even spoke to each other these days except to discuss forensics. What sort of life could we offer a child? The likelihood was we'd both end up Inside, I'd be giving birth in chains and the child seized before I'd even had a chance to hold him or her and put into care – and from Xanthe's stories we all knew what that meant: rejections from a string of would-be foster parents, violence, abuse…

How could it be right to give anyone that start in life? And would the child ever want to find me when they were older if they knew what I'd been in prison for? I'd explain that it was a miscarriage of justice but surely most criminals say that?

It was a stark choice. Everything in my religious

140

upbringing screamed at me an abortion was wrong. And I balked at the idea of getting rid of a healthy baby, of doing something so violent to something so innocent and dependent, especially after the circumstances of the conception.

That I was even considering it made me think seriously about whether I was developing a callous attitude to life – becoming more and more like the person who'd killed Bob. Or Oskar as we now had to think of him.

And yet what chance would I have to move on from this ghastly mess if I had the baby? I hadn't been at the company long enough to be entitled to maternity leave and I couldn't pay the mortgage if I didn't have a job, which could mean we'd all lose the house.

And then there were other, bigger questions. Was I mature enough to bring up a child? My track record with keeping plants alive was woeful. And neither of us had any money and I knew Stuart would go ballistic to find there was yet another complication in the way of meeting the mortgage payments.

I knew I wouldn't be able to expect much involvement from Zak. He was sincere in what he said, and I could see him being a doting dad for a few weeks or even months but what if things got serious with Chiara? She wasn't going to want him fussing over a child he'd fathered with someone else.

And yet at the same time I couldn't help a little fantasy of me and a tiny person united against the world. About all of us housemates sharing the childcare so that people on the outside didn't even know whose child it was. And I couldn't stop thinking that it would be the one good thing that had come out of that whole awful experience – that in some way, however hard it was, it would be a way of atoning for what we'd done.

I began to think about names like Hope or Phoenix. But then I had a horrible vision of Zak picking up the baby's lifeless body and sticking it out on the street just like he'd done with Rufus and it all felt horribly wrong and irresponsible.

I brushed a hand across my face and he pulled me towards him. He was kissing my hair and it felt nice, but I had to remind myself that this had nothing to do with love or even desire and we were never going to get back to where we once were.

He was very considerate in the next few days, stopping by my desk to check how I was and jumping up to take a chair from me when he saw me carrying it across the office. He refused a drink when I did and ate a brie sandwich Xanthe had made me. But I knew it was going through his head all the time to ask if I'd made a decision.

I felt Chiara looking at me suspiciously as we played Scruples that evening and wondered if he'd told her. Better to wait because he might never have to, but I knew Zak. He found it hard to keep secrets. Which was a concern in other ways.

But in the next few days whether by accident or design he kept Chiara away from the house, going over to hers or meeting her at the pub. They went to see *Scandal* at the local cinema and the rest of us saw The Waterboys at the Colston Hall. Zak seemed a bit shy of mentioning her name in front of me as I guessed he probably was of saying mine to her.

Before the sickness started it was relatively easy to keep it under wraps but there's a limit to how many trips to the bathroom you can laugh off as the result of a dodgy curry.

"You're like a cat on a hot tin roof this morning," said Imogen. "Where did you go in the middle of shorthand?"

"I had to go to the bathroom." It was lunch time and we were wandering around the maze of stalls at St Nick's Market, with their hand-made jewellery, quirky clothes and street food that would normally have tempted me, but that day was making me nauseous. I must have complained about the food smells once too often because Imogen swung round, her hand flying to her mouth. "Oh God, you're not."

"That's right, tell the whole world."

I hadn't planned on telling anyone else until I'd decided

what to do about it, but her suspicions were clear, and I felt guilty enough lying to her about the Bob thing without concealing this too.

"Not Zak?" She winced when I said it was.

"At least I think so. It might have been that man from the Brussels press trip, but I don't think it will be because he used a condom."

Her eyes stretched even wider. "And Zak didn't? Didn't you ask?"

I threw my hands out. "It wasn't a planned thing."

"Surely you had some idea when you got into bed together?" Put like that it did sound stupid, but I could hardly tell her the circumstances. We went down the steps and along the cobbled quay back towards the office.

"One night?" she kept saying. "What are the chances? Are you sure you only slept with him that one time?"

I bit back my annoyance. "I'm pretty sure I'd have remembered."

"But how could you be so unlucky?"

"It happens."

She had to concede that. "Does he know?"

"Yes – he says he'll support me either way."

The quay was busy with office workers out for some lunch and sea gulls hoping to get some scraps. The air was thick with the smell of hops from the brewery across the river. Sun spiked our eyes and flashed off the boats.

She laughed. "Support? What does that mean exactly? He doesn't have a bean and he's not even slightly reliable. You'll wake up one day and he'll have disappeared on that stupid little bike to God-knows-where. And what about Chiara?"

"What *about* Chiara? It's got nothing to do with her."

"Hmm, not sure she'll see it like that. She isn't going to be over the moon about Zak and you having a child together."

"I know that but I'm not going to do something just because it's convenient for them." We sat down on a bench. Imogen started eating the sandwich she'd just bought. I

143

dropped my face into my hands. "I know, I know, you're right. It's a mess."

She put a hand on my arm, then drew me into a hug. "It'll be all right," she said in a softer tone. "We'll sort this out."

Her voice changed again as she said, "You're not thinking of keeping it?"

"I haven't decided."

She drew back. "What? You must be out of your *mind*."

"I said I haven't decided."

Between bites she said, "God, Emily, it would be career suicide. What's Donald going to say? How are you going to afford childcare when you can barely pay the mortgage? You realise you won't get maternity leave? You've only been in the company five minutes."

"Yes, I know. But I was thinking possibly we could sort something out between us…"

Her voice rose. "Us? Oh, wait a minute, you mean like we did with the dog? Because that worked a treat didn't it?"

"Zak's not allergic to children," I pointed out.

The trouble was, I'd already started imagining what the child would look like when she was five or six. I tried not to, but I couldn't help it. I knew that if I ended the pregnancy I'd always be thinking "this would be her birthday, this would have been her first day at school, this would have been the day she got her exam results, got married…

Imogen balled the empty sandwich bag and offered me half a Twix, but I didn't feel like eating. Brandishing a stick of the chocolate at me she said, "You'd better be sure it's Zak's baby. If he and Chiara split up over this and then it's born and it's obvious from the colouring it was the Belgian…"

She stopped. "Oh God, Em, no don't cry. Look. It's bad but it's not the end of the world. Well, not quite anyway."

She promised at any rate not to tell Stuart because it would send him into a panic which, if I decided not to keep the baby, would be needless. He was so worked-up these

144

days you never knew if something like this might just tip him over the edge.

***

The identification of Bob as Oskar would have received a lot more attention if an awful thing hadn't happened in April. The front pages of all the papers were full of pictures of football fans crushed against the fence at a football match in Hillsborough. It was unimaginably awful – a family day out which had ended in tragedy.

But seeing a father talk about his son dying in such a pointless way brought back the shame and guilt about what we'd done.

Whoever he was and whatever his reason for being there, Oskar had deserved a better end and so had his family. For weeks they must have been in agony clinging onto the hope, however small, that he would one day be found alive. In that situation people always seemed to say the hardest thing is the not-knowing. But when they did know surely, they must wish they could unknow it again?

And Oskar's family still had no idea how he'd died. The most likely reason would be suicide and that must cause them pain because it was a type of rejection. They must carry a sense of guilt and shame because they hadn't spotted the signs and they hadn't been able to stop him. They hadn't understood him well enough to help him. These things played on my mind the whole time like background noise.

The postcard was waiting for us on the mat one evening when we got in from work. Xanthe picked it up, questioning why someone would bother to send a card when they hadn't even written on it. My stomach squeezed as I glimpsed the seaside photo on the front. The words said *Cornish Greetings*.

Xanthe dropped the card in horror. "That's too much of a coincidence, isn't it?"

Zak took it from her. "No stamp."

A few days later Imogen walked into the living room

holding a postcard of Leeds. "Who sent this?"

We managed blank faces but after she'd gone Xanthe asked, "Do you think she's doing this? To make us come out and say it?"

I couldn't believe Imogen would do that, but it was hard to think straight.

"Whoever it is wants to scare us," said Zak.

"But what if it's more than that?" I said. "What if they're doing this as a warning? To make it look as though we're the ones who killed Bob?"

Someone was playing with us, biding their time.

***

Zak tapped on my door later that evening and brought me in a coffee. The smell of it made me nauseous but I didn't want to seem ungrateful. For several minutes he attempted to make conversation about other things but eventually came out with, "So, have you thought any more about…you know?"

I blew out my cheeks. "I've thought of nothing else."

"And have you made a decision?"

"I've made an appointment. Friday afternoon. I'll have to take a sickie."

I could tell he was relieved although he did his best to keep his features neutral. "I'll take one too. I'll go with you."

"No, you don't have to do that."

"I want to."

I probably should have said no. Imogen had already said she'd come with me but, petty as it might sound, I felt Zak ought to share in some of what I was going through.

***

He borrowed Xanthe's car to take me to the clinic. There was nowhere to park, but he stopped by the entrance to let me out.

"Wait while I find a space, then I'll come in with you."

"No," I said. "Thanks, but honestly I need to do this myself."

We sat for a few moments without speaking. He looked at his watch and cleared his throat but just stopped himself from asking if I was intending to get out. I reached for the door, but it swept in, the enormity of what I was doing. I couldn't make myself move.

"I'm sorry, I don't think I can do this."

I expected him to look angry or frightened but all I saw was relief and at the same time he was saying, "Is this really what you want?" And then "Good. It's a good decision."

He pressed a tear away with his thumb, drew me towards him and somehow we ended up kissing – not like the last time when he was just kissing my hair. I wanted it to go on although I knew it wasn't real. We were both emotional – and look where that had got us last time.

"Are you sure this is a good idea?" I asked him. As soon as I said it I wished I hadn't.

He pulled back, leant over the wheel and mumbled, "You're right. No, I shouldn't have done that. Sorry."

Neither of us spoke on the way back. I suppose he felt guilty and we were both overwhelmed by the decision we'd made.

When we got back to the house Chiara was waiting for Zak. She threw her arms around him and gave me an odd look over his shoulder. I couldn't tell if she knew about the pregnancy or if she somehow suspected about the kiss. I felt a bit sorry for her – she was going to feel a lot worse when she found out I was keeping the baby. And I felt frightened for the future because it was impossible to imagine, and I'd just made it even more complicated. But mostly I felt relieved.

Chapter Thirteen

May

"They've found my car."

Stuart was standing in the hallway, still holding the telephone receiver although the dull tone told us the call had already ended some moments before. We'd not long got in from work.

Zak popped his head out of the kitchen with a half-eaten sandwich in his hand. "Found it? Where?"

Stuart managed to keep his voice level as he said, "A place called Sandy. It's in Bedfordshire. They want me to come and identify some stuff that was in it."

But despite the casual tone, his eyes flickered with fear. I thought we'd checked to see nothing was left in the car. My insides turned to liquid. What had we missed? Zak was nodding but didn't seem to be able to trust himself to speak.

"They've found it after all this time?" said Imogen throwing her bag down by the door and shuffling through some post. "Better not get your hopes up though. It'll be a wreck by now, won't it?"

"Yes, probably."

"Sandy? That's miles away, isn't it?"

"Yes, it is. Well…I'd better go."

And it was obvious that he didn't expect to see us again or at least not this side of a prison gate. I tried to make my 'Bye' sound as casual as it should be, but he caught my eye as I said it and managed a small smile. Xanthe jumped up from the sofa where she'd probably spent the day and threw her arms around him. She clung to his neck until he cleared his throat and disentangled himself.

"Aw," said Chiara wonderingly at what she evidently saw as a touching farewell. She crept up behind Zak and helped herself to a bite of his sandwich which he surrendered to her with a forced smile, but I doubt he had any appetite now anyway.

"Catch you later," he murmured to Stuart, but he looked away.

For the next few hours the four of us sat waiting for the phone to ring or Stuart's name to pop up on the TV news. A game of Scruples helped take our minds off it a little bit but it was hard to get worked up about whether you'd go back and pay for a meal you'd forgotten to get the bill for or tell your friend you didn't like their outfit when your real friend was being interrogated down at the police station.

When Stuart came back several hours later he looked done-in. "They let you go, then," said Zak in a low voice, nodding his head towards the kitchen to signal that Imogen was in there.

"For now." Stuart slumped into a chair. "Christ, I never want to go through that again. I very much doubt this is the end. They'll want to talk to all of you – I think we need to warn Imogen."

Zak frowned. "On the other hand, she'll be more convincing if she doesn't know anything."

"But what if she drops us in it without meaning to?" I asked.

"How can she? She doesn't know enough. Even if she remembers Oskar Bramley being at the party she doesn't know he died here or anything about us moving the body."

After some discussion we agreed that she shouldn't be told unless the situation changed – which happened sooner than we imagined.

The following day Xanthe phoned me at work.

"They're in the house," she whispered barely loud enough for me to hear.

"Who are?"

But I already knew. "The police. They said they wanted a

149

look round. I had to let them in. I should have insisted on them getting a warrant but he said it wouldn't make any difference, it would just take a bit longer. And I didn't want them to think we had something to hide."

Stuart saw my expression and was by my side in an instant. I could tell he was itching to take the phone off me.

"Are you okay? Do you want me to come back?" I asked Xanthe. "I think I might be going down with something – something I ate."

Stuart frowned and shook his head. He was mouthing something. I made out the word "suspicious".

"Better not," whispered Xanthe. "I'll be all right." She took a shaky breath. "They're in the kitchen at the moment."

Stuart was making cutting motions through the air. He wrote STOP on a piece of paper and held it under my nose. I waved it away.

"Probably better not give me a running commentary," I said.

"How many of them are there? Do they have dogs with them?" So many more questions crowded my brain but Stuart leaned over and pressed down the little button on the phone cutting the line.

He insisted we carry on as normal but it was agony trying to carry out our work knowing they were going through our things. Daft things go through your mind, like how you wish you hadn't left that heap of laundry on your bedroom floor but nothing compared to them lifting away the boxes and bikes in the cellar and examining the new floor, perhaps finding Oskar Bramley's finger prints or a stain we hadn't noticed. The day passed in a blur.

When we got back to the house after work Xanthe said they hadn't taken long and were polite enough but they gave no indication of what they were looking for or if they had found anything. They had ways of detecting blood spots you couldn't see with the naked eye, didn't they? I kept thinking back to that time Rick had noticed the redecoration in the basement and wondering what Xanthe would say if they asked about it and how convincing she'd be.

The first thing Zak did when we got in was take apart the telephone handset.

"Maybe they weren't looking for something so much as bugging the place," he said.

"Are you sure?" It all sounded a bit paranoid, but I had to agree it was possible.

We all knew how easy it was to bug a phone – we'd installed little microphones inside our handsets at work, so we could prove we'd quoted someone accurately if, as quite often happened, they denied it afterwards when confronted by their words in print and threatened us with court action. It was officially banned by the company, but they turned a blind eye to it for their own sake. Whether it would have been admissible in court is another matter, but it seemed to do the trick.

There was nothing inside the phone. We went a little crazy checking all the light fittings, crawling under furniture, lifting rugs, turning the house upside down but didn't find anything.

"But we'd better be on the safe side – if you want to talk about Bob save it for when we're out of the house," Stuart said.

***

Even after Oskar Bramley had been identified it sometimes still felt like we were normal housemates, going to work, sharing the chores, splitting the bills. Money worries generally took priority because they were more immediate and in an odd way they were a welcome distraction.

It was Imogen who noticed Xanthe's new shoes. "She says her sister gave her the money to buy them. If her sister really wants to help why doesn't she let Xanthe stay with her? Then we could rent out her room to help with our repayments."

I shrugged. "She prefers it here. Anyway, apparently her sister's joining a convent. Perhaps she's giving Xanthe her worldly wealth, so she doesn't give in to temptation although I don't suppose she can have much. She's only been working a couple of years, hasn't she?"

"So where else is Xanthe getting the money from?" Imogen asked.

We speculated, naturally. I thought the most likely explanation was that she'd become an escort, something she'd cheerfully admitted she'd do during one of our evenings playing The Truth Game; or failing that a drugs mule, whereas Imogen was convinced Xanthe was running a sex chat line from the house while we were at work. Determined to find the answer she went searching for evidence.

"Look what I found."

I was coming up the stairs to the shower when I saw her holding something that made my blood freeze.

She was standing in the doorway of Xanthe's room. The backpack in her arms was horribly familiar. The ink stain and the smily face logo jumped out at me. I saw Xanthe at the party jerking her head back to avoid being hit in the face by the same backpack as the man we came to think of as Bob swung round. I heard him ask where Fitz was.

I could only watch as Imogen opened the bag. I couldn't say anything. I just kept thinking about her fingerprints that were getting all over it. We drew in a collective breath as we glimpsed the contents. It was an obscene amount of money. I watched in horrified silence as Imogen took out handfuls of notes and laid them out very slowly in piles around the room. This couldn't be happening.

"There must be thousands of pounds here," she murmured.

The stairs shook as someone bounded up them. Imogen tried to stuff the money back into the bag and slide the backpack under the bed, but she was too late. The next thing, Xanthe was in the doorway.

Her eyes looked all green and glittery. They darted from the money to Imogen and then to me.

Imogen held up a stack of notes in each hand. "Where the

hell did you get this?"

I could see the panic in Xanthe's face, but I was still trying to work out how she could have the backpack and not have mentioned it to us in all this time. "Please," she said, "please don't tell anyone. Put it back. Don't touch it."

Imogen ignored her. "Did you steal it?"

Xanthe seemed to have lost the power of speech.

"Did someone give it to you? Did you earn it? And if so, *how?*" Xanthe made a couple of attempts to say something and failed. At last, seeing she wasn't going to get an answer, Imogen said, "Fine, I'm taking it to the police."

She started stuffing the notes back into the bag. Xanthe's eyes were twice their usual size.

"No," I said. "You can't do that. Put it down."

"No?" Imogen looked from one to the other of us. Her expression changed to one of incredulity. "Emily, do you know something about this?"

I found myself as lost for words as Xanthe. So many questions crowded my head, but I couldn't ask them in front of Imogen.

"Why are you defending her? She's going to get us all into trouble."

"Not nearly as much as you'll get us into if you do this," I said. "Much, much worse than you can ever imagine." My voice was wavering. I felt like someone was stamping on my chest.

Imogen looked disgusted. "Did you have something to do with this?" She looked from me to Xanthe and back again and whispered, "What have you done?"

She was on the verge of exploding. "For God's sake you two, just tell me."

We couldn't look at each other. In the end Xanthe mumbled, "It's not ours."

Imogen threw her hands up. "I know it's not bloody yours. You're always whinging that you don't have enough money to pay the bills and suddenly it looks as if you've won the pools. So, what is it – a present? A legacy from some long lost relative? A sugar daddy?"

Xanthe looked at the floor and mumbled, "I found it."

Imogen looked so disgusted she didn't even answer, just waited for a more plausible explanation. A look of recognition crossed her face and she started nodding. "Of course. I get it. It's his, isn't it?"

Xanthe looked at me and said, "Whose?"

My heart was jabbering. How could Imogen know about Bob? How on earth could she have worked it out? And if she had who else might have?

She rolled her eyes. "Zak's. You're covering for him. He's been dealing, hasn't he? I always suspected. Those disappearances, the late-night flits, the weird friends. So, did you just find it, or did you know it was here?"

I caught Xanthe's eye. There was a chance we could get away with this. We could leave her thinking Zak was running a drugs business and tell her we'd persuade him to stop if she just backed off. At least it would buy us some time.

"Stuart's going to kill Zak for this, you know that?" she said.

"Why's that?" Zak's quiet voice made us all jump. He was standing there in the room behind us. His eyebrows shot up when he saw the money. His expression froze as he recognised the backpack. "Where did you find that?"

Xanthe was shaking her head, trying to communicate by telepathy that Imogen wasn't aware of the connection, but he swung back to me. "How the fuck did you get hold of it? And since when has *she* known?" He nodded his head at Imogen. "I thought we had an agreement not to tell anyone unless we all approved it. We agreed it was too much of a risk."

"She doesn't know," said Xanthe waving her arms but he wasn't listening.

"I'm not doing this. I'm not taking the rap for everyone. I said that at the start."

Imogen's eyes narrowed. "How I know doesn't really matter does it? It's what you've done that's important. I can just about believe you'd be stupid enough to do it – but involve the rest of us? Expect us all to keep quiet about it? Put us all at risk? That's something else."

I was trying to signal to Zak to leave it. "I'll explain later," I mouthed but I could tell he was furious and frightened. His nostrils were flaring, and his eyes were filled with a strange energy.

"You think I did it on my own? Then you're thicker than I thought. How do you think I carried him to the car by myself? And who do you think cleared up the mess?"

"Eh?"

I thought I was having a heart attack.

"Shut up!" screamed Xanthe.

I saw it pass over his face, the look of confusion and then the horrible realisation that Imogen hadn't known after all. But she would now.

"What are you talking about?" Imogen asked slowly.

"The dog," I said. "He's talking about Xanthe's dog."

She looked incredulous. "What's the dog got to do with this money?"

Xanthe started crying. I wasn't sure if she was doing it on purpose or whether the mention of poor Rufus had upset her.

"You're not making any sense."

Imogen made towards the door. Zak jumped in front of her, and barred her way, gripping her by the elbows.

"You can't go to the police. You can't tell anybody."

"Don't talk to me like that. Get off me."

She kneed him in the groin and wriggled free leaving him slouched in the corner. For the first time I saw fear cross her face.

"What's this all about?"

"Please just trust us," I begged. "If you go to the police you'll ruin all our lives."

"Does Stuart know about it?"

We nodded. A look of hurt and anger overtook her.

"I see. So, it's just me who's been kept in the dark then. I'll ask him. I should have known I wouldn't get any sense out of you lot."

She was gone before we could stop her, leaving a silent scream in her wake. Zak sank onto his knees cradling his head. "I thought she knew," he kept saying. "God, I thought she knew. I'm so sorry."

There was no point shouting at him now. The damage was done.

"What's the backpack doing here?" I asked Xanthe.

But before she could answer Stuart's voice penetrated the air. "House meeting. Now."

It was the sort of command that usually resulted in a rude response from Zak but on this occasion, he cleared his throat and said, "Coming."

***

Down in the kitchen Stuart was standing at the sink looking out of the window, his hands clasped behind his back. I expected him to be in one of his rages where only a tranquiliser dart would have stopped him, but he was frighteningly calm. Turning, he demanded to know how the backpack came into Xanthe's possession.

Xanthe slumped into a chair and drew her knees up, pulling her skirt over them like a small child. We all sat around the table, Imogen's ice blue eyes were filled with confusion and shock.

"I found it in my room under the bed. I've no idea how it got there."

"When was this?"

She shrugged. "A couple of weeks ago."

"But we looked," said Stuart. "We looked everywhere that night. Don't you see? If someone put it there they did it as a trap."

I looked hopefully at Imogen, but she said, "I still don't know what the hell you're talking about."

"Why didn't you tell us?" I asked Xanthe.

She looked desperate. "I didn't know what to do. I was going to burn it. But then I was fired, and I needed the money."

"Have you been spending it?" Stuart asked. "How much have you used?"

She looked up at the ceiling and then down at her knees. She started picking at a loose thread. "Only small amounts. Nothing that would draw attention. I used some to buy a train ticket to Brighton and some that night we went to the fair on the Downs. I bought some clothes to wear to the trade show in Milan. And I put some in my bank account to pay the mortgage until my money from the DHSS comes in."

Zak was staring at her, his face frozen in shock. "You *stupid...*"

"I want a list," said Stuart. "Everything you've used it for. The police might be able to trace the notes."

"How could they trace them back to Xanthe now she's already spent them?" I started to ask but he cut across me.

"We need to think. We need to come up with an explanation as to how that money came into our hands. And to answer your question Emily it depends where she spent the money and how many times she visited the same place."

"Can't we just say we found it after the party?" Xanthe said miserably.

He laughed. "And kept it? That's a crime in itself. But do you think the police will accept that and move on? It will lead them straight to the body. It's one thing to move a body, quite another to move a body and be found in possession of thousands of pounds that belonged to the victim. Because that suggests a motive for murder."

Imogen who'd been listening white-faced clasped her hands over her cropped hair. "Can someone please tell me what's going on?" She looked terrified. "You *killed* someone?"

"No, not that," I said. After a pause I added, "We didn't kill him. We only moved him."

Her face was screwed up in confusion.

"Who?"

Stuart recounted the evening we'd found Bob. Imogen stared around us white-faced and wild-eyed. "This is a wind-up isn't it?" When she saw that it wasn't her features screwed up in revulsion and horror. "You treated him with less respect than you'd give a dead animal. *Like a piece of rubbish.*"

"Calm down, please, for God's sake," said Stuart. "We didn't want to do it, but we couldn't risk the police thinking we'd killed him."

"But don't you see?" Her eyes flickered with tension. "What you did made things so much worse."

"Not helping," murmured Zak.

"And you didn't tell me? All this time you've been keeping it from me. Why the *fuck...?*"

"You weren't here," I said. "And after, well, we thought it was better for you, not knowing. We wanted to protect you."

She was looking at me as if she no longer knew who I was. It had sounded better in my head.

"Don't. Don't ever say that again. You did it to save your own skins. Because you didn't trust me. I liked you, Emily. I actually thought you were okay but..."

"The fact is, whether it was the right or wrong decision, it's the one we made," said Stuart. "It's where we are now. And now you know, I'm afraid you're part of it. For all we know you did it – or Rick did."

Imogen was still shaking her head. "No. Not me. I am nothing to do with this. Don't involve me. I wasn't even there."

But you could see it sinking in. She was involved now whether she wanted to be or not. She'd have a hard job convincing the police we'd acted without her or at least without her knowledge, that she'd lived with us all this time and known nothing about it. And her alibi for the weekend wasn't much stronger than Zak's and mine.

You could see it catching up with her – all the thoughts that had gone through our heads, how even if she wasn't sent down her job would be on the line and her chance of a perfect family home would be further away than ever.

She swore she wouldn't tell anyone, not even Rick or her

father. Perhaps I was naïve, but I believed her. In a way it was a relief now that she'd found out. She was a strategist and she was normal, and she was convincing. I began to hope she might have a brilliant idea that could see us through this nightmare.

But she clearly wasn't in the mood to talk about strategies just yet.

"When I first met you in the training room," she said, "I thought you were all a bit odd. I sat there asking myself if I was ever likely to be friends with you. But I never, not for a moment, thought you'd do something as fucked-up as this."

She made a sudden decision, sprang out of her chair and raced for the door. A bolt of fear shot through me. I jumped up too, but Stuart pushed past and threw himself against the door.

"Get back."

Something gleamed in his hand. He'd grabbed the kitchen knife off the worktop.

"You're not going to the police, Imogen. We're not going to let you."

She looked round at us, disbelieving. We stared back. We had to make her understand.

"You're not going to stop him, are you?" she said weakly.

As though we'd rehearsed it we shook our heads, never taking our eyes off her face. I've often gone back over that moment in my head. I like to think I was convinced Stuart would never have pushed that knife in and that's why I didn't intervene. But I have to live with the fact that if he had we'd all share some of the blame.

Chapter Fourteen

In some ways it was easier once Imogen knew about Bob. She at least stopped accusing us of being strange and secretive all the time. To tell the truth I think she was scared of all of us. The way she'd looked at me that evening when Stuart was brandishing the knife at her played on my conscience. I replayed it in my head, tried to see it in some different light but it was hard to get away from the fact that we'd all made her feel threatened and she now obviously thought she was living with four psychos instead of four weirdoes.

Chiara had become more watchful of me too. I tried to make it clear she had no need to be but perhaps that made things worse. She was possessive of Zak, sitting up close to him and holding his hand. She also ruffled his hair quite a lot which I knew he hated, and I sometimes thought he looked a bit hunted when someone told him she was on the phone.

Once or twice when he laughed at something I said, or we exchanged a look about something I noticed Chiara's eyes resting on me, but I couldn't tell what she was thinking.

Finding the backpack with the money inside had added a new slant to the Bob story. We had no idea if the money inside the bag had been brought by Oskar to give Fitz or whether he'd received it from Fitz. We'd been thinking of Oskar as the victim but what if he'd really been the aggressor? I hoped the money was a blackmail payment or perhaps a hitman payout – in which case Oskar wasn't such an innocent victim after all. Not that it counted as justification for what we did, and it was hardly something we could use to explain our actions without getting us into a load more trouble.

***

June

By the beginning of June it was impossible to conceal the pregnancy any longer. As predicted Stuart went ballistic when I confirmed it. I think he'd had his suspicions for a while but on a lazy Sunday morning when we were all sitting around in the kitchen drinking coffee, listening to music and reading the papers I took off my jumper without thinking. I saw his eyes fix on my stomach.

"You know this affects all of us?" he said. "How are we going to manage when you stop working? You will have to stop, you realise that, don't you?"

"Only for a few weeks," I assured him. "There's a woman on *The Designer* who had a baby at Christmas and was back by the middle of January."

"Yes, but she probably has a nanny or a house-husband or helpful parents around the corner – or all those things."

I told him it was all under control. I'd be off work for such a short time it would only be like taking holiday leave. Zak said he'd take time off after me and we'd sort out childcare and split the cost.

He shook his head. "You make it sound easy. But babies cry a lot. They keep you up all night. They can't be left on their own, ever."

"We do know what babies are, thanks," said Zak but he looked a bit green.

"And what does your girlfriend think about this? You have told her, I assume?"

Zak looked a bit embarrassed. "I'm working on it."

"Well you'd better hurry up."

It turned out Stuart was right about the difficulties. When I started researching it, childcare turned out to be horribly expensive and quite hard to arrange. Nurseries had long

161

waiting lists and childminders were very picky about taking newborn babies.

Xanthe came to the rescue. "I'm great with babies," she assured us. "And it will fit with working freelance from home."

"Are you sure you know how much work it involves?" Zak asked but he got a very sour reply about her making a better job of looking after his child than he had of caring for her dog.

Stuart still wasn't happy because the situation would leave three people struggling to pay the spiralling mortgage, but we didn't have much alternative.

"I don't know," said Zak after she'd left the room. "Are you sure we can trust her?"

"She'll be fine," I said, largely to convince myself. "She's not as scatty as she seems – not when it's something important."

I caught a strange look in his eyes. I could tell he wanted to say something but couldn't decide how.

"Have you thought that Xanthe might have done it? Killed Bob, I mean."

I almost choked on my coffee. "Xanthe? Come on, she's so puny she couldn't punch a hole in a paper bag."

"Yes, but how strong do you have to be to push someone downstairs in the dark?"

I thought about it, but I just couldn't see Xanthe doing anything so violent. "Remember how upset she was when she found Bob?"

"She was traumatised, yes. But that could be because of what she'd done."

"She was screaming for help though. Why would she want to alert us all to what she'd done?"

"Because she needed help – someone stronger to move the body."

"You think she used us to do her dirty work?"

"It's possible, isn't it? She had to go to the basement when Stuart asked because it would have seemed odd if she'd refused. Perhaps it was a relief to her because she'd been waiting for one of us to find him and no one had. She then made out she'd just found the body. And I'm sure her shock was genuine – seeing him as a corpse, she was confronted with what she'd done. Maybe she'd been hoping he wasn't that badly injured and had got up and walked away."

It still sounded far-fetched "I don't know. She can't kill a mosquito."

He considered this but then said, "So, I'm not saying she did it on purpose. She might not even have realised she'd killed him. You saw how he was hitting on her and she pushed him away. Perhaps he tried again later or perhaps he was angry and wanted to take it out on her. She was trying to get away from him. Perhaps she pushed him away and he lost his footing."

"And walked back into the party as though nothing had happened?"

He shrugged. "We were all pretty out of it, would we have noticed if she was behaving a bit strangely? And then there's the money. We searched the house thoroughly that night for the backpack, didn't we? I looked under Xanthe's bed. It wasn't there then."

Something cold crept up my limbs. "Are you sure?"

"Of course, I'm sure. Think how long she managed to keep the backpack from us – she's an actress. And there's another thing – I know it's minor but that Tenerife air crash – I looked it up and neither plane was flying to the UK."

I froze, my mug of tea halfway to my mouth. I had to accept it was a bit odd. "But it might have been scheduled to stop over in England. Anyway, you can't always believe what you read in the papers – as we know all too well. Why would she make up something like that? And even if she did it's hardly on the same scale as killing someone is it?"

"No," he conceded, "but it makes me question how truthful she is."

***

The phone call came when I was at work. Sometime in the afternoon between booking a photographer for a cover shoot and checking some page proofs I picked up the receiver expecting it to be a marketing manager coming back to me with a quote I'd asked for or a PR with some figures. Instead it was the police asking me if I could come down to the station and help them with an enquiry about a stolen car belonging to one of my housemates, Stuart Mountford.

"Am I under arrest?" I asked, reeling. I was horribly aware of how sound carried in the open-plan office. Around me people were typing stories, pulling out filing drawers, conducting telephone interviews and shouting about deadlines but I felt eyes on me from all corners.

"Not at all. You're free to leave whenever you like. But we'd appreciate your cooperation. You're entitled to free and independent legal advice if you want it."

I agreed to go along straight after work and made my goodbye as cheery as I could in the hope people would believe I was just a helpful witness to something minor. There was no chance to speak to the others about it, but Zak caught my eye as he left the office during the afternoon and I guessed he was heading to the same place.

The duty solicitor who saw me before the interview looked as if she'd had a life of privilege and I couldn't imagine she'd ever been in trouble of any kind. Her golden hair was smoothed into a long, shiny pony tail and she eyed me through preppy, dark-framed glasses.

She went through the details with me. "My advice is just to answer the questions that are put to you. Don't volunteer anything. If you aren't comfortable with the questions you can always reply 'No comment.'"

"Do people really do that?" I'd thought it was something that only happened in TV series.

The room looked pretty much like the ones on TV too – I mean there wasn't much in it, just the desk, three chairs and some recording equipment. My heart thumped at the prospect of my words being committed to tape – replayed, mulled over, thrown back at me in court.

The female detective constable was joined by a sergeant who looked frighteningly like my Uncle Derek – pouchy-faced and bald except for copious ear hair and black eyebrows. He seemed to enjoy making an entrance and for a few moments we sat looking at each other.

"I must caution you that this interview is being recorded," he said and the words that followed were depressingly familiar. "You do not have to say anything, but it may harm your defence if you do not mention when questioned something you later rely on in court. Anything you do say may be given in evidence."

I felt like I'd somehow fallen into a TV crime drama and had to keep reminding myself that this was real, and I wasn't playing a part.

For the benefit of the recording he announced the date and time, introduced himself, his colleague and the lawyer, and asked me to give my name. I cleared my throat but the words still came out as barely more than a whisper.

"Can you speak up a bit?"

"Emily McKinlay."

"We're here to talk about the theft of a car on January 8th, 1989 belonging to Mr Stuart Mountford."

I waited, wondering what was coming next.

"We've found the car."

"Oh, congratulations."

As soon as the word left my mouth I realised it was the wrong thing to say. It sounded too bright, sarcastic, and from the expression on the detective's face it was a bad start to the interview. Sometimes when I'm at my most terrified a strange calm washes over me and I speak with an ease that evades me at other times. I heard Stuart hiss in my ear, *"You're sounding flippant, Emily. Stop it."*

The DS continued, "So what we need to do now is establish who took the car and for what purpose."

"Ah, I don't think I'll be able to help you with that," I began regretfully.

"Well, let's see, shall we?" said the DC.

The sergeant asked if I'd ever been to Sandy and I said I

hadn't. I wasn't sure where it was. He unfurled a map and planted his bony finger on it. "It's right here, you see, in Bedfordshire. Very close to the A1, about halfway between Milton Keynes and Cambridge. Does it ring any bells now?"

I frowned as though I didn't follow. "And that's where you found Stuart's car? But it's miles away from here."

He nodded. "A hundred and nine miles to be exact."

I was doing my best bewildered expression, mainly because I was bewildered. How had they only just found the car or only just worked out that it belonged to Stuart? And how, assuming this was what we were leading up to, had they made a connection with Oskar Bramley?

He asked if I remembered Stuart's car being stolen. I said that I did.

"And do you remember where you were that night? It's the weekend after New Year if that helps."

I told him our well-rehearsed story.

"Whose party was it?" he asked.

I ran through the details we'd been over so many times – I had the name of the party giver fixed in my mind – only the first name of course. I'd never known the second name and we hadn't kept in touch. I couldn't be sure of the street, but it was quite near the station – one of those Victorian semis in Wimbledon – or was it Wembley? I didn't know London very well. I had no idea if they were still living there.

Stuart's voice sounded in my ear. *"Careful, Emily. You're sounding glib again."* It helped that we'd practised our lines so many times in front of him. He'd anticipated most of the sarky queries and the aggression, the swings in direction and the killer question dropped in among the trivial ones. I bit my lip and did my best to look anxious to help without being over-anxious. I felt panic rise as I found myself wandering from the script and reined myself back in. I'd already broken the solicitor's rule of not volunteering anything. She looked impassive but must have been despairing.

166

"Did Mr Mountford ever lend you his car?"

I told him I'd never borrowed Stuart's car, that I'd never learned to drive because of my epilepsy. He asked when I'd last had a fit. That worried me. I didn't want him to make a connection with that night but I didn't know what Zak had told him. In the end I told him I couldn't remember.

He frowned. "The funny thing is, we have a record of a car with the same registration being stopped that night near Okehampton. Do you know where Okehampton is?"

When I shook my head he sighed and pointed it out on the map again. "I take it your degree wasn't in geography? It's right here on the edge of Dartmoor. That's the road you'd take from here down to Cornwall."

I might have imagined it but he seemed to say that last word more loudly than the rest. My mouth felt dry. I wasn't going to risk saying anything. I could only sit there like a fool and wait for what was coming.

"An officer spoke to Mr Mountford about a rear light that needed fixing. He was with a young lady apparently. Was it you?"

My lips felt dry and cracked and my tongue too big for my mouth. I held out for as long as I could but in the end I had to lick them.

He pointed to the tape. "Could you answer the question, please? Don't just shake your head."

"No, it wasn't."

That policeman who'd told Zak off about the broken light hadn't asked my name. My looks were hardly unusual, and I doubted he'd have taken a description at the time. How many young women with bobbed hennaed hair must there have been at the time? They couldn't be sure it was me.

"The officer recalls that she seemed very nervous. *Terrified* was the word he used. Why do you think that was?"

He was offering me a chance to say I'd been there, but it hadn't been my fault – that I hadn't wanted to help Stuart, but he'd made me. Tempting but I mustn't fall for it. I swallowed.

167

"I don't know. I suppose if they'd stolen the car she would be frightened to see the police."

He turned his mouth down, acknowledging the point, or letting it go for the time being. "The officer remembers that the driver spoke with an Irish accent."

My heart beat fast. "A lot of people do, I suppose."

With a patient smile he said, "Yes. But Stuart Mountford, the owner of the car doesn't, does he?"

"No. But the car was stolen."

A glint of triumph showed in his eyes. "The description the officer's given us of the driver and the details of the owner don't match. At all. Even for a dark night. They do however match your house mate Zachary Brooke. He's Irish, isn't he?"

I swallowed. "Yes."

"And you're telling us that the car was taken by people other than you and Zachary Brooke?"

The words hit me like a punch in the stomach.

"Of course I am. Why would we want to steal Stuart's car?"

"Let me ask the questions if you don't mind. So, let's talk about Zachary. Zak, is it? How well do you know him?"

I shrugged. "We share a house. We work together. We play Scruples around once a week."

"You do what?"

The female constable cleared her throat. "It's a game, sir. You take a card and answer a question – a moral dilemma."

He snorted. "I know what it is. I'm just rather surprised it counts for getting to know someone." He turned back to me. "Are you in a relationship with him?"

"No, I'm not."

He looked surprised. "But you're having his baby, aren't you?"

I felt my face flood with colour. How could he possibly know that?

"I'm having *my* baby. Look, I'm sorry, I don't know what this has…"

He sat back and folded his arms. "I'm assuming you

know who the father is."

I was tempted to shout that it was none of their business. They couldn't prove anything by it after all. But then I thought that if by some means I couldn't even fathom they knew I was lying about that they might think I was lying about other things. And remembering how Stuart had reacted to finding out Zak and I had spent the night together after our drive to the Cornish coast, I definitely didn't want them making that connection.

The solicitor put a hand on my arm. "My client's not obliged to answer that question. Unless you can explain what relevance it has to your investigation."

The DS must have decided to let the matter lie but I wondered what conclusions he was drawing. He asked a few more questions about the car. He seemed to be working on the theory that Stuart had got his friends to fake a car theft. This wasn't so bad. As long as they had no idea what it had contained. I began to think this might be quite straightforward after all.

"Do you know how much the car was worth?"

"I don't know anything about cars."

He sighed. "You don't know much about anything do you Miss McKinlay? It all seems rather convenient. Well, let me tell you that the car was worth nothing at all. Which makes an insurance scam rather improbable, doesn't it?"

Reluctantly, I agreed that it did – assuming the people involved knew anything about cars.

It was then that he produced a clear plastic bag, which he introduced for the benefit of the tape as exhibit CLJ/1. The bag contained a battered trainer.

"Have you any idea who this belonged to?"

I shook my head, but I was screaming inside. "I don't recognise it. It could be anyone's."

His expression hardened. "Oh, we know whose it was."

I didn't like the use of the word *was*.

I had to keep reminding myself about what Stuart had said about the police laying traps. *"They'll plant something and say you dropped it. Don't fall for that one. Don't admit to anything unless they have incontrovertible proof."*

"Oh, for fuck's sake, this isn't an episode of *The Bill*," Zak had said but it didn't seem funny now.

This was incontrovertible wasn't it? Unless the shoe had been planted. Perhaps it had. Surely it would have been burned to a cinder if it had been in the car?

I shrugged as if to say I'd like to be more helpful but wasn't able to. I had to keep it together now. I reminded myself *It's not over until it's over.*

But I could feel both pairs of eyes on me as he said, "It was found on a cliff in North Cornwall, close to where a body of a young man was found."

Then oh so casually he placed exhibit CLJ/2 in front of me – a photograph

"Do you recognise this man?"

And there it was. The game was up. I felt a crushing pain in my sternum as I looked at the photograph. Imaginary insects crept over my skin.

"Sorry, I don't."

"Oskar Bramley, aged twenty-four, from Leeds," said the female DC. "Does that help?"

My breathing was all over the place. I was fighting desperately to keep it under control. Images were crowding in of Zak hoisting the body out of the boot on that windy cliff, asking me to help with the legs which kept getting stuck. It was so dark and so noisy. Would I have noticed a shoe coming off?

But I still didn't see how they could have made a connection to the burnt-out car in Sandy which was so far away. It wasn't over yet. I had to keep going until the last drop of luck ran out because what else was there? I was caught on a precipice – I could hold on or let myself drop. It wasn't much of a choice.

I shook my head – although it felt more like a twitch.

"We found something inside the car too," said her colleague.

My heart stalled. But that surely couldn't be right.

"You said the car was destroyed by fire."

The sergeant frowned. "I didn't say it was destroyed, did I?"

The constable shook her head to confirm that he hadn't. Something cold crept over my scalp. I felt the roots of my hair lift. I concentrated on trying to look impassive but as I tried to speak my throat had swollen over.

"I meant because it had been set on fire, I just assumed that it was."

Every so often one of them would leave the room, hold a whispered conversation with someone outside the door, disappear for a while and then return. I couldn't help thinking about Zak sitting in a similar room. What were they telling him or implying about me? Had I ever told him about the firework incident? That would come as a surprise.

And Xanthe, wide-eyed and tripping over her words. What would they be asking her about that night and would she remember everything Stuart had told her? I could imagine her going off at a tangent giving them information they hadn't asked for. Stuart had lost his temper so many times about her inability to keep a straight face. But this was different – this was real.

"Do you know which materials are most capable of surviving fire?" the sergeant asked.

"Glass?" I ventured at last. It came out as a whisper.

"Glass can withstand high temperatures, yes. But not as high as some metals – gold for instance. Diamonds are even more resistant. So, a distinctive piece of jewellery can sometimes be identified after a fire."

A pain seared above my eyes. I pressed my fingers against my brow.

"Miss McKinlay, are you all right?"

I nodded. My head swam. My brain felt huge and heavy. I was thinking back to the party. Oskar tapping me on the shoulder and asking if I'd seen Fitz. I could still feel the imprint of his bony fingers. Had he been wearing a ring? I had no idea. Now I thought about it he might have been.

"Oskar Bramley had an ear piercing. Did you know?"

"I didn't know him," I reminded them, relieved to have at

least avoided that trap. "But I don't understand. Lots of people wear ear rings."

"They do, don't they?" he agreed. "But they don't all look like this."

He produced a third exhibit – another clear plastic bag, this time containing a tiny but very distinctive ear ring – a scorpion with a diamond at the centre. I'd never seen one like it before.

"Does this look familiar to you?"

I could honestly say that it didn't. But it had been dark at the party and Oskar had been lying on his side on the basement floor – probably the wrong side for me to spot an ear ring, and it was very small. It must have snagged as we were hoiking him out of the car. A picture crept into my mind of Zak swearing and fumbling in the boot after we'd thrown the body over. I'd asked him hadn't I what he was looking for? Had he known? My ears roared.

"I'm going to ask you again," said the DI. "Were you in Stuart Mountford's car that night?"

"No."

He watched me as he said, "Really? Zak says you were."

Indignation swept through me. I nearly fell for it. I nearly said, "He's lying."

But that was what they wanted. To drive a wedge between us. To get me to say that Zak at least had been in the car. I heard Stuart's voice in my head. "Don't believe that any of us have said something about you unless you know for sure it couldn't have come from any other source. Do not react to slurs."

The inspector sat back and crossed his arms. "Why would Zak lie about that?"

I wanted to throw up but somehow I held his gaze and said, "He wouldn't lie. He wouldn't have said that because it's not true."

The DS waited for a more satisfactory answer. When it didn't come he said, "And now you see what I'm wondering is how did this ear ring end up in Stuart Mountford's car on the same night that Oskar Bramley died?"

The solicitor reminded me I was free to reply, "No comment" but I didn't want to appear difficult and as though I had something to hide.

"I really don't know. It must have belonged to whoever took the car or someone Stuart had given a lift to - I mean, who says it was that night?"

All I could think of was that I had to get through this interview at least long enough to see Zak again, long enough to tell him that I hadn't betrayed him, however it might look if they were playing similar tricks on him.

"Oh, it could have belonged to someone else, of course," he said in a tone that was far too agreeable.

I sensed what was coming.

"Except that this piece is unique. Oskar Bramley had it made. We've had it confirmed by the jeweller. And we know he was wearing it the day before your New Year's Eve party. You do know he was at your party, don't you?"

I swallowed. "Was he? I don't remember him."

They both stared at me, watching my expression. I could only turn up my hands in a helpless gesture. "I don't know – there were so many people. Perhaps he was there, and saw the car and came back a few days later and took it."

Their faces told me they didn't believe a word of it. And then a change in direction took me by surprise.

"How long have you known Mr Mountford?"

This was easier, at least but my words weren't coming out as easily as I wanted them to. "About a year – the beginning of the training scheme. We've been sharing the house since August."

"How would you describe him as a person?"

I didn't think I'd better mention Scruples again. "Good. He's kind, honest, works hard."

I talked about Stuart's consideration for others – how he was scrupulously fair when it came to sharing the bills and other household expenses, the way he took on responsibilities like emptying the bins without making a deal out of it and the way he'd given us lifts when he'd had the car and never quibbled over petrol money.

I stopped, wishing to hell I hadn't brought up the car, but the officer motioned for me to go on.

I recalled the way Stuart cried over *Kramer versus Kramer* during one of our video nights, how he'd dived across the room to stop Xanthe being electrocuted when she tried to hook her toast out of the toaster with a knife, the way he'd begged Imogen not to lean over the balcony because he thought it was dangerous and the way he'd stayed up all night trying to catch a mouse under a mixing bowl because he refused to set traps.

Unmoved, the sergeant asked, "Would you say he was easy to live with?"

"Yes." Everything was relative, after all. "I mean he's a bit particular about some things, but we're used to him."

"Does he have a temper?"

I tried to think what Zak would have already told them. He might have mentioned the episode when Stuart broke the door and bust Zak's lip. In the end I told them Stuart had fallen out with people a couple of times that I was aware of, but they'd always made it up afterwards. "It's just that he sets high standards for himself and gets disappointed when other people fall below them."

He looked at me thoughtfully. "What do you know about his past?"

I knew what he was getting at. "Look, I know about his sister," I said. "It didn't happen the way people said. It was an accident. She was swept off the rocks."

"His sister?"

An awful feeling curled inside me as I said it. The detective tried to keep his features neutral, but it was clear I'd told him something he hadn't expected to hear.

"Are you aware he almost killed his stepfather with a cricket bat?"

I felt a cold, spreading sensation in the pit of my stomach. I shook my head.

"Gave him brain damage. Stuart got six months in a nice, comfy detention centre. His stepfather unfortunately wasn't so lucky – he'll need care for the rest of his life."

It was a shock, but I wasn't going to let them use it to trip me up. "No, I didn't know that. But I know his stepfather was a bully."

The policeman raised his eyebrow.

"I mean, of course that doesn't make it all right, I'm not saying that. But Stuart doesn't lose his temper without a lot of provocation."

The sergeant's expression took me by surprise. It looked like concern.

"I have daughters the same age as you," he said. "All I'm saying to you Emily is be careful. I wouldn't want them sharing a house with Stuart Mountford." I had no idea if he was genuinely worried or if it was a ploy but he reached inside his jacket. "I'm going to give you my card. If you have any reason to be concerned, give me a call."

Something in his tone made my hand shake as I took the card. I couldn't shift the sick feeling inside me and wondered if I could make it out of there in time to get to the bathroom.

As I got up to go he said, "Just one final thing about Stuart – you do know Mountford's not his real surname, don't you?"

I couldn't help myself. "No. What's his name then?"

"Fitzwilliam."

He must have seen it. However much I tried to control the blush creeping up my face it kept spreading. I stood there uncertainly. He looked surprised. "You're free to go. Unless there's anything else you want to tell me?"

Coming to my senses I told him there wasn't.

"Is that it?" I asked the solicitor as we walked down the stairs.

"It should be," she said. "It doesn't look as though they have enough to charge you with anything. But keep yourself available just in case they need to interview you again."

Chapter Fifteen

Back at the house recriminations flew. The air was heavy with suspicion. It had been a hot, sticky day and the French windows were open. The setting sun filtered through the curtains, casting a golden light on the upholstery – it was a perfect evening for sitting in the garden with a bottle of crisp dry white but instead we huddled on the sofas with some cans and packets of crisps we'd grabbed at the petrol station. None of us had eaten and we were all ravenous but there had been no time to buy anything to cook. Stuart insisted on a full post mortem, picking over what everyone had said.

"I can't believe you thought it was okay to tell them I was having a baby with Zak," I said to Xanthe.

She looked anguished. "I'm sorry. But you didn't have to tell them I kissed Oskar."

"That was me," said Zak. "For your benefit. To explain any trace of him on your clothes. But you didn't have to mention the dog, did you? You know it was an accident and I told you I was sorry."

"Sorry?" She looked up at the ceiling and shook her head as though it was pointless talking to him.

He turned to me. "And did you really have to tell them about the sect?"

Xanthe was crying softly, smudging her eyeliner. Imogen just sat quietly in the wing chair, looking perfectly, almost frighteningly, composed. I had no idea what she was thinking – but I knew she wouldn't take the blame for any of us, not after the way she'd been deceived.

"Playing with fireworks?" said Stuart. "That has to be one of the stupidest…"

"I wasn't playing," I said, wondering how something I'd done at school had even come up and if I had the energy to go through it all again. "That boy was always laughing at me because of my fits, asking if I was about to throw a wobbly. I'm not proud of what I did but I didn't think. I didn't see what it was."

His face twisted in incredulity. "But you don't have fits. And how could you not realise what it was?"

It was the way I'd always remembered it but hearing Stuart say those words I wondered if maybe I had known all along and just for that microsecond I'd chosen not to know. It made me question a lot of things about myself, about truths I might have created because they made a more comfortable environment.

"And you two both assured me there'd be no more surprises after the broken light," said Stuart. "You promised me you'd checked to make sure nothing had been left in the car. But then it turns out not only did you miss one glaring item but two."

I'd had enough of questions being thrown at me. "Fine, but why didn't you tell us your real name?"

The others rounded on him. "After all you said about mutual trust, and telling each other everything," said Zak. "The way you lost it when you found out about the traffic ticket – and yet all along you were lying about who you really are. So, tell us – was Oskar Bramley looking for you that night?"

Stuart gripped the sides of his head. He looked done in after all the police questioning, but I couldn't feel entirely sorry for him after the way he'd deceived us. There had to be a reason.

"No, he wasn't. And Fitzwilliam isn't my name, it's my stepdad's. I didn't mention it because I knew you'd jump to this conclusion – and it's the wrong one."

"Is it?" Xanthe said. "You've been in prison. You didn't think we had a right to know that?"

"It wasn't prison, it was a young offenders institute."

"What difference does that make?" Zak checked himself.

177

"No, all right, I mean, what difference does it make to why you lied to us?"

Stuart threw his hands up. "I didn't kill Oskar Bramley, all right? For God's sake, I didn't know him. I never set eyes on him before that night. Emily, you must remember I spent all night talking to you."

I swallowed. "Not all night. Not before midnight."

The skin round his eyes looked tauter than ever. "Come on, you can't think…"

My chest was tight and painful, but I had to hear his answer.

He slumped. He was pressing his fist against his mouth as though he was afraid he'd say something he regretted. We waited. "All right," he said at last. "I changed my name. Or rather I went back to using my own name, the one I was born with – my father's name. I refused to use my stepfather's after everything he'd done."

He started to describe his stepfather as he'd done for me that time I'd been in his room. Zak gave an impatient snort.

"You smashed his skull with a cricket bat. How many times did you have to hit him for that to happen?"

I felt Stuart's body stiffen beside me and was glad to be surrounded by other people. I shifted in my seat. He'd obviously lost it with his stepdad. I remembered the ferocity with which he'd attacked Zak just for teasing him. He must have done so again with Bob-Oskar. He could do it again at any time.

He shouted, "I've been over and over this with the police. My God, you're as bad as they are. Emily knows why I did it. She understands, don't you? Go on, tell them."

I cleared my throat. "I'm not sure I'll get the details right. It might be better if you told them yourself."

The look Stuart gave me was one of disgust. I suppose he thought his story had mattered to me so little I'd forgotten it but after all I had promised to do just that, and it was probably better than admitting I hadn't been listening.

No one interrupted him this time. He talked a bit about his school, how he'd hated it, how he'd been treated, how he blamed his stepfather for persuading his mother to send him there.

"I told my mother I wasn't happy. She didn't listen. She just said I should stick it out for a bit longer and the "teasing" would stop. At the beginning of my second year she drove me back. I was crying my eyes out, pleading with her to turn round but she was ignoring me, putting her lipstick on in the rearview mirror. She didn't seem to care that she was delivering me into their hands, she was so determined not to listen she turned the radio up."

No one knew what to say so we just let him talk.

"I thought I'm not having this. She might be happy to let him control her life but he's not going to dictate mine. So, I kissed her goodbye and went in the front door of the school - and ran out the back. I walked five miles to the station and took the next train back home. I was going to say to her, 'You can't make me stay there.'

"It took ages to get home, but I thought when I did she'd understand that I wasn't just being difficult. She'd see how determined I was.

"But as soon as I let myself in the back door I knew at once something was wrong. You could always feel it when Paul was angry. The air was heavy with danger. The downstairs rooms were empty but there was blood on the stairs. Something crashed above my head and I heard her scream."

"Your mother?"

"No, Skye. My sister."

"I crept up the stairs. She was cowering in the corner of her bedroom – pleading for her life. He was wielding his belt. I hadn't realised until then what was going on although I had seen bruises on her arms and there was an occasion when she'd said she'd walked into a door. I suppose he must have timed his attacks for when I was at school."

"What did you do?"

"I only had a split second to think. Her eyes met mine and he turned round. I still had my cricket bat in my hand. I brought it down on his head."

I felt cold all the way down to my fingers.

"Couldn't you have just shouted at him to stop?" I asked.

He looked at me disbelievingly. "Don't you think I haven't thought of that? I've replayed it so many times in my head. But if I hadn't physically stopped him he'd have done it another time and then another. And I'd have been at school, so I wouldn't have been there to do anything about it."

He crumpled "I didn't think I'd hit him that hard. But the way he looked at me as he registered what had happened - I could see he was going to get me back. He lunged at me and wrested the bat out of my hands – he did it so easily.

"He was a strong man and he was furious. He'd hit me enough times in the past. I knew I wouldn't get away with it now."

"And so you hit him again?" prompted Zak.

Stuart kneaded the skin above his eyebrow with a crooked finger. "No. Skye did to stop him throttling me. I don't know how many times. I lost count." He flinched at the memory.

He stretched his fingers out in front of him. I could imagine he was seeing them covered with blood.

"After she stopped she dropped the bat. I looked down at it and for a moment I didn't even know what it was. Skye was screaming. She was drenched in his blood."

We were all silent, picturing the scene.

"I wrapped the duvet around Skye – she was so cold. She didn't speak, she couldn't say anything at all. I said, 'It's all right now. He won't hurt either of you anymore.'"

"At least she knew she was safe," I said.

His face twisted into a smile. "But I was wrong you see."

His features twisted into an incredulous sneer, as though I hadn't been paying proper attention. I thought I might be about to be sick.

"She shrank away from me and whispered, 'I shouldn't have done that. I love him, you see. He's going to marry me.'"

My hand went to my mouth. "Oh. God."

"So of course, she wouldn't stand up for me in court. She denied he'd done anything wrong and went along with the police's theory about me freaking out because he'd tried to send me back to school."

I was still digesting this. "So, you took the blame? What about your mum? Didn't she try and stop you?"

He gave a long, shuddering sigh and made a face that was halfway between a frown and a smile. "She went with Skye's version. She just kept saying, 'Why did you have to get involved? You made it so much worse.' But the truth was, she had to make a choice between me and Skye and I can't really blame her for that. She knew she was going to lose one of us and Skye needed her more than I did. I think she'd had an idea he was interfering with Skye but hadn't faced up to it and she felt bad about that.

"The judge described me as cold and calculating." Stuart stopped talking but his features kept moving minutely as though he were going over the words in his head, trying to make sense of them.

"Is that what you think?" he asked at last. "Now you know?"

I was taken back to the conversation we'd had on the living room floor at the New Year's Eve party. He'd said those same words, believed that at last someone understood and yet all I'd been able to think about was how uncomfortable I was and how I couldn't see Zak any more.

"You're not those things," I said although I hoped he understood that wasn't the same thing as saying what he'd done was all right.

"It hurts," he whispered. "It physically hurts. It's like being torn apart."

None of us knew what to say. At last Xanthe took his hand and said, "Was it really that bad in the detention centre?"

He curled his hands into fists. "Whatever you're imagining, it was worse. Anyone who tells you these places are like holiday camps is lying. You could be beaten half to death right in front of the staff and they'd turn a blind eye.

Sometimes they even encouraged it – it was a bit of fun for them like watching a dog fight. And sometimes they were the ones beating you anyway."

"The rules changed all the time to suit them – they cancelled visits, cut short exercise time – you never knew where you were. They told you every day you were worthless, a failure, nobody cared about you. If someone tells you those things enough times you start to believe them."

"They punished you until you broke. But some of those boys were in for the most trivial stuff like receiving a stolen gift – and it didn't just break them, it killed them."

"So how can you vote for the government that brought in the Short Sharp Shock system?" asked Zak, his face screwed up in bewilderment.

But it didn't seem like the right time for a political debate. So much for the "nice, comfy detention centre" the police inspector had talked about in my interview – although perhaps in comparison to an adult prison, it was. I shuddered at the thought of a young Stuart with his angelic appearance and perfect vowels finding himself in such brutal surroundings. I could only imagine how he'd have fared among the more violent inmates, let alone predatory staff.

He didn't seem the typical ex-offender, kicking back against authority at every turn. Instead, he'd gone the other way – obsessively sticking to structure as though if he broke just one rule everything in his reconstructed life would fall apart. But thinking about it, that made a kind of sense too.

His voice dropped to barely more than a whisper as he said, "My cellmate, the only boy in there I saw as a friend, killed himself by swallowing razor blades. A prison officer told me it was my fault. That it was because he couldn't stand being banged up with me."

He turned his face away, so we couldn't see that he was fighting back tears.

Xanthe threw her arms around him. "Have you kept in touch with Skye?" she asked.

He shook his head. "She's in sheltered housing somewhere. I saw her once. We hadn't seen each other for so long it was difficult to know what to say to each other. She doesn't understand she did anything wrong. But I have to live with the fact that every time she closes her eyes at night she has to see what I see – hears the smash, feels the spatter of blood."

He got up to leave the room but as he reached the door he gripped it, turned and said,

"I'm not going back. It'll kill me. This is why we can't afford to make mistakes."

Chapter Sixteen

After a stomach-churning few days following the police interviews I began to think perhaps the solicitor had been right and despite their suspicions the police didn't have enough evidence to charge us. Our lives regained a semblance of normality although you never knew if the phone call you were about to answer would be from the police again or whether they'd turn up at the office or the house and take us all in.

Sometimes I just wanted it all to be over. I thought it would be better if we did get caught. At least it would bring things to an end instead of this unrelenting adrenalin overload. At least we'd be able to explain and there was a chance a jury might believe us.

But then I'd be reminded of the life inside me. Being pregnant made me feel fiercely protective but also vulnerable. I couldn't move fast so I had no chance of making a quick getaway, and I worried that all the stress would affect the baby.

Once we'd told Imogen about Bob, Rick started coming over more often. He'd meet her after work on Friday evening and get the first train back on Monday morning. Whether she'd asked him to I didn't know but he seemed determined not to leave her on her own with us and who could blame him?

But we'd always know when he'd been in the house. We'd find his shoes by the door or his tie draped over a chair and get that sinking feeling.

He'd take phone messages for us but couldn't resist adding his own bossy instructions: *Your mum rang for the THIRD time. Call her!!! Chiara wanted to know if you had any plans this evening. I said you didn't.*

Xanthe went mad when she found him throwing out her only pair of trainers on the grounds that "nobody could want those disgusting things."

"I swear to God I'll kill him," said Zak, shoving the tin pyramid that Rick had arranged on the counter top. "I'd rather stick needles in my eyes than have him as a house mate."

But our immediate concern was Imogen. The way she'd reacted to the news about Bob meant we didn't feel safe. We kept an eye on her all the time. When she went out one of us always asked if she wanted company. We followed her to work and back home and listened on the landing when she was on the phone down in the hall.

Once as we joined her in the office canteen she rounded on us.

"Look are you going to stop this? Because it's unbearable. No offence but we see enough of each other at home."

We had no choice but to back off although we still watched from a distance. She tried to evade us, going for lunch with her editorial team and volunteering for lots of trips. But it made you wonder, what would happen if she drank too much at one of these events and unburdened herself to someone about the people she lived with? The only hope I could cling to was that people wouldn't believe her and would dismiss it as drunken rambling.

But when she came towards you with people you didn't know you had to ask whether she was being a Judas, about to betray us to the police.

Shouts and crashes woke me late one night. I could picture the police storming the house, dragging each of us out of bed, shining a light in our faces. Then an even bigger shudder passed through me as the thought sunk in that it might not be the police. Whoever Fitz was, there was always the possibility that he or she would come to the house trying to retrace the money Bob had owed him.

But opening my door a crack, I saw Rick on the stairs.

185

He gave me a hate-filled look, ran down and slammed the front door. Imogen yelled something out of her window above and banged it shut. In the morning her face was puffy and stretched around the eyes. It wasn't something you could easily ignore.

"So, are you going to tell us what happened?" Zak asked, although he didn't sound like he cared much.

Imogen spooned yoghurt into a bowl and squeezed honey over it in a long, deliberate swirl.

"He lied to me."

"About what?"

"His past."

We exchanged looks across the table. "Surely as long as it's in the past," said Stuart. "Or are we talking about unfinished business?"

She shook her head. "No. It was when he was at school. For three whole years and he's only just thought to tell me."

"Didn't he go to a boys' school?" I asked.

Stuart cleared his throat. "It doesn't necessarily mean anything. I mean I don't think it's that uncommon."

Imogen rolled her eyes. "I realise that. He isn't gay. They used to look at magazines with pictures of women while they were doing it."

"So, what's the problem?" asked Xanthe, her features scrunched in confusion.

"The problem?" Imogen exploded. "Oh, I don't know. Just this little thing called AIDS – perhaps you've heard of it? I'm not angry because he experimented or let himself be experimented on or whatever. But I'm furious that he concealed from me that he's a glaring health risk when all the time I thought I was safe."

She flung her head into her arms and her shoulders shook and heaved. Then she ran out and slammed the door.

"That was harsh," said Xanthe.

"What's new?" said Zak.

"This isn't good," said Stuart. "We need him on our side."

We had to admit we were all relieved to see the last of

Rick. If it really was the last. But these days we couldn't afford to fall out with people. You never knew where it might lead.

Chapter Seventeen

"I'm collecting my stuff."

The change in Rick's appearance in just a few days shocked me. He was unshaven and instead of his usual sharp style he was wearing tracksuit bottoms and a rumpled t-shirt. He looked as though he hadn't slept in weeks, but he mustered his usual condescending smile.

"Right. Imogen's not –"

"I know. She said it would be fine. I won't be long."

I stood back to let him past, remembering the time he and I had been on our own in the house and he'd discovered the new-look basement. It seemed a long time ago now and I was reassured by the presence of three others in the house this time, but I still found it hard to trust him.

He put his head in at the living room and nodded at Zak and Stuart.

"Hey, how are you doing?" asked Zak, barely disguising his surprise.

"Good. Hope I'm not interrupting anything."

I stood watching him as he went up the stairs, but he turned halfway up and gave me a withering look. "I know my way, thanks."

I went back to watching a video with the others – *Midnight Express* which on reflection wasn't a good choice.

"How much stuff did he leave here?" Stuart asked after a while. "I never saw him bring much with him at weekends."

Above our heads came a series of dull thuds and the sound of furniture being trundled around. I could imagine Rick sliding open drawers and rifling through wardrobes. He was obviously looking for something.

Zak shrugged. "I don't envy him trying to find anything

in that mess."

"Do you think we should make a note of what he's taking?" Stuart asked. "Imogen won't be too pleased if she comes back and finds he's gone off with something of hers."

Eventually we heard him coming down stairs. Stuart popped out of the door. "Were you looking for something?"

We heard Rick's terse reply. "Thanks, no, it's okay."

We all came out into the hall. Rick had gone a peculiar colour. There were sweat patches under his arms. He looked from one to the other of us. He seemed agitated.

"Got everything?" asked Zak, casting an eye over the bin bag. "Can I give you a hand out to the car?"

"No, I'm fine."

Short of demanding that he turn out the bag there wasn't much we could do. Zak stood back to let him pass.

"All right, well, see you around, I guess."

"I doubt it," said Rick. He stopped halfway to the door, perhaps tried to rein himself in from saying something and then found he couldn't stop himself. "You've made sure of that haven't you? You turned Imogen against me – got me out of the house which is what you wanted, wasn't it? Well done. I hope you're happy."

"We didn't do anything," said Stuart. "Whatever it was, you did it yourself."

It seemed to be the last straw. Rick exploded. "Do you think I don't know what you lot have done?"

Silence fizzed between us.

"I've no idea what you're talking about," said Stuart.

Rick put down the bag he was carrying. "No? You realise I could go to the police? Tell them that Oskar Bramley – or Bob as you like to call him – spent his last night here and leave them to draw their own conclusions?"

I caught my breath. We did our best to look confused, but it probably wasn't convincing.

"We didn't touch Oskar Bramley," said Zak at last.

Rick gave a triumphant snort. "That's a lie isn't it? His last hours were spent in this house. He was here at your

189

party on New Year's Eve. He never left. You see, I know that you, Zak, and you, Emily, drove his body to that clifftop in Cornwall and threw it over. That doesn't sound to me like not touching him."

We exchanged looks. This was awful. We'd been expecting all this time to be found out and the moment we'd taken our eye off the ball it had happened.

"I meant we didn't touch him while he was alive."

Rick narrowed his eyes. "I'm not sure I believe you."

My stomach squeezed until I could barely breathe. This was worse than the police interview because Rick wasn't just fishing for information – he seemed to know things.

"You can think what you like," said Zak doing an impressive attempt at looking unconcerned.

"Oh, can I? Thank you. I'll tell you what I think then. After you dumped the body you did a massive detour via Bedfordshire where you left the car and then got a train to London, so you could get another train back from London to Bristol to make it look as though you'd been staying the weekend in town."

None of us said anything. We were finished. Either Rick was a brilliant detective or Imogen had been a lot less discreet than we'd thought. She'd shopped us to her boyfriend who had the power to bring everything crashing down.

"How do you know?" asked Zak at last.

Rick smiled. "Because I have this." He dug around in the bag and produced a tiny tape recorder.

"That's Imogen's," said Xanthe. "She's been looking for it for weeks."

She snatched for it, but he held it out of her reach. "I knew you were up to something. I hid this in the kitchen. Imagine my surprise when this is what I heard."

He pressed the button. I felt sick as our own words filled the room: *"Even if she remembers Oskar being at the party she doesn't know he died there or anything about moving the body..."* He pressed the button again, selecting other conversations.

"Be my guest," he said to Xanthe as she made a second grab for the device. "It's all backed up on another tape anyway."

"It was you who sent the postcards then?" said Zak.

He nodded. "I wanted to see what you'd do – whether any of you had the guts to come out and admit it."

"Why didn't you go to the police?" asked Xanthe.

He smiled ruefully. "Because of Imogen. I wanted to protect her. I didn't see why she should get dragged into it all. That doesn't matter so much now, of course."

"Look, come on, you know we didn't kill anyone," said Stuart, his voice breaking with emotion. "Can we please talk about this?"

Somehow, he managed to persuade Rick to go through to the living room which at least felt less confrontational than standing in the hall.

"All we did was move his body because it had nothing to do with us," said Zak as he sank into a chair.

"Yes, and in so doing you perverted the course of justice." Triumph flickered in Rick's eyes. I could imagine him in court wearing his robes, strutting about and grinding down a witness, congratulating himself afterwards on reducing them to tears while the rapist or mugger or murderer walked free.

"You must know that because of what you did you've made yourselves number one suspects?" he said with an incredulous laugh. "You were in close contact with the victim on the night he died and certainly among the last people to have seen him. They'll be able to produce lots of witnesses who saw you with him. And, even worse, you actively tried to prevent a police investigation taking place."

Stuart searched desperately for something to say. His face was pink and he wiped a line of sweat from across his nose. "Surely you can see we had to do it?"

But Rick laughed. "No. You chose to do it. Concealing a crime doesn't become any less serious because you thought you'd get blamed for murder."

"But what else could we have done? You've said yourself

191

we'd have been number one suspects."

Rick spoke as though he were addressing a child. "You know what you should have done. You should have gone back up those stairs without touching anything, called the police and told them exactly what you'd found. What you actually did makes you look guilty, but it's also more than likely destroyed any evidence which might have helped prove your innocence. I'd say your chances of being convicted of murder *now* if the police find Bramley was killed here would be close to a hundred percent."

Zak inhaled sharply. "Thanks. That's a big help."

"Well don't tell me you're surprised. Conspiring to prevent a lawful and decent burial of a body is very bad – you could each end up spending a couple of years in prison. But *disposing of a body* with intent to prevent a coroner's inquest – that's a lot worse. If the post mortem finds the death was unlawful and a motive for murder or manslaughter can be established, you could be looking at a life sentence."

It was the worst of the worst. My stomach tightened again. I felt something move inside me. It felt like a kick. I'd been starting to get them recently, but it just brought home to me how unlikely it was that I'd ever be able to keep this child. Would I even be allowed to hold her before they took her away?

"What do you think we should do?" I asked. We could at least take advantage of Rick's legal knowledge.

He blew out through his cheeks. "That's up to you. But I do know one thing – courts are more lenient when people give themselves up and spare the public purse from a long trial. "An early guilty plea can shave a lot off a sentence – so I'd get on the phone now and tell them what you've done."

He got up to leave. As he reached the door he added with a smile, "Oh, and pray."

"We're not going to give ourselves up," said Stuart.

There was a catch to his voice. I didn't like where this was going. It reminded me of the time he held up the knife to Imogen. We all knew that if Rick walked out the door our secret was well and truly blown. This was what I'd been afraid of – that in trying to escape justice for a lesser crime we'd end up committing a much worse one.

"Where are you going?" he asked Rick.

Rick didn't reply. He was leaving and there was nothing we could do about it. We'd lost control of the situation. If only there was something, anything, we could do to stop him.

"Wait," said Xanthe. "What were you doing in my room just now?"

He laughed and tried to deny it. "I wasn't in your room."

"Yes, you were. Imogen's room's above Stuart's but we could hear you right above our heads."

He stopped and turned. He continued to deny it, but he was starting to look rattled.

"You were looking for something. It wasn't a backpack by any chance?"

I felt all my energy drain away. What was she thinking? Now we were surrendering information he might not have had in the first place.

"Of course not." I could have sworn his face flushed.

"Liar," she said. "The reason you haven't gone to the police isn't because you wanted to help Imogen - you just wanted to save your own skin. Why don't you tell us that you knew Oskar before the party?"

Our heads flicked back to Rick. A strangled laugh escaped him. His face was white mottled with pink now and his eyes filled with a strange light. "Because I didn't."

"Really? You mean you don't remember bribing him to lie in court?"

I had no idea where Xanthe was getting this from or whether she was just feeling her way and I could see Zak and Stuart were as surprised as I was, but it seemed best to let her carry on.

"Oskar wasn't a stranger to you, was he? He came to the party to see you."

"No, you're mad, you've got that wrong." Rick looked

around the rest of us, appealing for sympathy but the look of alarm was unmistakable and all he got in return was stony looks. I think he could see it was useless.

"He came to the party because you promised him money. Just like the last time. What did he have to do for it this time?"

Stuart, who had thrust out a restraining hand to stop Xanthe, dropped it and stared at Rick. Zak moved in front of the door and stood there with his arms folded.

"Is there something you're not telling us?"

He cast a look back at Xanthe as though to say, "I hope you've got your facts right." Her eyes flickered with energy.

"Perhaps it isn't us who should be careful," she said. "Perhaps it's you – *Fitz*."

"Hang on, you've lost me," said Stuart.

"Rick isn't just short for Richard," said Xanthe, shaking her hair back. "It can be short for lots of things. Like Erik, Warrick, Leofric…"

"Yorrick," said Stuart.

"Baldric?" I suggested.

"Yes. But in this case it's short for Fitzpatrick. Isn't that right?"

In the space of a few moments everything had turned. Now Rick was the one on the defensive and we were the ones demanding answers.

"All this time you've been acting as though we were the guilty ones," said Zak. "Is that what this is about? You wanted us to take the blame for what you did?"

"I didn't do anything," Rick protested. "I met Bramley, yes. I agreed to lend him some money. That's all. We'd been good friends once – we were at school together. But we were caught with cocaine. He got thrown out after I confessed, I was allowed to stay on. Our lives took very different paths. He got in touch out of the blue a few months ago. I couldn't turn my back on him. I felt sorry for him – the way things had turned out. After I gave him the money I went back to the party. Whatever happened to him afterwards has nothing to do with me."

"You'll have a hard time convincing a jury of that," Zak said.

There was a moment when I thought Rick might run at the door and a moment when I thought he might hit Zak. But in the end, he said,

"I only wanted to help him get back on his feet."

Zak scoffed at the poor choice of words. "That's just it, though, isn't it? He never did get back on his feet, did he? You killed him, didn't you?"

"Of course I didn't. Absolutely not." All the colour seemed to have drained from Rick's face. "I promise you he was alive when I left him. I didn't lay a finger on him."

The air was charged with suspicion and disbelief.

Stuart's face was white and dangerous. "You'd better tell us what happened."

Rick evidently hadn't anticipated this turn of events. We were all fuming at how close we'd come to thinking this was all about us when in fact he had been trying to save himself. His voice was quieter than usual, and you could see the tension in his hand when he went to push his hair back.

Sweat shone on his forehead. "I didn't touch him. Come on, think about it - I was only with him a few minutes. The time it would have taken to go to the toilet and get another drink. I went straight back to Imogen afterwards. Don't you think she'd have noticed something different about me if I'd just killed someone?"

He stopped as though something had just occurred to him or he'd just remembered it. "And I'm not the only one who knew Oskar, am I?"

He pointed his chin at Xanthe who looked down at her knees. Her hair curtained her face but her hands were shaking. I inhaled until I thought my lungs would burst.

"I didn't hurt him," she insisted. "All I did was put him in touch with you, Rick. What you did was much worse. I had no idea he'd come to the house – or that it would lead to this."

"Why in the world didn't you tell us you knew him?" Stuart demanded.

Xanthe turned her large green eyes on him. "Because what would you have thought? You'd have jumped to the wrong conclusion."

"Would we? Or the right one?

She clutched her head in her hands. "He was in the squat. After we were evicted we had nowhere to go. We were practically starving. But while he was on the streets Oskar was questioned about a murder case. Someone offered him money to lie in court about something he'd seen – a man's coming and goings from a flat across the road from where Oskar used to sleep. It was a lot of money – enough for us to pay a deposit and the first month's rent on a room somewhere.

"Those few weeks gave us the chance to sort ourselves out. Oskar got cleaned up and got a job. And I signed up for college, and from there I got a place on the training scheme.

"Oskar had been in trouble a few times, so he didn't have much faith in the justice system and he was quite happy to help someone put two fingers up at the judge. But he only went along with it because they convinced him the man was guilty."

She turned to Rick. "But you didn't care, did you? It was all a game to you."

All the arrogance had drained away as Rick said. "I promise you it wasn't. I've learned from that experience. I wouldn't do it again."

He was still evidently reeling from discovering that Xanthe knew about his past. I was still getting over it myself although I could see why she hadn't wanted to tell us that she'd known Oskar.

"It wasn't my idea," he said, appealing for our sympathy. "I was the junior, learning the ropes. I didn't want to rock the boat. It was how they did things. The way it was put to me was that they were a hundred per cent certain the man was guilty and if he got put away, the case would be closed and everyone would be happy. All I had to do was encourage one of the witnesses to make his evidence a bit more compelling – be more precise about the timings. I wasn't totally comfortable with it to tell the truth, but I wanted to keep my job. I'd worked so hard to get it."

He looked round, desperate to make us understand.

"I'm not sure we care," said Zak. "Do we care?" We shrugged our indifference but Rick ploughed on anyway.

"If I'd blown the whistle no one would have believed me, I'd have been dropped from the firm and they'd have made damned sure I wouldn't be able to get work with anyone else."

"So, you paid Oskar Bramley to lie?"

He looked up sharply. "About the timings and some descriptive details, yes. It just proved that the murder could have been committed in the timeframe."

"And so you were the golden boy for winning the case," said Xanthe. "Except you were wrong, weren't you? That man was innocent. And thanks to you the investigation was closed and the real killer was free to go on and kill Lily Ambrose. Wow. And you thought we were despicable."

Rick at least had the decency to blush. "You've no idea how bad I feel about it. I believed he was guilty. It was my first big case – it was so important for me to win."

"Was it really?" I asked, unable to contain my anger any longer. "More important than a girl's life?"

His expression hardened again. "Come on, you know how it works. Lawyers can only do so much. All they do is present the evidence. It's the jury who decides if a person's guilty and the judge who passes sentence."

"Yes, but in this case the evidence was false," I pointed out.

He shut his eyes and nodded. It turned out that after being convicted of killing Lily Ambrose the killer had confessed to the earlier murder and one or two others.

"Oskar was horrified," said Xanthe. "He felt partly responsible for Lily's death and he lived in fear of being picked up by the police and sent down for perjury. It had a huge effect on him, sent him back into that downward spiral. He was looking over his shoulder all the time and injecting himself with all sorts to help him forget. It really

197

messed him up.

"But he realised the lawyers must be terrified too because if he told the truth they'd all find themselves in prison."

"So, Oskar threatened to spill the beans about the bribe?" said Zak.

Rick nodded. "I had no idea how he'd managed to track me down. He said he wanted more money in return for keeping quiet. A lot more."

"And you didn't see that coming? For God's sake, I thought lawyers were clever." He shook his head in disbelief.

"A common misconception," said Rick with a pained smile. "I didn't want him coming anywhere near our offices. I thought it would work best if I met him in a crowded situation like a party where we'd be quite anonymous."

"But why would anyone take Oskar's word against yours?" I asked. "Why didn't you just take the chance that nobody would believe him about the blackmail? Surely if the worst came to the worst you could get yourself a good lawyer?"

He shook his head. "There was no chance of that - Bramley had the whole thing on tape."

"So you know how that feels," said Zak with a bitter grin. He turned to Xanthe.

"When you realised who Rick was you decided to help Oskar get back at him?"

She shrugged and nodded.

"For a cut?"

"Yes. But it wasn't just about the money. He'd been good to me and I wanted to help him. I told you, I never thought it would lead to this. Honestly, I didn't. I had no idea Oskar would come to the house."

She was looking for assurance that we understood but none of us knew what to think.

"But none of this explains how Oskar died," said Stuart. "There's something you're not telling us. Which one of you took the back pack?"

"You know I didn't," said Xanthe, her voice full of hurt.

Our eyes turned to Rick. He looked wretched. "Of course I didn't. I'd just given him the money. Why would I take it back?"

No one knew what to say. "Perhaps you changed your mind," I said.

"I promise you – I didn't think anything of it. Just closed the cellar door and came away and rejoined the party. I assumed he'd wait a few minutes and then come out too and go home."

"And you spent the rest of the night with Imogen?"

"Yes."

"You'd better hope she backs you if this comes to trial," said Zak.

Rick glared at him. "Well, that's the thing isn't it? We'd better back each other."

I couldn't believe his arrogance. "We don't owe you anything. You tried to pressure us into going to the police because you knew there was a good chance we'd get charged with murder."

"No, you're wrong. I just wanted a bit of bargaining power, that's all. If I'd wanted to I could have gone to the police any time since I heard that recording."

"Then what did you want?" I asked. "You know we don't have any money."

A glimmer of hope returned in his eyes. "The house – in return for keeping your secret."

Stuart seized him by the throat. "Get out."

Chapter Eighteen

After I'd made the decision to keep the baby I went back up to Scotland for the weekend and broke the news to my parents. They were appalled of course and apoplectic when they realised the father wasn't going to be around.

They said – or shouted – a lot of things I really didn't need to hear like how only stupid girls "got themselves knocked up" at twenty-one, how I'd screwed up my future, thrown away my degree and the career I'd dreamt of since I was eleven.

Their language instantly regressed a few centuries in line with their antediluvian views. All the old-fashioned words tumbled out – "out of wedlock" "old maid" "on the shelf" "shop-soiled", "used goods" – even "bastard child"

My mother came back from the bathroom telling me the effect on her had been "instant diarrhea". I was genuinely worried my father was going to have a heart attack. The neighbours were used to his outbursts but this one was impressive even for him. I doubt there was anyone in the street who didn't now know why I'd put on weight.

My parents asked again and again if I realised how selfish it was to have a child outside marriage. What sort of future could I give him or her? They wanted to know if the father was married, or if I even knew who he was.

My sister attempted to come to the rescue saying being a single mother wasn't that unusual anymore but somehow while doing so she came out about her sexual status. They went nuclear. But if they'd had even the faintest idea of what else was going on in my life right then they'd have realised how ridiculous they sounded and how pointless this all was. It made me think about how they would react if they ever found out. Would they cut me off? I couldn't imagine not being able to speak to them again or being turned away on the doorstep.

In the end, after we'd all shouted ourselves hoarse, I went out into the garden. It had been raining. The sky was the colour of grubby underpants and everything was dripping but it smelled of sweet grass and wet bark and, well, childhood.

I had a sudden urge to visit our old Wendy house at the bottom but when I got there I found Jess had beaten me to it. We lay side by side like two Alices in our tiny surroundings, with our feet up on the walls. It felt strange after all those years, remembering ourselves camped out here for sleepovers as children, chewing gum and planning our next adventure.

"Are you all right?" Jess asked me. "You know what they're like. It'll blow over."

I grimaced. "It's not just the baby."

She turned to face me. "There's something else? Worse than getting pregnant?"

I wanted so much to tell her, but I couldn't risk it. "I need to know if you'll help me – if it comes to it."

She smiled. "Of course. You know I will."

"No, I'm serious. You don't know what it is yet. This is a big thing. A really huge, horrible thing…"

She looked at me quizzically. "Nothing's that bad, surely." Then seeing my expression, she said, "Or maybe it is. Tell me."

"I can't. But I need to know if you'd have the baby if I'm ever not able to look after her. Or him."

Jess laughed. "You'll manage. Everyone does. Wait. You're serious, aren't you?

"The thing is, I might not be able to look after her. For a while I mean. Or maybe ever. And I don't want her taken into care."

Thinking about it there in that place where we'd spent so much of our childhood with our T-shirts stained with mud and blackberry juice, battle-scarred legs in Wellington boots, guinea pigs lolloping over us, it made it all so much worse.

Jess propped herself up on her elbow. "That's not going to happen Em. You're a bit daft, I grant you, but you're not a total loon. They won't take your baby away."

Her expression changed. "Or are you ill? Oh my God, how ill?"

"No, it's nothing like that. I'm just worried about something." I was struggling to hold back the tears.

"All right, so what have you done? What are you not telling me?"

"I can't. There are other people involved. I would if I could but please trust me, it's better if I don't."

"Oh God, it is bad, isn't it?"

"I can't say. I can't. But I didn't do it, okay? Whatever they say and however it looks I didn't do it. At least not the really bad thing. Please remember that. And tell Mum and Dad."

She looked alarmed. "Just tell me, is this worse than the firework thing?"

I shut my eyes. The firework thing – it seemed minor now.

"Yes. But it's not how it looks."

"Oh my god."

I thought back to Stuart trying to confess to me at the party and a new wave of guilt washed over me. He'd needed my approval so badly.

Jess sighed. "Without you telling me more it's hard to know what to think. But whatever it is if you say you didn't do it then I believe you."

This was my little sister. When did she get to be so wise? I'd almost not noticed how amazing she was.

"If it happens," she said, "which it won't, but if it does - I'll take care of the baby for you. I'd love to. And when you come out you can have him or her back. I promise you."

"Are you sure? Babies are expensive. And noisy. And messy and time-consuming and they play havoc with your social life."

"We'll cope."

"What about Ali? Don't you have to ask her first?"

Jess looked appalled. "No way. If she didn't support me in this I wouldn't be with her. You're my sister. That tiny person in there is my niece or nephew – the closest I may ever get to having a baby of my own."

"Thanks. I can't thank you enough."

She looked at me wonderingly. "Don't be an idiot."

I felt a load had been lifted. It was only a solution to one part of my hideous situation but at least I knew now that I'd done one responsible thing and if the worst happened, the baby would at least be safe.

Chapter Nineteen

I told Donald about the pregnancy. Most people in the office had noticed by then and rumours were bound to have reached him. He went ballistic as I'd expected, spitting out phrases like "I'm disappointed," and "you've thrown away a place another trainee would have given their right arm for" but at least he didn't fire me. Once I'd convinced him I was serious about staying in the company he said I could take all four weeks holiday leave at once and he'd turn a blind eye to a week's sick leave which should give me time to sort out child care. Zak said he'd take off a couple of weeks after me and with Xanthe at home all day now the prospect of being a single mother didn't seem so lonely and frightening after all.

In August a pleasure steamer called the Marchioness which had been hired for a birthday party collided with a dredger in the Thames and 51 people drowned. The fact they were young people enjoying a party hit us – although it inevitably led to another row when Zak said the tragedy wouldn't have received the coverage it did if the people on the boat had been less posh and Stuart saying he should be ashamed of himself.

On one of those sun-filled weekends I was coming back from a visit to my sister when I met Zak and Imogen who were also walking back up to the house from the station.

"Em! Are you all right? God, it's so good to see you." Zak drew me into a crushing hug which took me by surprise.

"All good," I replied, "No news yet." He was obviously keeping an eye on the dates. It couldn't be much longer now. I was so heavy and uncomfortable I wanted it to be over but at the same time I wanted to put off the moment for as long as possible because I had no idea how I'd cope.

"Aren't you cold?" he asked, feeling my arms.

I laughed. "Never, these days. Which is just as well – none of my coats fit anymore."

"We should get you a bigger one."

"Thanks but I've got my own hot water bottle right here," I said, feeling my pregnancy bump.

I could feel his heart thumping through his jacket. When I pulled back from his embrace I winced as Zak turned his head, revealing a black eye, and what looked like a carpet burn on his cheek and a swollen and bruised lip.

"What happened to you?" But it was already dawning on me. "Oh wait – you told Chiara about the baby?"

He grinned painfully. "She wasn't over the moon."

"She did that to you?"

I put my hand up to the scars. I'd suspected she had a temper and could only guess at the level of anger and hurt she must feel at finding out about the baby but hadn't guessed she'd be violent.

"She doesn't believe there's nothing still going on between us."

"I could talk to her if you think it will help."

He shook his head. "It definitely wouldn't. Thanks, but there's no point now – it's over. She wanted me to move away with her and promise I'd never have anything to do with the child – or you."

"Oh God, Zak, I'm sorry."

He shrugged. "No, in a way it's a relief. She scares me when she's angry. It's bad enough living with Stuart."

"She's done this before?"

His face flushed. "She usually goes for the areas that don't show so much."

I didn't know what to say except, "Why didn't you tell us? And why did you put up with it?"

He looked away. "Because when she wasn't hitting me she was lovely to be with. And I thought after what I'd done

– you know, with Bob and everything – I was lucky to be with her and didn't deserve any better."

"You know that's not true."

He took my hand. He seemed a bit agitated. "And in any case…"

Imogen who'd gone on ahead turned round and shouted, "Are you two on a go-slow today? Let's get some food."

"What were you saying?" I asked.

"No, nothing."

We called in at Spud U Like and walked up the road together eating our baked potatoes and sharing stories from our weekends. Zak was still laughing about something as he pushed open the door to my room.

"Shit."

He slammed it shut again. He wasn't laughing anymore.

"What is it? Let me see."

He was looking at me questioningly. Finally, he shrugged and stepped aside with a strange look on his face. Opening the door again, I stood trying to make sense of what I was looking at.

Stuart was lying on my bed, his naked body twisting and straining at the silk scarves that held him. His mouth was stopped with a sock. His eyes bulged. His face was streaked with tears, but he was exhausted. A sweet, cloying smell filled the room blending with body odour and urine. His body was caked in something dark. It was a relief to discover it was chocolate. And there were snail trails of cream that had soured in the over-heated room.

We stood filling the doorway, taking it in. How long had he been there like that? He looked at us wildly, desperate for our help but at the same time apparently resenting us for catching him in such an undignified state.

"For God's sake, Emily."

Imogen was the first to come to her senses. She picked up my dressing gown, threw it over Stuart's midriff and started picking at the knots. "Scissors," she demanded, snapping her hand out.

I scrabbled around in my washbag, glad to have

something to do. Stuart was groaning and fuming. Zak stood there looking incredulous and amused. Imogen attacked the knots with her teeth. Stuart's ankles and wrists had angry, weeping sores where he'd obviously struggled for ages. I was calculating back to when we'd last seen him. Nobody had been in since Friday.

"Look, I…" I began.

"Don't," she said. "I don't want to hear it."

"No but hang on. I didn't do this."

"Emily. What part of 'don't' are you not getting?"

Zak ripped the sock from Stuart's mouth. "This may seem an obvious question but what the hell were you up to?"

Stuart brought up his freed left arm to nurse the bruised corners of his mouth. His arm shook and didn't seem to be able to go where he wanted it to. His voice trembled with emotion and exhaustion and incredulity. He tried to talk but it came out as a rasp which turned into a coughing fit. Zak grabbed a bottle of water from the floor by my bed that was probably a few days old but in the circumstances that didn't seem important, removed the top and held it out for Stuart who downed it in a few noisy gulps and pushed it back at us for a refill.

I stumbled off to the bathroom, ran the tap and handed it back to him. I guessed he hadn't eaten or drunk anything all weekend. Stuart looked round at us and sank his head back against the rails.

"Xanthe," he wheezed.

"Xanthe. Why would she leave you like this?"

It seemed a joke too far even for Xanthe. Stuart had always had a soft spot for her, but she must have had better acting skills than I'd thought to have got him to go along with this seduction scene. But to leave him for so long, knowing that we'd find him like that – I'd thought of her as mischievous but never cruel.

"She said it would be fun," he said rubbing his wrists and scrabbling at his skin.

Selfishly, I couldn't help thinking about the smears and

flakes that were ending up on my sheets and my dressing gown right next to his skin and whether they'd ever come out. I hadn't planned on spending the night in the launderette.

His whole body shuddered. "I wanted to see what it was like. It *was* fun at first. Then she said she'd be back in a moment and disappeared. I waited, thinking it was all part of the game. But ten minutes passed, and the house was silent. After half an hour it was obvious she wasn't coming back. Then it started to really hurt. I thought my limbs were going to be starved of oxygen. I actually thought I was going to die."

A tear escaped down his reddened cheek. "I'm such an idiot."

"No you're not," I told him. "But why on earth hasn't she come back? I can't believe she'd leave you like this even for fun. Something must have happened."

"She's gone to Sweden to see Erik," said Imogen. "That Swedish PR guy she met at the trade fair. She told me on Friday she was going to the airport after work."

There was a silence as we digested this.

"She could have called," I said. "She could have at least let us know what she'd done, made sure someone would come and untie him. I know she's forgetful but how can it slip your mind you've left someone tied to a bed?"

And why for God's sake had she chosen my bed? I didn't say those last words, but Stuart must have read them in my expression.

"I'm sorry about the bed. Mine has an upholstered headboard."

And Xanthe's was a futon with no headboard at all. But she could have asked.

"You don't understand." He clutched my arm. "She's gone to the police. She knew I'd have stopped her going. This was all a ruse to incapacitate me. We need to get away. I thought you were them."

"What are you talking about?"

As if I couldn't guess.

"She's dropped us all in it, hasn't she?" said Zak. "Gone and told them everything. She picked a time when most of us were out. She knew Stuart would stop her, so she found the only way she could to restrain him, given that she's five foot nothing and you're what, six two?"

Stuart nodded weakly.

"But she must have forgotten the rest of us were going to be away this weekend. I suppose she thought one of us would be back yesterday or this morning."

Never assume. It was what they drummed into us every day during our training. I couldn't believe Xanthe would make such a basic mistake.

"We should leave," said Stuart.

"That will only make us look guilty," said Zak.

"Which we are," I reminded him.

"Yes, but not of everything. They'll pin the lot on us if we run now."

Chapter Twenty

The police didn't come that day or the next. But each morning we woke wondering if they would. Xanthe's disappearance was a worry but my mind was taken off it a few days later when I went into labour as I was carrying some shopping back to the house. The others were all out at work but Mrs Parker next door must have spotted me hobbling into the house because she seemed to appear out of nowhere, made all the arrangements, waited with me until the contractions were close enough, put me in her car and drove me to the hospital.

The birth was pretty horrendous in my opinion but the midwife recorded it as "standard" so I suppose it could have been a lot worse. But the baby was perfect. Her skin was paler than Zak's but darker than mine. She had a lot of black hair and the cutest nose.

From the moment I saw her I knew that I had someone in my life who I would always love unconditionally. This tiny person whose life had started in such an unpromising way, who was separate from me but a part of me. I just hoped I'd be able to stay with her long enough for her to remember me.

Zak came as soon as he got Mrs Parker's message at work. I could tell as soon as he took the baby in his arms he'd fallen in love with her as deeply as I had.

"Do we have a name?"

"I was thinking Olivia. Liv."

Because she was all about life – something wonderful that had come out of that terrible night.

"Liv it is." Zak looked down at her sleeping in his arms. His eyes glistened as he said, "This is the most amazing thing that's ever happened to me. You know I never knew who my father was – or my mother either for most of the time I was growing up. I don't want it to be like that for this little one. I'd do anything for her – and you. We may not be a conventional couple but we're Livvy's parents, you and I, and no one can take that away from us."

***

It's amazing how such a tiny being can make everything else in your life seem unimportant. Those first few days with Livvy were all-consuming. Night ran into day and I became morbidly fascinated by how I managed to function with so little sleep. It was strangest during the day when everyone else was out. I felt even more cut off from reality than I had over the past few months. I wondered each day if Xanthe was going to turn up. She'd said she'd help with the baby after all. I also regretted telling her she could borrow my clothes that didn't fit while I was pregnant because she'd obviously helped herself to my coat before she left and it was getting chilly. Who knew if I'd ever see that again?

I was pushing the pram up Park Street a week later. It's a very steep road that leads from the cathedral up to the university tower and pushing a pram up it is no easy task. I had my head down and was telling myself with grim determination that the burn in my thighs was better than a gym session when Chiara appeared, seemingly out of nowhere. The pavement was crowded, and the traffic was flying past and there was no way to avoid each other.

She looked into the pram, noting how like Zak Livvy looked and asked rather stiffly how things were going.

She looked horrified when I told her about Xanthe's disappearance. "God, such a shock for you all. I'm sure they'll find her though."

We walked in uncomfortable silence for a few moments. She was on her way back from a client meeting and her heels clicked on the paving. I caught sight of our reflection in shop windows as we passed and thought how elegant she looked compared to me in my old clothes and trainers.

"I thought I'd found the perfect partner in Zak," she said. "He was smart, funny, kind – and I loved the poems he wrote. But sometimes it was like coming up against a locked door. There was a barrier I knew I'd never get past. He'd never let me in. As though he had a guilty secret. He confided in you, though, didn't he?"

I felt her eyes searching mine but busied myself with adjusting Livvy's blanket, so I wouldn't have to answer.

"When I discovered the baby was his, it hurt so much. Not that I want one – not yet anyway - I want to live my own life first. But he could have told me earlier. I understand why he didn't, but it made me feel shut out – discovering there was something so huge in his life that he wouldn't share with me. I know it happened before he met me. I know he wasn't unfaithful, but he's still deceived me for a long time. You all did."

"I'm sorry, Chiara."

"All I wanted was for Zak to put it in the past and come away with me. He said I was forcing him into a corner, giving him an impossible choice. He said there was nothing to discuss. So you see I couldn't stay. Not in a relationship where I had to take third place. If I did I was just going to get more badly hurt.

"I never understood his obsession with your house – it's a nice enough place but really it's you guys he couldn't drag himself away from. I couldn't compete."

"Honestly, we didn't plan for any of this to happen."

She shrugged.

"Perhaps I'd have been jealous of you anyway Emily. It's not a looks thing, obviously, but something in the way his voice changes when he speaks to you. The shared looks, the way you finish each other's sentences, the things that for God's sake nobody but you two seem to find funny. I might seem confident, but I've never had what you have between you."

"What we have is probably different from what it

seems."

She gave me an odd look. "Whatever you say. But as it turns out, the baby was such a minor thing. It didn't seem possible that he could have a worse secret than that."

She must have seen my expression because she said, "Yes, I know about the body in the basement. Xanthe broke down one evening and told me what you all did to that poor man. I couldn't believe you could be so callous…"

My heart stalled. How could Xanthe have done this to us? Why had she betrayed us? I tried to explain the circumstances, but she didn't want to listen. When we reached a cross roads she went off in a different direction for her bus.

She said good bye but as I turned to go she mumbled something like, "Say hi to Zak. You're welcome to each other."

Chapter Twenty-One

November

"And then there were three," muttered Zak as we watched the police car slide away from the church yard after Xanthe's funeral, weave through the yew trees and disappear out onto the road.

A middle-aged man with a limp asked half-heartedly if we'd like to join the family for refreshments after the service but I got the feeling he was trying to make the directions as difficult as possible to follow. In any case, the last thing any of us felt like was standing around making small talk to a family Xanthe had clearly turned her back on years ago with gossip circulating about the tall, blond man who'd been bundled into a police car back at the church – hadn't he been with us?

And of course, we had things to talk about.

The car we'd hired for the day stood in the lane by the church where we'd left it.

"I suppose I could…" began Zak.

"Don't even think it," Imogen said. "In any case, Stu's got the key."

Not knowing the Essex village where Xanthe had grown up, we walked for ages past Camberwick Green-style village greens, duck ponds, farm fields, cute little thatched cottages and modern housing developments and even the odd windmill in the hope of finding some public transport. It was November. The wind cut across the low-lying land and the ground was thick with leaves. I was worrying about how long it would take to get back to Livvy and our next door neighbour who was looking after her.

"They must know something about Stuart that we don't," said Imogen, wrapping her coat around herself. "They wouldn't make an arrest unless they were certain. They must think they've got enough evidence for a trial."

"But he can't have killed Xanthe," I said. "I can just about believe he killed Bob/Oskar in a fit of rage but not Xanthe – even if she made him look like an idiot. He couldn't have got to her. We know where he was that weekend. We all three came back together from Spud U Like and found Stuart tied up which makes it impossible."

"Although that doesn't necessarily mean he's not responsible," Zak said, digging his hands into his pockets. "I've thought about this a lot. What if Stuart asked someone to tie him up to give him an alibi because he'd already killed Xanthe?"

I held my hair back from the wind. "Are you serious? Stuart wouldn't do that. Not to Xanthe. He loved her – in a way."

"Yes, but she was going to destroy his future. You heard him talking about his time in the detention centre. He'd do anything to avoid getting sent back into the system. Getting a place on the training scheme – he must have felt he'd turned his life around. But if Xanthe found out he killed Oskar and was going to the police he'd lose everything."

"I don't know," said Imogen. "I still don't think he's got it in him to do it. Although I suppose it's just possible he could have arranged for someone else to kill her."

"How would Stuart know how to organise a hitman?" I asked. "You don't just put an ad in the paper, do you?"

Imogen shrugged. "He's been Inside remember? He knows people. I'm guessing it's just a question of having the right contacts."

It still didn't seem believable.

"First Xanthe gone and now Stuart. It feels as if we're being taken out one by one. Who's going to be next?"

Chapter Twenty-Two

In those weeks after Stuart's arrest we barely slept. I sat up all night hugging Liv to me, not knowing how I could let them take me from her. Every time I picked her up I thought it might be the last time. Sometimes Zak got there before me. He was much better at this baby business than I'd expected, handling the nappy changes and bottle paraphernalia without question. Listening to him sing to her and seeing her strung exhausted across his chest as he slept gave me glimpses of a future in which we were a conventional family and our life at number 17 a distant memory like a bad dream.

I didn't dare do any Christmas shopping – I felt it would be tempting fate – except for a few items for Liv which I wrapped and wrote labels for. I also bought eighteen cards and wrote on them for her in case I wouldn't be around to give them to her in person and left them with Jess just in case the police found them and saw them as an admission of guilt. But in the end the four of us spent Christmas together in the house and kept ourselves busy on New Year's Eve to try and take our minds off the events of a year ago.

The trial took place the following spring. It was chucking it down as we travelled by taxi to the court, the streets merging into a wash of colour as fallen cherry blossom slushed like snow under the tyres. Outside, people scurried under umbrellas that lifted in the wind, and took refuge in the bright shelter of the shops. All that stress about what to wear, how much to spend, which size to get – if only they could see that none of it actually mattered.

It was a shock to see Stuart sitting isolated in the box at the back of the courtroom when I was called up to the witness stand. It had all happened so suddenly after Xanthe's funeral and we hadn't even had the chance to say goodbye. We'd visited him while he was on remand but had clung to the hope it would never come to this. My mouth was dry. I answered the questions as best I could, not knowing what had been said before me, but whatever I said seemed to be taken as confirmation of Stuart's guilt and a couple of times I caught his reproachful, hate-filled stare.

We'd hoped of course that Rick would help Stuart but he refused. Now that Xanthe and Oskar were both dead there was no one to corroborate our story that he knew Oskar, had bribed him to commit perjury or had anything to do with him the night he died. Besides, we'd agreed to keep Rick's secret in return for him guarding ours – it was the only way.

"One of you has to fall so the rest can walk."

We only chose Stuart because the police already had him and his alibi was the weakest. They knew he'd lied about his car being stolen, they knew it had been used to transport Oskar and they knew about his temper. In his original statement he hadn't said anything about being tied up but was now relying on it to prove his innocence.

Stuart was wearing the suit he'd bought for the trade show in Birmingham that was slightly too short in the arms. His scarlet neck portrayed the stress he was under.

He caught my eye a few times during the proceedings and I understood something of the horror he was feeling and I wished there was something more we could do.

The jury didn't have to be told about Stuart's previous conviction but for some reason the Defence thought it wise to bring it up at the start so there would be no surprises later. It seemed a risky strategy. He laid it on thick that Stuart was a reformed character. The one awful mistake he'd made in his youth had been punished. The short, sharp shock system had been effective, taught him a lesson he'd never forget and having tasted the penal system once he'd never let himself go down that road again.

To give him his due Donald did admirably as a character witness, praising Stuart's dedication to his work, respect for interviewees, his chivalry towards colleagues and ability to remain calm under the pressure of news deadlines.

The lawyers spent a long time conjecturing over whether Stuart could have untied himself, done the deed and tied himself up again. The prosecution had some escapologist demonstrate it could be done by tying one knotted loop first, then all the other knots and putting his hand through the loop last, pulling it tight with his teeth.

"This is a joke," said Zak and earned himself a glare from the judge.

When it was Stuart's turn to speak I waited for him to drop us all in it which he could easily have done but he didn't. His voice sounded clipped and his face went taut, his mouth slipping to the side as he spoke. He drank sips of water between questions.

I studied the jury and wondered what they made of him. I tried to imagine I was hearing the details in the same way that they were. Would his posh voice and terse replies count against him or would they see through the pride and anger to the vulnerability and the honesty in his expression?

But other things came out too at the trial – things we hadn't been aware of. A witness had overheard Stuart tell Oskar to get out of the house and he'd been seen pursuing Oskar down the hall towards the cellar door. One of the advertising team on *Golfing Weekly* said that they'd heard him arguing with Oskar in the basement.

When asked if he was sure it was Stuart shouting, the man said, "A hundred per cent."

"Bloody liar," murmured Imogen.

But blood particles had been found on one of Stuart's hoodies which matched Xanthe's blood and a motorist had seen a man of Stuart's height and build wearing a matching maroon hoody emerging from the grassy bank onto the road close to where Xanthe was eventually found, brushing leaves off his trousers. I saw sweat glistening on Stuart's forehead as he admitted he had no explanation for these things. I kept my eyes on him but he wouldn't look in my direction. I began to wonder if we, rather than the jury, had been misled.

The trial went on for a couple of weeks but there was a horrible sense of inevitability about it. Addressing Stuart at the end the judge said,

"You told one lie after another. On both occasions your deliberately misleading actions interfered with police investigations and left two families in the agony of ignorance. You showed a callous disregard for your victims, one of whom not only knew you but counted you as a friend.

"You gave no thought to the feelings of those families. Your only concern was to save your own skin. You've shown no remorse for what you did and despite the evidence you chose to plead not guilty. As you must have realised this has led to a lengthy trial which has not only cost the State a considerable amount of money but put the families through the needless additional suffering."

I watched Stuart's pale face empty of expression as the sentence was passed. Life imprisonment. He closed his eyes. A member of Oskar's family cheered and a woman I recognised from Xanthe's funeral said she hoped he'd rot in hell. Stuart had no relations present.

Oskar's family read a statement outside the court saying that Stuart's sentence was minor in comparison to theirs. "He'll be out in a few years, living his life. But he hasn't given the family any explanation as to why he killed Oskar and nothing can bring Oskar back to us. So how can we call it justice?"

Xanthe's family's lawyer read a statement as her parents clung to each other for support.

"Charlotte's only mistake was in being too trusting. She thought she'd found a friend in Stuart Mountford and the other people she bought the house with. For that lapse in judgement she paid with her life."

"What happens now?" I asked our lawyer at the end of the trial. "Will they come for us?"

"My hunch is that if he was going to charge you with perjury he'd have kept you there today," she said. "It could

219

still happen but for now that's it. I suggest you make the most of your lives. Have you booked a holiday yet?"

We stepped out into the late afternoon sun. People were streaming out of offices and congregating outside the pubs along the river. I felt drawn to it all in a nostalgic way but all I wanted to do was get home to Livvy.

Chapter Twenty-Three

After the sentence we travelled back to the house in silence. Mrs Parker was looking out for us, holding Liv who was fast asleep and blissfully unaware of the events going on around her.

"She's been an angel," said Mrs Parker. "I'll miss her if you move away. I suppose you will now, won't you?"

It seemed the only solution. We couldn't get out fast enough. The mortgage rate had gone up to fifteen percent and the chances of being able to rent out Stuart and Xanthe's rooms to cover their shares were miniscule now everyone knew what had happened. The only people who were likely to be attracted by a house like this weren't the sort you'd want as housemates.

Mrs Parker followed us next door, giving us a rundown of the baby's feeds and nappies.

Liv woke up as soon as we crossed the threshold, as if she knew it was a bad place. The house seemed so much bigger and emptier than before and her cries filled the space. I picked her up and soothed her. It felt so good to be reunited after a day apart.

"I don't know how you can bear to sleep here," said Mrs Parker. "I have to say we were rocked by the news. We both thought – and no offence to the rest of you – that he was the trustworthy one. Just goes to show doesn't it?"

I found myself apologising for our behaviour – the noise and the parties. Now we knew our neighbours better I felt a bit ashamed of what we'd put them through.

"It hasn't been so bad lately," she said.

We stood in Stuart's room which seemed cleaner and starker than ever. It was impossible to believe he wasn't coming back, that he wouldn't be striding around calling us "my furry friends", ordering house meetings and shouting at us for leaving our underwear drying on the radiators or not taking our mugs back to the kitchen.

Over the next few days we'd have to pack away his scant belongings. I picked up the picture of Skye that I'd been looking at that time when Stuart found me in his room. It was the only time I'd felt frightened with him and I'd convinced myself afterwards that it had all been in my head.

"I still can't believe it either," I said. "I know he had a temper and I know he was going to pieces but I thought I knew him. I thought he was basically good."

"Why on earth did he do it?" asked Mrs Parker. "He hasn't given any explanation. Was it the usual?"

I was distracted by checking Livvy's nappy. "I'm sorry? What's the usual?"

"Oh you know – jealousy. Sexual rivalry."

"No. We don't know what it was but I'm sure it wasn't that."

"Only I thought there might have been a falling out between him and that dark one."

"Zak?"

"No, no. The other chappie that used to be around a lot, with the dark hair. We could never work out how many of you there were to tell the truth."

"You mean Rick? Tall, wears a suit most of the time?"

"That's the one. Perhaps they had a row over Charlotte, you know."

"Xanthe – Charlotte - wasn't going out with either of them," I said. I could imagine this sort of conjecture going on in houses around the country. When would it stop?

"Well she got into his car. The dark one's."

My hands froze. "Sorry, when was that?"

"The very last time we saw her. We were just going out. She was about to go off in that funny little car of hers when he turned up and she went off with him."

"Wait. Can you say that again?"

Olivia was still crying when Mrs Parker left.

"I'll take her." Zak lifted her gently out of my arms.

I went back to Stuart's room where Imogen was still standing looking out of the window at the space where Xanthe's car used to stand before her parents had collected all her stuff.

"What if she's right?" she said. "What if Rick did come to the house on the night Xanthe disappeared?"

"We don't know it was the same night," I said.

She turned and I saw the fear in her eyes. "But I remember he rang me at work the day I went to the press trip in Harrogate. He said he was going to call round – he wanted to talk. Only I didn't get the message until the Monday. But what if he did come and what if he hurt Xanthe?"

"Killed her you mean?" Zak stepped into the room. "Why didn't you tell us this before?"

"Because I didn't think it was important. I didn't know he'd come. He didn't say anything about it. And well, I was still angry at you lot because you didn't tell me about Oskar. I was still trying to sort it out in my head."

"You think Xanthe went somewhere with Rick that night?" I asked. "Why would she have done that? You don't think they were seeing each other, do you?"

Imogen smiled at the idea. To be fair I couldn't think of any two people more mismatched. "No. I reckon Xanthe was going to the police just as Stuart says. She tied Stuart up so he wouldn't be able to stop her, but Rick overheard their conversation and went after her. I don't know what happened. Something must have gone wrong."

"Jesus, I hope you know what you've done," said Zak.

"But I don't think he could have killed her. You heard what they said today about Xanthe's blood particles on Stuart's hoody." She wrapped her arms around herself. "You know, I thought he was the love of my life. Now I wonder if I was just an alibi."

***

The following day we paid Rick a surprise visit in his Richmond office. His face brightened when he saw Imogen and paled when he saw us. He agreed to talk in more discreet surroundings, so we walked down by the river. It was too cold for most people to be walking except for one or two with dogs who moved briskly, ears muffled by woolly hats although it was spring.

"We want the truth," Zak told him. "And don't piss about this time."

Rick sat down on one of the benches and we stood around.

"I didn't touch her. All right, maybe I clutched her, tried to stop her getting away. But I didn't hurt her. I wouldn't have. I saw her in her car outside the house. She was trying to get it started. I could see she was agitated. She was crying, shouting, thumping the steering wheel. I offered her a lift to wherever she was going. She said she was visiting a friend. But she asked me to drop her off when we were just around the corner from the police station. I got suspicious. I speeded up and drove away.

I wanted to talk to her, just needed her to calm down. I drove out past the football ground. I thought if we could go for a drink somewhere quiet I could talk her round. I don't know if she thought I had other intentions, but she was hysterical, she wouldn't listen to me. We were passing the woods, driving at forty, and she opened the door. I hauled her back in. She started hitting me.

I pulled off the road, down a small lane. We came to a stop. I told her all I wanted to do was talk. I thought I was getting somewhere, persuading her that yes there was a chance the police would believe Oskar's death was an accident but there was a bigger chance they wouldn't, and it wasn't worth the risk for any of us.

"She said she couldn't take the pressure any more – the guilt. And she was going to drop me right in it – pin everything on me. I had to stop her. Everything I'd worked so hard for would have been taken away. What future would I have? I worked my arse off for this career. I'd already lost

Imogen and lost the house. I couldn't have her throw away what little I had left.

"I was trying to explain that she couldn't do it without implicating herself and the rest of you. She grabbed the door again. I tried to stop her. She broke away. I jumped out and ran after her through the trees. It was pissing down and the ground was slippery. I tried to catch her but she ran out towards the road below. I couldn't risk being seen so I retreated back into the woods."

"So you didn't see," said Zak at last. "But you must have heard."

Rick pressed his fingers into his head. "Of course I heard. I heard the brakes screech and the noise of the impact. I heard someone scream. It was probably her."

"For fuck's sake, you know it was her."

He looked up, his eyes bloodshot. "All right, but I didn't kill her. It wasn't me. Much as you don't want to believe it, the police got the right man."

Chapter Twenty-Four

"Surely Stuart would have grounds for appeal now?" I said.

I'd brought it up a few times since we got back to the house but Zak never seemed to want to talk about it. "Even if Rick denies it, the Parkers saw Xanthe getting into his car."

Zak was in the kitchen, cooking in a cloud of turmeric that would have sent Stuart up the wall if he'd been there. He said the stains never came out. I'd just fed Livvy and put her down for a sleep.

"I just want to forget about it now and move on," he said.

"So do I. But what about Stuart?"

He turned down the power on the hob and filled the kettle. "Stuart was there, Em. You heard what they said about the blood particles. They were Xanthe's. And he was seen coming up the bank from the ditch where she was found."

"I know but there must be another explanation."

He set two coffees down, sat at the table and rubbed the sides of his head. "We can't keep having this conversation, can we?"

"But-"

"Emily, for God's sake, give it a rest. Xanthe's gone. There's nothing we can do to bring her back. At least it was quick. She didn't suffer. She came out of the trees so fast and hit the bonnet before she had time to be surprised."

Everything went still. I couldn't hear anything except the hum of the fridge and the clicking of the clock hands.

"What did you say?"

He was staring at me, his face frozen in horror at the realisation he'd said too much.

226

"No, that's not what I meant."

"How do you know she hit the bonnet?"

"No, I don't, I was guessing."

"No, you said 'she wouldn't have had time to be surprised.' You were there, weren't you?"

I got out of my chair. My legs almost gave way. His face filled with alarm.

"No, Em, listen to me. Sit down. Please. Let me explain."

But I couldn't sit there. All this time I'd been blinded by my feelings for him, my bruised pride, my envy of Chiara. I'd made excuses for him, overlooked the obvious things like the way he'd kicked the corpse off the cliff as though it were a piece of rubbish, the way he'd set fire to the car so casually as if it was something he'd done many times before.

I was suddenly horribly aware that we were alone. The Parkers wouldn't hear – they couldn't even hear their own television. The neighbours were all at work and the phone had been cut off days ago as yet another red bill went unpaid.

I backed away. He lunged for me. "No. You can't leave. I can't let you leave. You can't do this."

I dodged to the side, grabbing my chair and obstructing his path. "I can."

I shoved the chair at him and ran. I heard him jump over the chair. He reached for me but I wriggled out of his grasp.

I ran down the hall. He caught me. We fell against the wall. I got up again.

"Emily, stop. You don't understand."

"That's the problem, though – I do understand, don't I?"

He slammed himself against the front door. I turned round. I knew the back door was locked. That only left one option. The basement. All my instincts screamed no. But there was no other choice.

I pulled open the basement door, grabbing the key from the lock as I did so. I swung round the door. Immediately, he was there. He grasped the handle on the other side.

"Please, Em, we need to talk." His voice had softened,

taking on that tone that had fooled me for so many months. I'd been an idiot, let myself be blinded to his lies.

I almost fell for it. Just like I'd fallen for all the other things he'd told me. This man who wrote poetry, wore a Rainbow Warrior T-shirt, didn't eat animals, this man I'd shared a bed with, had a child with, had killed Xanthe.

"No Zak, we've talked enough. I can't trust anything you say."

He wasn't going to give in. He'd been found out and he wasn't going to let me go. I had to get the key back in the lock on my side at the same time as putting all my weight against the door. My breath caught as the door rattled and shook.

"Emily. Stop this. Open the door. Open the bloody door!"

Everything about him had changed. I fumbled with the lock. A sickening clink as the key fell from my hand and bounced down the steps in the darkness. I squatted down and groped for it but couldn't find it.

I flailed in the disorientating darkness for the light switch. I could see nothing at all. I had visions of losing my footing and plunging down the steps, landing on the floor below just like Oskar.

I found the switch. Thank God. I'd feel safer once I could see. Then I'd be able to make my way through to the passage door that led out to the outside steps. I jabbed the switch back and forth. No light came on.

"How could you do it?" I asked through the door, just resisting his attempts to break through. "What could Xanthe ever have done to deserve that? There must have been other ways to stop her going to the police. How did it feel when you realised you'd killed her? She was a friend, Zak. She'd have done anything for you – even after what you did to Rufus."

As the words left my mouth it was obvious I should have realised at the time. The way he'd created a different reality about how the dog died. That's what he'd done with Oskar and unwittingly we'd helped him. Now he'd done the same to Xanthe.

And it was what he'd do with me.

A cry erupted from upstairs. Livvy. I'd left her upstairs. What kind of mother must I be to leave her on the wrong side of the door? Who knew what might happen to her if he took her with him? He'd displayed only kindness to her so far, but I hadn't seen it either until now.

"Please Zak – think about Livvy. She needs me. I'm not going to tell anyone. Just let me take her and go. I can keep secrets better than anyone, you know that."

I heard footsteps on the gravel above me. Through the slit of window at the top of the basement I saw boots and the bottoms of a pair of jeans pass in front of the house. With relief I realised Imogen was back which made me feel safer. Surely Zak wouldn't do anything to me while she was in the house?

She must have let herself in very quietly because I didn't hear the door slam or her feet on the stairs but at least Livvy stopped crying so I guessed Imogen must have gone to her.

"I'm not going to hurt you – or Livvy," said Zak. "You must know that. You're the two people that matter most to me in the world. Will you just listen to me? I didn't do it. I wasn't there. But I think – I'm pretty sure – I know who did."

I wanted so much to believe him.

"Tell me then."

"I can't…Oh God, I can't tell you."

"Zak, tell me now."

After a long pause in which I thought he might have given up and left he said, "Chiara."

"Chiara? Why?"

"You must believe me, I didn't know until after it happened and even then I didn't make the connection – not straightaway. Chiara was driving away from me after the row we had when I told her about the baby. She was in a state – you saw what she did to me. I told her she shouldn't drive until she'd calmed down but to be honest I didn't want her to stay."

I heard him slump down to sit on the floor. I sat gingerly

on the step on the other side of the door. I pictured him with his knees drawn up and his head back against the door, eyes closed. I still didn't know if I should trust what he said.

"I stayed in her flat because I didn't want to go back to the house looking like I did, and she'd said she'd be away until Sunday. But later that evening she was back. She was in a bad way, I'd never seen her like that before. Her car was smashed in at the front. She was so distressed she could hardly speak. Gradually it came out that she'd hit something.

I felt a chill spread through my body. "Or someone? She hit Xanthe?"

"I don't know. I think – yeh." His voice dropped to a whisper. "I think it was.

"She was driving faster than she should. It was dark and raining so hard she could barely see. The bank's steep up to the woods. It's a blind bend even on a good day. She was half blinded by tears and the rain was coming down in sheets, too fast for the wipers to have much effect.

"As she rounded the bend something burst out of the trees. A dark shape. She didn't have time to register what it was. She tried to brake but she didn't have a chance.

"She knew she'd hit something. It happened so fast there was no time to think. She must have swerved, tried to stop. But all she could remember was the impact – like the car was exploding but it was all her cassettes being thrown up into the air and landing like glass shards. And then everything went black. Something landed on the bonnet, blocking the windscreen.

"It was dark, she was scared, and she knew there'd be another car along soon. She couldn't risk being seen. Something took over. It was probably at the back of her mind that she'd had a couple of drinks and if that came out she'd lose everything. So somehow, instead of pulling over, she put her foot down. She pushed on through and the windscreen cleared again."

I felt sick picturing the scene.

"So it was an accident," I said slowly.

His voice dropped. "That's what she said. But afterwards I realised Xanthe was wearing your red coat, the one you couldn't fit into when you were pregnant…"

I caught my breath. "She hit her deliberately? Because she thought it was me? She meant to kill me?"

For some moments he didn't answer.

"At that moment, yes – but not really. She wasn't thinking. You should have seen her when she got back to her flat. I said to her 'You know it's illegal to drive off without stopping after hitting someone?'

"She just laughed. Pointed out I'd broken a few laws myself – and I realised nothing in life was as black and white as I'd used to think.

"I went back with her to the spot where it happened. It was a bit lighter by then but the road was still wet, rain dripping off the trees. The road was thick was sodden leaves. I looked for tyre marks but couldn't see anything. We walked up and down with our torches. There was nothing. No sign of an accident. I began to think she'd imagined it.

"And then of course when I went back to the house I met you coming up the hill from the station, and you were fine."

A memory flooded back of Zak's joyous reaction when he saw me that night. I'd put it down to relief at having split with Chiara but now I began to see it was more than that.

"You weren't hurt. You hadn't even been in Bristol on Friday night when she'd had the accident. So we managed to convince ourselves she'd been mistaken – that she really had hit a tree. Or a fox or a deer or something." He paused. "Yes, I know that's bad too. But then we found Stuart tied to your bed and everything got crazy. And with Xanthe going missing things moved on.

"As far as we were concerned Xanthe was in Sweden so we never thought this had anything to do with her. It was only weeks later, after her body had been discovered, that I started to piece it together."

Every time I thought this thing couldn't get worse, it got worse. I thought I'd heard everything by now, that there couldn't be any more shocks to come but like some dreadful, diseased thing, every time you poked it another awful rotting truth spilled out.

"You knew, and you didn't say anything?"

"Don't you see, I couldn't? A secret for a secret, a lie for a lie. Just like with Rick. Just like we've done all through this bloody awful mess. I wasn't in the best position to set terms. I promised to keep her secret if she kept ours. That's why she hasn't gone to the police about what we did."

He was quiet for a while and I heard him shifting position, trying to get comfortable. "And at the time I felt responsible. I knew Chiara wasn't thinking straight. And afterwards I told her I never wanted to see her again – that's really why we split up. But I didn't tell the police because I felt it was partly my fault."

I could hear him breathing on the other side of the door. His voice was close as though his face was up against the wood.

"I can just about understand why you didn't go to the police but for God's sake didn't you think I had a right to know?"

"Yes, you did. And I'm sorry. I don't like it either – this whole thing is shit. I can't stand it any longer. I just want it to stop."

I thought I heard a sound from upstairs. Like any new parents our ears were tuned to Livvy's little noises. We stopped and listened for a moment but the house was quiet except for its usual creaks and hums.

"But how come Stuart had Xanthe's blood on his hoody?"

"Xanthe must have injured herself earlier in the evening. It was only in the past few days that I understood why there was no body there anymore. Rick must have heard the impact, like he says, but instead of getting back in his car and driving away he must have come out of the woods, checked for signs of life, realised there was nothing he could do, and then panicked, thinking if anyone saw him, they'd think he was responsible. So he rolled her down the bank."

Another noise – definitely a cry this time. What if Zak was lying? But I had to get to Livvy. As I pulled open the door Zak scrambled up and raised his hands as though I were aiming a gun at him. His eyes were filled with shock, fear and confusion.

"I'll go," he said.

"No, I will."

But in the hall we froze, staring up at the staircase levels. Livvy's cries were louder now. My heart dropped as I saw who was standing on the top landing holding my baby.

Chapter Twenty-Five

I rushed forward. Zak stopped me.

"Don't do this, Chiara," he said.

Chiara's face was streaked with tears. "You promised," she said. "You promised me you wouldn't tell."

She looked down at Livvy. "Shh, shh shh."

"Please put her down," I said. "This isn't fair."

She nuzzled her face in Liv's silky hair. "A lot of things aren't fair though, are they? Like, let me see – lying, cheating, keeping secrets. None of it's fair. But you thought it was all right to treat me like that didn't you?"

She smiled and then her mouth made an O. "Whoops."

I cried out. She was holding my precious baby, standing dangerously close to the bannister.

"Pretty pattern on the floor," she whispered in a baby voice to Livvy. Livvy gurgled back.

"Please, please put her down," I said. "I'm not going to tell anyone."

"Chiara, you've made your point," said Zak. "I'm sorry. Just please, for God's sake be careful. Give her back."

"Oopsadaisy." Chiara bounced her once, twice, three times in the air. "Oh, isn't this fun?" Livvy burbled, unaware. Chiara's voice hardened. "You should have told me about her at the beginning Zak. Just like you should have told me about the man in the cellar. Did you enjoy stringing me along?"

"No of course I didn't. I told you I'm sorry. Look, we've all kept secrets from each other and now we're all keeping them *for* each other. I never meant to hurt you. Just put her down."

"Down?" Chiara raised her eyebrows. "Are you sure?"

She gave a little smile. "Oh all right then."

The bannister creaked as she leant over, dangling Livvy in front of her. The baby blanket fell to the floor, floating and tumbling before landing in a heap.

We both screamed. We couldn't help it.

"I wish you hadn't made me do this," Chiara said.

"You wouldn't," I breathed.

"Wouldn't I? I didn't mean to hurt Xanthe. She was the best of you. But actually, I don't think I killed her. Stuart hit her after I did. If he'd been more careful she'd probably have survived."

"Come on, you know Stuart never left the house," Zak said.

It sounded ridiculous but I wasn't going to argue and tell her about Rick. I didn't think she really meant to hurt Livvy only to scare us, to be the one in control, but the way she was behaving, I could imagine her losing her grip. I could only whisper while trying not to cry,

"Please. I'm sure you're right. I won't tell because there's nothing to tell. Like you say, you didn't do it."

Chiara laughed. "If only I could believe you. If I really thought you'd keep quiet, it would be different. But you've shown me you're not to be trusted."

Zak's face was screwed up in horror. "Stop. Just fucking stop this."

"You're not giving me any choice," she shouted. "Can't you see, this is hard for me? Don't make it harder than it is."

She bounced Livvy up and down again. What happened next seemed to take place in slow motion. The bannister creaked. It gave way in a series of creaks and folds. Chiara screamed. I saw the panic on her face. She grabbed the remaining part of the rail but it also started to collapse. We rushed forward. She fell.

My vision clouded and went dark.

Chapter Twenty-Six

I was conscious. My eyelids flickered. Opening them, my gaze met Imogen's. Denim blue eyes, barely blinking. I flinched.

"Why aren't I dead?"

"Don't be an arse," she said. "You'll have a few bruises, that's all. The staircase collapsed. I came in with Mr and Mrs Parker just as it happened – the place looks like a bomb's hit it. We heard a scream and then all the noise."

"Where's Livvy?"

"With Mrs Parker."

"And Zak?"

"He stayed with her until the police came. He told them what Chiara did."

"Is Chiara okay?"

Imogen rolled her eyes. "Don't waste your energy worrying about her. She's probably concussed but she's not dead. She's in the hospital under police guard. You broke her fall and she broke Livvy's. Stuart will get his appeal now."

***

An hour later we sat eating takeaway pizza in the midst of the ruins. The hall smelled of dust.

"I thought I loved her," Zak said. "But I don't think I ever did, not really. I was in love with some things about her but only because I made myself close my eyes to others. The only person I've ever really loved is you, Em."

I smiled. "I'm sorry about earlier. I got it so wrong. Is there any way you could forget I said those things about you?"

It was a long time before he answered. "I don't know. I want to say it's all right, but you called me a murderer. I can't believe you didn't even trust me with my own child. I don't know where we can go from here."

"But I…"

"I need to think about this. I don't know if we'll ever be able to put it behind us. I keep thinking we're out of the shit but then it starts happening again."

When he'd finished the pizza he took off on his bike. I thought it might be one of those situations where he'd relent. For several weeks I expected him to turn up just like he had after the night we'd moved Oskar's body.

But when I answered the door one Saturday morning expecting to see him I found myself looking at Xanthe's father. He accepted my invitation to come in but looked uncomfortable as though the house was somehow to blame for what happened to Xanthe.

He took in the wreckage in the hall as we passed through to the living room. I made him tea which he drank without milk or sugar.

"Everything that was said about Charlotte at her funeral was true," he said, looking down into his tea. "Until her teens she was a model child. Perhaps we pushed her too far. We just wanted to see her settled but that was the last thing she wanted. She wanted a life that was more exotic, more exciting, than the one we gave her. Even as a little girl she used to dream of joining a circus.

"As she got older she had dreams of being a dancer but we wanted her to have a good education first. As a teenager she started challenging the way we did things. She refused to come to church anymore, stopped eating meat, got her ears pierced – she found us embarrassing most of the time.

"She made a mess of her GCSEs, dropped out of school and got in with the wrong crowd. She made accusations against a dear family friend which I was convinced was all in her head. But one day we found a note on her pillow and she'd gone.

"The police were wonderful at first but after a while they scaled down the search. For a year we had no idea if she was alive or dead. I hired a private detective who eventually found Charlotte living in a squat using a different name. I suppose she thought that life was more exciting.

"She refused to come back. That was harder for us to hear than being told she was dead. But we just hoped she was happy. I still don't understand how she could do that to us. My wife's health's never been the same. But to hear she'd been getting back on her feet, going back to education, starting a proper job. It looks as though she'd started to see sense. And that man took it from her…

"I'm very sorry," I said.

He drained his cup. "I don't suppose you knew what he was capable of. You had a lucky escape."

He took something from inside his jacket.

"I noticed this among her things we collected. I don't know if it's important but it has your name on. It was tucked inside one of her books."

He handed me an envelope. I wondered how we could have missed it all those times we'd gone through Xanthe's things looking for a clue to her disappearance but like he said it must have been stuck inside a book. I had no idea what it might contain. It felt strange to have some communication from Xanthe after all this time as though she was speaking from beyond the grave.

After her father had gone I opened the letter. My fingers trembled as I smoothed out the page.

In case this all goes wrong, I just want to explain what I did and why I can't keep quiet about it any longer.

I've already told you I put Oskar in touch with Rick. I gave him Rick's phone number which I got from Imogen's diary. I thought he was going to arrange to meet him in London so it was a shock when he turned up at the party. He'd promised not to tell Rick how he'd found him so we pretended not to know each other at the party but I did point Rick out to him.

I saw Oskar going into the basement, followed a little

while later by Rick. I waited until Rick had come out and gone back to join Imogen in the living room. I went into the basement and found Oskar counting the money. I asked him for my share but he refused. He was angry with me for rejecting him earlier when he tried to kiss me. He wanted me to go back to him but I didn't want to. I had to tell him that had never been part of the plan as far as I was concerned. My life had moved on. I felt I was finally getting somewhere and I didn't want to be dragged back down.

He hit me. I grabbed the backpack and ran up the steps. He followed me and was wrestling it off me. He grabbed me by the hair and was pulling me backward. I was losing my balance. I kicked out. He stumbled back on the stairs. I seized the chance to get out and lock the door.

It never occurred to me he was badly hurt. I assumed he'd get up, run back up the steps and start bashing on the door. Someone would let him out. The key was still in the door. But now that I think about it, the music had been turned up full blast so it would have been hard to hear him unless you'd been right next to the door.

I was convinced he'd come after me for the backpack. All I could think of was getting away. My room was full of people. I pushed through all the bodies in the hall and kitchen and went out into the garden. I hid the backpack in the old coal store so I could come back for it later.

I was about to go back in when other people started to spill out into the garden. Someone offered me a smoke and we started kissing. I thought Oskar wouldn't dare confront me if I was with someone else. And eventually I thought he must have given up looking for me and gone home.

It wasn't until we found the body that I realised he must have fallen harder than I'd realised, and that it was my fault. I should have told you but the way Stuart took control of the situation, I thought no one need ever know. I never meant to get anyone else into trouble.

At first it seemed as though everything was going to be all right but now the police have started questioning us I'm sure it's only a matter of time. It's been torturing me and I can't keep quiet about it any longer. I've put off going to the police until now because I know it might lead to you all getting convicted for the things you did. But I can't bear it any longer.

I folded the letter up and put it back into the envelope.

Chapter Twenty-Seven

2000

"Emily, we need to talk."

I recognized the voice immediately. Ten years fell away. As if we were back at number 17. Imogen was sitting sideways in an armchair, her legs slung over the arm. The French doors open, the curtains lifting in the evening breeze. Golden light filtering through, making patterns on the floorboards. I forced myself back into the present, to the council flat I shared with Livvy.

"What do you want?"

"Stuart's out. Look it up. The appeal went through this time."

All I could think of to say was, "He can't be. The judge said…"

"He said a lot of things Emily. But they've used new technology apparently which makes his trial unsafe."

Things were whirring through my head – the trial, the way the Prosecution barrister had been so scornfully certain, the looks on the jury's faces. And Xanthe's father looking as though he were about to throw up and being helped out of court.

"And my guess is he'll be heading over to see you soon."

My stomach sank. I had no idea how to deal with this. In fact it was another few days before he found me up in Edinburgh. We walked through the gardens – I'd thought it would be better to meet on neutral territory. His hair had receded, he was skinnier, his face sunken. He blinked more often than I remembered.

"How are you?" I asked.

"Good. At least not bad. At least better than I have been."

"Stuart, I'm sorry."

"What for?"

"For not being able to convince them earlier. Rick would never admit to them what he eventually told us – that it was him who rolled Xanthe's body down the bank. And Chiara denied everything of course. It isn't fair that you took the blame for everyone."

Stuart lifted his shoulders with a forgiving smile that made me feel worthless. "It's what we agreed. There was no need for everyone to go down for it."

"I can't believe you're not angry about it."

He twitched. "Oh no, I'm angry. I'm angry about the things I missed out on. Like getting married, having a family. A decent career. My life will never be what I hoped it would."

A couple of children trundled their bikes past and a small dog bounded up to us.

"I'd have liked a normal life. Liked a family."

"There's still plenty of time for that," I said. "Most people our age haven't started thinking about having children."

But I thought about Liv who was in her final year of primary school – hair that wouldn't be tamed, socks that never matched, always with her nose in a book. I couldn't imagine my life without her. Stuart had been Inside her whole lifetime.

He shook his head. "I don't think it will happen, not now. I'm a different person. Not easy to love. And people have preconceptions, don't they?"

For a while neither of us said anything. I found him looking at me.

"We agreed we wouldn't drop each other in it. But some of those things you said in the witness box – you didn't need to say them."

"I'm sorry. I didn't want to. But I had to answer the questions. I was under oath."

His voice took on a sharper note. "Did you? Did you

really? Or were you trying to save yourself by making sure I was put away and the case closed up and forgotten?"

I sighed. "The Bob plan was yours," I reminded him. "None of it would have happened otherwise. I never wanted anything to do with it but none of you would listen to me."

"Then you should have spoken up."

"I know. That's one thing the experience taught me. I grew up such a lot in those few months. And it's what I've taught Livvy - to think for herself and never to go with the crowd."

"You knew that by making me sound unhinged you were increasing the chances of me being found guilty. Which increased the chances of you walking away. And you did, didn't you? You all walked away."

"We didn't think it would end like that. Afterwards we didn't know what to do."

Then out of the blue he came out with it. "I thought maybe it was you."

"I'm sorry?"

"The reason I didn't say, the reason I didn't speak up for myself at first, is because I thought you'd done it. Did you?"

I shook my head. "Of course not."

He looked at me. "You've nothing to lose, Emily. Just admit it to me if no one else. I've done time for you. They won't waste money reopening the case again now. The least you owe me is the truth."

"Stuart, I think you're confused."

"I knew Xanthe couldn't have left in her own car. I'd fixed it so it wouldn't start – I was so worried she'd go to the police. So someone must have given her a lift. I thought perhaps you and Zak had seen her and she'd jumped in the car with you but then you'd had an argument and either lost control of the car or hit her or something."

I had no idea what to say except that I was sorry and grateful and he was a better person than all of us but that he was wrong.

He sat absorbing this knowledge for a long time before

he left. I didn't see him again.

2019

Number 17 looks much the same as I remembered it. The garden at the front where Stuart and Xanthe used to park their cars has been paved over and there are pots of bright tulips around the edge. There's a rocking horse in the window of Xanthe's room.

For a moment I think I see her leaning on the window frame and calling out to someone below. I picture Imogen in her room, closing the Austrian blind, and Stuart in his, shooting the sash up to get some fresh air even when it was freezing.

But all that's gone.

There have been times when I've been tempted over the years to visit the town, but I've made various excuses not to. If a friend hadn't begged me to drive her to Bristol for a literary festival perhaps I wouldn't have been standing here now looking at the place, daring myself to stand firm.

I'm so tempted to ring the bell and ask if I could have a look around.

I can smell the spices from Zak's cooking, Xanthe's cigarette smoke, Imogen's bath oil and the magnolia in the garden when the French windows are open.

I wonder if I'd have the courage to look in the basement.

But I don't. I don't want to inflict my story on the people living there now. They have the right to live their lives unencumbered by the past. I don't want to give them nightmares about finding a body in the basement or seeing a baby falling through the air in the stairwell.

The house is something different to them.

I turn to go. But I think I'll take one photograph just to remind me – give me closure. I rummage in my bag for my phone – I can never find it when I need it. Livvy's always telling me to get a brightly coloured case - I walk back across the street and stand against the wall opposite.

The curtains twitch in number 15. Mrs Nosy Parker still

up to her tricks. No that can't be right. How old would she be now? Well over a hundred.

While I'm standing there the door of number 17 swings open and someone I don't know walks out to their car. I feel my face flood with colour and drop my phone. I'm scrambling for it when a voice I recognise says, "Oh my God, it's you isn't it?"

Everything slows. Even the street noise fades out around me

"Zak?"

He looks older, of course he does. He still has a good head of hair but it's greying, and his face is thinner, pinched around the mouth.

But essentially, he's the same person that climbed on his bike right there thirty years ago and never even looked round. He must see that I've changed too. I no longer henna my hair and I've put on a stone or two since those days when we used to live on toast over a weekend. It's different when you have a family – you have to feed them somehow.

"I can't believe you recognised me," I say to mask the awkward pause.

"You haven't changed that much," he says with a shrug. I draw back from his appraising look. "In any case I've seen your pictures on Facebook."

"What are you doing here?"

"Same as you I expect. It's not the first time I've been back. Sometimes I walk past, sometimes I stand and look. It helps a bit. Were you on your way somewhere or do you have time for a coffee?"

It's tempting. But this is the life I turned my back on. I always felt that by making contact with any of the other house mates I'd be letting some of the past back in.

"Five minutes?" he says with that hopeful raise of the eyebrows.

We walk down to the docks to where the publishing house used to be. It's a café bar now. Some of the old shops and restaurants remain but a lot has changed. We walk through a broad, paved square that has a continental feel, cross a small bridge across the river, festooned with padlocks. Students more affluent than we were but who remind me of my own daughter – our own daughter although it seems funny to think of Livvy that way after all this time.

"Do you still think about it?" I say as we order our coffees at a table overlooking the water, and some expensive-looking flats on the other side. "Everything that happened?"

He pulls a face. "I try not to. But you know how it is."

I do. He was and will always be the person who knows me best. I don't say that I've spent moments here and there thinking what if…? What if we'd stayed together? What if I hadn't accused him of killing Xanthe and trying to kill me? As if I've said it aloud he says at the time it wasn't the accusation that hurt but the fear – the suggestion that he had it in him to do something like that. Perhaps we all have.

"I felt like King Midas in reverse – everything I touched turned to shit. I didn't want that to happen to you – or Livvy. I thought if we stayed together it would always be there and we wouldn't be able to move away from it and we'd end up hating each other."

"So here's a question," I find myself asking. "If you could go back in time knowing what we know now would you still take that place on the training scheme?"

"I would." I'm taken aback by his lack of hesitation. "I'd still move into the house with you, too."

That's a bigger thing. A much bigger thing

"You didn't keep in touch with Livvy," I say.

"I wanted to. You've no idea how much I wanted to. But I honestly thought she was better off not knowing me, not being a part of what we did."

It turns out he knows a lot about her. He's been stalking us on Facebook for years. He knows about her birthdays and our holidays, her jobs and her tattoos. He knows she's been bungee jumping and sky diving and about the six months she spent in Australia. He talks about her as if he knows her.

And yet he doesn't. He's missed so many things. He doesn't know what her laugh sounds like, the faces she pulls, the way her hair has a life of its own. He doesn't know the real Livvy, only the Facebook one.

"What have you told her about me?" he asks.

I know Livvy didn't mind not having a father when she was growing up, but I don't know how to tell him without sounding as if I'm attacking him. She's always accepted that we were a small team. For a while during my brief and not too successful marriage she was part of a conventional family and I was able to convince myself that redemption was possible.

But when David left he said being married to me felt lonely. He always felt I was keeping him out. There was a part of me he'd never be able to reach.

"How's life treated you?" I ask Zak. What's he done with all the years of freedom that he might have lost out on? Years that Oskar Bramley never got to live. Years that Stuart spent in prison.

He's been a travel writer, a charity worker and more recently a website designer.

He's lived in Prague and then in Sarajevo. When it got nasty there he moved to Palermo for a while. We talk about the others. Imogen's working for the UN. Stuart's out of prison now. Who knows where Chiara is?

"Sounds like everything worked out for you," I say.

He shrugs. "I'd have traded it all in if I could."

"What for?"

"You need to ask?"

"But you left, remember? You said you couldn't live with me because I hadn't trusted you."

He nods. "And I meant it – for a few days at least. I was hurt and angry. I thought about getting in touch but I didn't let myself. I thought it was for the best. I spent a few weeks trying to work it out. When I went back to the house it was empty and there was a For Sale sign outside.

I told him how we'd handed in the keys to the building society. He didn't seem surprised. It was what everyone was doing back then.

"Then a few years later when Facebook started up I found you. I wanted to get in touch but your profile says you're married and I didn't think you'd welcome me turning up."

Perhaps I shouldn't say it, but I do anyway.

"I'm not anymore."

When we leave he keys his number into my phone. "In case you ever want to get in touch."

I watch him walk back over the padlock bridge and along the quay. I keep watching until he's nearly disappeared. And I realise I can't let him go, not this time. I text Wait.

I see him stop and look down at his phone. He turns, smiles, and weaves his way back towards me.

THE END

Fantastic Books
Great Authors

CROOKED
CAT

Meet our authors and discover
our exciting range:

- Gripping Thrillers
- Cosy Mysteries
- Romantic Chick-Lit
- Fascinating Historicals
- Exciting Fantasy
- Young Adult and Children's
  Adventures

Printed in Great Britain
by Amazon